Only rarely does a novelist appear like Robert Hudson with a voice that is singularly distinctive in style and ravishingly absorbing in subject matter—in this case the difference between knowing God and knowing about God. *The Beautiful Madness of Martin Bonham* is an accomplished and seductive book you will never forget.

—Leonard Sweet, best-selling author, professor, publisher, and founder of SpiritVenture Ministries

———

Whether it's nonfiction, poetry, technical writing, adaptations of Renaissance texts, or (now, wonderfully) fiction, Bob Hudson can take the obscure and somehow turn it into a universal parable of the good, true, and beautiful. In this instance, a small religious college becomes the backdrop for exploring whether or not you can truly love God with all your mind if you fail to love your neighbor as yourself. Hilarious, thoughtful, and thought-provoking: a true delight!

—Sarah Arthur, author of *A Light So Lovely: The Spiritual Legacy of Madeleine L'Engle*

———

Hollywood has mastered the art of dramatizing the tropes that play on repeat in our mundane, modern lives. But what might it look like to live today the drama that has captivated the attention of the spiritual masters of the Christian tradition? *The Beautiful Madness of Martin Bonham* answers that question in a way that's both invigorating and refreshingly down to earth—a theophany that you can imagine happening in your own town, with the people who populate your everyday life.

—Jonathan Wilson-Hartgrove, spiritual writer, preacher, and community cultivator. He serves as Assistant Director for Partnerships and Fellowships at Yale University's Center for Public Theology and Public Policy

---

Hudson tackles a religious topic as relevant in our world today as any other, orthodoxy (beliefs) versus orthopraxy (practice). Or in this case, theology (the study of God) versus theophily (loving God). Hudson's approach is thoughtful and full of its share of shenanigans. A good reminder for all of us, don't take yourself too seriously, but humbly seek to get things right.

—Traci Rhoades, Bible teacher and author of *Not All Who Wander (Spiritually) Are Lost* and *Shaky Ground: What to Do After the Bottom Drops Out.*

Finding a book that does everything this novel does is like finding a unicorn. It is genuinely funny, scores many good-natured jabs at sacred bovine, and—rarest of all—has an earnest search for an honest and meaningful faith at its tender heart. Robert Hudson has written a novel I wish I had written —and yet this is better, because I get to enjoy it..

—John R. Mabry, author of *Ash Wednesday* and *Growing into God: A Beginner's Guide to Christian Mysticism.*

THE BEAUTIFUL MADNESS
OF MARTIN BONHAM

CUPPERTON
UNIVERSITY

CUPPER TINUS

GRADIBUS PARVULIS
AD ASTRA

ALSO BY ROBERT HUDSON

Kiss the Earth When You Pray:
The Father Zosima Poems

The Further Adventures of Jack the Giant Killer:
Southern Retellings of the World's Oldest Stories

The Poet and the Fly:
Art, Nature, God, Mortality, and Other Elusive Mysteries

The Monk's Record Player:
Thomas Merton, Bob Dylan, and the Perilous Summer of 1966

Seeing Jesus:
Visionary Encounters from the First Century to the Present

The Art of the Almost Said:
A Christian Writer's Guide to Writing Poetry

The Christian Writer's Manual of Style

Four Birds of Noah's Ark:
A Prayer Book from the Time of Shakespeare
(Thomas Dekker, edited by Robert Hudson)

Companions for the Soul
(with Shelley Townsend-Hudson)

THE BEAUTIFUL MADNESS OF MARTIN BONHAM

A TALE ABOUT LOVING GOD

ROBERT HUDSON

ARTWORK BY
MARK SHEERES

APOCRYPHILE
PRESS

Apocryphile Press
PO Box 255
Hannacroix, NY 12087
www.apocryphilepress.com

Published in association with the literary agency of Credo Communications, LLC, Grand Rapids, MI 49525; www.credocommunications.net.

Please join our mailing list at www.apocryphilepress.com/free. We'll keep you up-to-date on all our new releases, and we'll also send you a FREE BOOK. Visit us today!

CONTENTS

Campus Map   x
Introductory Note   xiii

1. The Department of Theophily   1
2. The Forum on Faith   19
3. The Banquet   38
4. A Ministry of Profanity   54
5. A Visit from the Archbishop   72
6. Shoulder Angels   91
7. Ms. Westcott's Story   109
8. Night Class   128
9. A Walk in the Woods   148
10. The Disciplinary Committee   165
11. Ms. Lambert's Story   183
12. The All-Faiths Festival   205
13. Into the Labyrinth   225

Notes on the Text   235
A Note from the Author   259
About the Author   267

In memoriam

Clarence Hogeterp and Dennis J. Kopaz

Book friends

At the University ... I saw that there were things
in this world of which I never dreamed;
glorious secrets and glorious persons past imagination.
—Thomas Traherne, *Centuries of Meditations*, III, 36

A WHITTEMORE MUSIC BUILDING
B NORTH STREET
C CUPPERTEA CAFÉ
D ROMANCE LANGUAGES
E NORTH QUAD
F PHIPPS AUDITORIUM
G UNDERGRADUATE LIBRARY
H BOULDER
I SHEERES ART MUSEUM
J BEETHAM HALL
K WARNERS FINE ARTS BUILDING
L FACULTY PARKING
M STUDENT STORES
N CUPPERTON STUDENT UNION
O THE CUSS
P MURPHY CHAPEL AND RECTORY HOUSE
Q ADMINISTRATION BUILDING
R BANQUET HALL
S CRAMER BULDING AND LAB THEATER
T CAFETERIA
U SOUTH QUAD
V GARDNER-VAN HOUTEN LIFE SCIENCES CENTER
W ERICKSON HALL
X ARBORETUM AND LABYRINTH
Y OBSERVATORY
Z SOUTH WOODS

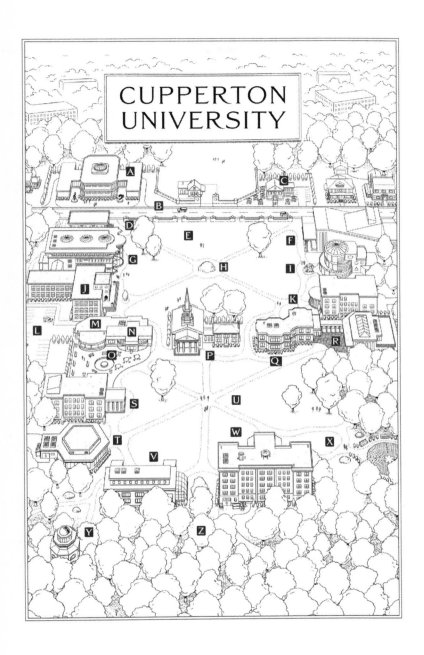

INTRODUCTORY NOTE

Sources of quotations are provided at the back of this book
—see *"Notes on the Text (by Dr. Martin Bonham)."*

CHAPTER I

THE DEPARTMENT OF THEOPHILY

In the valley of this restless mind
I sought in mountain and in mead,
Trusting a True Love for to find:
Then to a hill did my way lead ...
—*anonymous, 15th century*

"Bonham! Are you a complete idiot?"

The Rev. Dr. Cornelius C. Dunwoody, PhD, ThD, DD, chairman of the Cupperton Seminary and School of Theology, stood in the doorway of my office in Beetham Hall, looming like a diminutive colossus. His clenched fists were planted firmly on his hips, his stance wide and the top of his bald head turning Fuji-apple red. Even though I'd been expecting such a visit that gloomy January evening, his abrupt appearance startled me nonetheless. I knew how Poe must have felt when buttonholed by that raven atop the pallid bust of Pallas just above his chamber door.

"C-come in," I stammered. "Have a seat." I pointed to the well-worn leather chair on the opposite side of my desk.

Without budging from the doorway, he barked, "Have you lost your mind? Have you *completely* lost your mind? You'd better explain, Bonham—*now!*"

I'm not sure when in life Cornelius Dunwoody, renowned man of God, developed this penchant for indignation and imperiousness, for which he is known across campus, though I've long conjectured that it must have something to do with a childhood spent trying to convince his playfellows to call him Neil rather than Corny. That would sear the soul of even the most stouthearted, and it's a lesson to parents everywhere to consider well before choosing names for their offspring.

"Have a seat," I repeated. "We'll talk ..."

But none of this makes sense, I realize, without at least a brief recital of the events that precipitated this encounter, which proved to have so much import in the months and years to come.

I, Martin Bonham, am a gray-haired, single, bookish male of a certain age, of the species *Homo sapiens sapiens*, who is also a tenured professor of English at Cupperton University (a top third-tier Midwestern college, according to *US News and World Report*) and cofounder of the school's Department of Theophily ... but more about that later.

Decades ago I did my graduate work in Middle and Early Modern English, writing my dissertation on Florio's translation of Montaigne, the version Shakespeare read, and as far as dissertations go, a greater work of academic puffery than mine does not exist. I once joked that there were only ten pages of value among its two hundred, but that was a pompous overestimation. The whole affair casts book-burning in a strangely attractive light. I have since written two other works, an overview of Middle English grammar and an annotated anthology entitled *Religious Poets of the Fifteenth Century*, both mercifully out of print.

At Cupperton, I teach English lit, Chaucer through Milton, along with the usual battery of survey, grammar, and composition classes, though my greatest joy has been my two-semester senior seminar on the "Writings of the English Mystics": "401 (Fall)—Fourteenth to Sixteenth Centuries" and "402 (Spring) —Seventeenth to Nineteenth Centuries." Despite the complaints of the professors in the graduate Seminary and School of Theology who sneeringly refer to my seminars as the "Writhings of the English Misfits," a small but steady parade of curious students—graduate-level seminarians among them— files through my classroom.

Case in point: Ms. Westcott.

One cool, sunny September morning, right after Mystics 401, I was, like Wordsworth, wandering lonely as a cloud along the path that angles across North Quad, between the much-repainted memorial boulder and the Sheeres Art Museum, when I became aware of a presence at my side. It was Katie Westcott, a third-and-final-year seminarian and one of Dr. Dunwoody's favorites. For two weeks now, dressed perennially in black, she'd been attending my 401 class, and I don't believe I've ever encountered a more earnest or intense student—so intense, in fact, I suspected she could light matches by staring at them. At the far end of the classroom's oblong conference table, amid a half dozen bright-eyed senior English majors, she would sit silently, absorbing everything and twitching almost imperceptibly, like a puma in horn-rimmed glasses ready to pounce.

"Dr. Bonham," she said to me on this day, "can we talk?"— more of a demand than a question.

"Of course," I said and suggested that we wander in the

direction of the CupperTea Café, our local dispenser of latte and other equivocal beverages. Few places are more amenable to intimate conversation than a crowded coffee house buzzing with the low roar of small talk and the high scream of espresso machines. The day was bright and the semester young, so, I thought, what could be better? "My treat," I added with paternal indulgence. Little did I know that my entire life was about to be upended.

"Well, it's about seminary," she began as we took our seats in a high-backed booth by the front window, she with a triple espresso and I with an iced chai. With a penetrating look, she peered at me over the heavy rims of her glasses, and her severely cropped black hair seemed suddenly more severe. Feeling uneasy, I studied the many initials carved in the wooden tabletop. "Or, well, not seminary exactly," she said. "It's about me. There's a problem."

"Oh?" I said.

"I'm giving up," she said.

"Hmm," I said.

"I think I need professional help," she said.

"Huh," I said.

Whenever I hear the first halloos of an incoming confession I tend to respond in monosyllables. Though comfortable with complex early English orthography and syntax, I'm less so with complex people, and Katie was beginning to feel complex. My problem is that I'm highly empathic by nature, so that rather than easing sinking souls from their spiritual sloughs of despond, I tend to settle myself by degrees, as if in quicksand, into the same boggy place. I'm suggestible that way. None of my friends catches a cold without my thinking I've caught it too.

"You see," Katie continued, "all my life I wanted to go into the ministry. I read the Bible twice through in middle school, went to Christian high, double-majored in religion and Greek at Carleton, and minored in Latin and classics. I've read many of the Church Fathers and major theologians. After working for a year to save money, I came here ... where I realized something is terribly wrong."

Feeling myself slipping toward the slough, I asked, "Which is ...?"

"I don't love God."

Suddenly the CupperTea seemed to grow quiet. Seeing how serious she was, I knew enough to remain expression-less—pleasant but inscrutable, like Mona Lisa in a tweed jacket.

"Really," she said. "I don't think I ever have, and maybe I never will."

"Are you angry at God? It's okay if you are."

"No, no, it's not that, and it's not that I don't believe ... I do. It's just that I ... I don't *feel* anything. No awe or passion. No emotion at all. The Great Commandment says we're to love God with all our heart, soul, mind, and strength ... I can't imagine what that's like."

I pondered for a moment. "What about church?"

"I hate it. They sing all these gooey 'Jesus-we-adore-you' songs, like he's some sort of cosmic boyfriend ... like we're supposed to have romantic feelings or something ... and everyone gets so worked up. It's creepy! And the people who claim to love God the most quite often seem to show it the least."

I wondered how many triple espressos she'd already had that day.

"What do your profs say?"

"Well, that's the kind of thing you just *don't* talk about in seminary. They'd quote things at me like 'we love God because God first loved us,' which would only make me feel worse. The guilt's overwhelming. My minister at home told me just to *act* like I loved God ... and eventually I would."

"Fake it till you make it," I said.

"Something like that ... though Nietzsche called it the 'religious pantomime.'" Katie is the kind of student who, when you serve up a weak cliché, is likely to volley a well-placed Nietzsche back at you.

She said, "I understand the basics of salvation and grace ... and gratitude, but the feelings just aren't there." She gazed out the window as a long-boarder clacked past on the pavement. "It's like this. My sister dated a guy in high school. They went skating one winter, and she fell through the ice. The boyfriend pulled her out, wrapped her in his coat, and carried her a mile back to our house. He saved her life. The problem was that everyone, forever after—including the boyfriend—kept reminding her. Over and over. She was grateful, but eventually the obligation—the weight of it—sort of swamped everything else. They broke up. You can't oblige someone's feelings."

"What about Dr. Dunwoody ... you talk with him?"

She flashed a caustic eyeroll in my direction that seemed to say *puh-leez*. "Look, that's why Ms. Lambert in the library suggested I take *your* class. I was hoping the mystics would have some answers, but they just make things worse."

"How so?"

"Well, they've got feelings for God all right, but their feelings are all so severe and huge and incomprehensible—"

"Ruskin called it their 'beautiful madness,'" I said, which I only quoted to pay her back for the Nietzsche.

"Whatever," she snapped. "I obviously can't go into the ministry now. I'm sick of the whole thing."

"I'm so sorry," I said, after which came a long pause. She sipped her drink. I sipped mine.

Then she caught me by surprise. "So, tell me this"—her

incendiary eyes burned into mine—"can *you* honestly say that you love God, right now, this moment, with all your heart and mind and soul and strength?"

I paused ... and pondered. There are triumphant moments in life when one rises to the occasion, when one speaks words that are "as an honeycomb, sweet to the soul, and health to the bones."

This was not one of them.

I felt hollower than a bass drum and shallower than a tambourine, neither of which was making any noise at the moment. After thirty years of relishing old mystic texts with titles like *The Fire of Love* and *The Doctrine of the Heart*, I had to face facts. "No," I said at length.

"So, do you ever *feel* like you love God ... deeply and passionately?"

"I'm sure I must ... sometimes—"

"But when? *When* do you most feel like you love God?"

A fair question, but to my shame, all I could think of was Katie's grammar. Should I tell her that it should be *as though you love God* rather than *like you love God*? Honestly, I'm not proud of myself sometimes.

Katie didn't wait for an answer. She stared hard at me. "With no 'beautiful madness,'" she said, "how do we know we're not just part of the 'religious pantomime'?"

I BELIEVE it was Jean-Paul Sartre who, in one of his perkier moods, compared our life to being adrift in a rowboat ... on an endless ocean ... at night. It is in choosing a direction and rowing that we find meaning. And so it was, after meeting with Katie at the café after 401 the rest of the week, that we discovered something interesting: we had started rowing.

First, we sensed the need to broaden our field of inquiry. Why not pose Katie's questions to a few of the brightest *non-seminary* types who attend church? Although the university is more than an hour's drive from the nearest large city, it's nestled among three smallish, rural Midwestern towns in close proximity—Cupperton, Palmyra, and Ware, called the Tri-Communities, or Tri-Comms—which means we were able to conduct a series of field trips to the back row of nearly every religious establishment within a fifteen-mile radius, even including a mosque, a gurdwara, and a synagogue, to see which faculty members we recognized—an undercover operation, you might say. And we discovered quite a few. In the weeks that followed, we talked with Catholics, Baptists, Jews and Bible churchers, Muslims and Mennonites, a Buddhist, and more. We asked them, "Can you *honestly* say you love God with all your heart, mind, soul, and strength?" and "*When* do you most feel like you love God?" (I never corrected Katie's grammar.)

One of our first visits was to St. Athanasios Greek Ortho-dox, the home church of Cupperton University president Sirena Costa, whom, out of deference, we decided not to approach. But at St. Athanasios we also recognized Dr. Alice Mears, chair of the Psychology Department, to whom Katie posed her questions. Dr. Mears said simply, "I think I most love God when I love others ... and when I love myself. Remember, that's the other part of the commandment."

Another Sunday, we spotted microbiology professor Dr. Bill Fredericks at Word of Life Pentecostal, who stood out because he was the only person who didn't sway, shout, or raise his hands. Soft-spoken and reserved, he didn't fit the mold. But as we walked from the gathering that morning, Katie asked her questions, and he became rapturous about "oxidative phos-phorylation," "unicellular protozoa," and "photosynthetic prokaryotes." As he prattled on, Katie caught my eye and mouthed the question, "Glossolalia?" Delving into the microscopic world, the professor told us, is like peeking into the workshop of the Divine, and it fills him with awe and an almost crushing love for God's inventiveness.

Then there was Dr. Graciela Rojas of the Romance Languages Department, who I knew attended the small storefront Catholic Iglesia de María de la Paz in Palmyra. She'd arrived at the university two years earlier, and I'd had the privilege of being her faculty mentor. Graciela pondered for a moment and then said with sweet simplicity, "Katie, I know what you mean. I feel that too. I have so many doubts. But somehow, just knowing that God loves *me* gets me through." Katie stared at Dr. Rojas, then reached out for a hug.

We even managed to infiltrate a mysterious private meeting of the Assembly of Devout Planetarians, which we excitedly expected to be a UFO cult, but it turned out to be the monthly wine-and-cheese gathering for student volunteers at the planetarium. Still, it was there that we encountered Dr. Josh Fields of the Astronomy Department, who, as you might expect, had some interesting things to say about the "starry welkin" and the "the Bowl of Night" (referencing Shakespeare and FitzGerald respectively—always trust scientists who read literature). He had once toyed with the notion, he said, of teaching a January term on "God in the Universe" but dismissed it on account of his not being particularly religious. He'd been raised in, and escaped from, what he referred to as the "Implacable Church of Wednesday, Saturday, and Twice on Sunday." Still, despite himself, he couldn't resist the uncanny sensation that a Cosmic Top Dog of some sort was playing hide-and-seek around every corner of astrophysics.

And so it went. We talked with Carl Evans, my friend from the Theater Department, who attends St. Timothy's Episcopal;

and Dr. Soo-jin "Sue" Park in Biology, who's a deacon at the First Baptist Korean Church of Palmyra; and Dr. Naazim el-Atar at the Islamic Center in Ware; and Tom Fouchee of the Art Department, who worships at St. Linus Catholic; and my dearest friend in the world, Ms. Lambert, our head librarian, whom I occasionally accompany to the local Friends Meeting. Katie and I talked with people from nearly every department who told us stories of how their studies filter into their spiritual lives, who shared their thoughts and wisdom and the many ways they experience God's love and seek to return it, and who were grateful even to be asked such questions. As Katie grew a bit more hopeful, so did I.

Perhaps our only misjudgment was in approaching a street evangelist—somewhat of a fixture in the Tri-Comms area, known as Brother Jonas—on a whim one Saturday afternoon in October after Katie and I had attended synagogue. He was preaching as usual in the CUSS—an acronym for the large brick courtyard in front of the Cupperton University Student Stores. It's an appropriate moniker because the locale is a popular student hangout and a magnet for spontaneous expression ... like Speakers' Corner at London's Hyde Park without as many anarchists with Cockney accents.

This gentleman had perched himself atop one of the benches and, surrounded by a small crowd of curious onlookers, was delivering an emphatic preachment, denouncing those of us present as a "perverse and crooked generation," while punching his Bible into the air as if it were a first-place trophy. Like the children of Israel, we waited for him to descend from Sinai so Katie could ask her questions. His descent was soon hastened by a group of inebriated frat boys who sang a spirited rendition of "Onward, Christian Soldiers" as a way of compelling the preacher to conclude.

We approached. No sooner had the words left Katie's lips

than Brother Jonas declaimed (loudly, though we were no more than two feet away), "Yes, praise God, with every ounce of my being. No one can claim to be a Christian who does not feel that love burning inside them like a furious, holy volcano, for 'the Lord thy God is a consuming fire, even a jealous God' and will not tolerate those 'who have forsaken the right way and are gone astray,' and Jesus himself says in the book of the Revelation, 'If thou art lukewarm, neither cold nor hot, I will *spew* thee out of my mouth'! Amen and amen. And James, the brother of our Lord, says ..."

Somewhere Kierkegaard tells the story of a man who smiles and bows politely and waves hello, even as he's backing away from his interlocutor. That was precisely what Katie and I did.

———

One evening, the week of Christmas, Katie and I were huddled over espresso and hot chai in our regular booth at the Cupper-Tea. As snow sparkled under the streetlights outside and Andy Williams, on the overhead speakers, was crooning, "It's the most wonderful time of the year ...," we took stock of our research. At one point, I absentmindedly remarked, "You know what would really be wonderful? If we could somehow get all these people together in one place ..."

Katie's eyes got large.

Mine got large back.

"Do you think ...?" I said.

"I do think!" she replied.

"I think so too!" I said.

And that's how it began. We talked and talked, talking over each other as often as not, and the more we talked, the more excited we grew. We gabbled like teenagers forming a rock band, though in time we would feel more like saboteurs chucking our sabots into the machinery of the university.

The gist was this: what if there were an interdisciplinary curriculum devoted to the idea of loving God and better understanding God's love in return? What if there was an undergraduate religion department that studied wonder and awe and mystery *instead* of theology? Students could learn about seeing and sensing and knowing God in everyday, diverse, practical ways—in Nature, poetry, and music ... in science and art and in other people. Dr. Fields could teach about God in the universe, and Dr. Fredericks could share his spiritual passion for single-cell creatures. A trained psychologist like Dr. Mears could coach us in overcoming the obstacles to loving ourselves— which is often heavy lifting even for the most devout.

"Katie ... *theophily* ... that's the Greek word for 'the love of God,' right?" She nodded. "So, what if we called our department"—I was already referring to it as *ours*—"the Department of Theophily?"

Even as I asked the question, we knew the obstacles. The graduate Seminary and School of Theology had long opposed the establishment of any competing religion curricula— asserting that their graduate-level classes were open to undergraduates and already offered everything a student curious about religion could dream of: biblical languages, systematic theology, ecclesiology, church history, homiletics, ethics, patristics, and so on, to say nothing of brilliant professors with long strings of letters after their names.

"But, you know," I said, "that's why the university needs a Department of Theophily; it would cover all the spiritual territory that the seminary doesn't—literature, art, drama, history, philosophy, sociology, science, psychology—and even the writings of the English misfits! In fact, it would deal with about ninety-five percent of the rest of human experience. It would be the perfect minor or even a second major for students in music and nursing and social work and creative writing and poli sci and ..."

Katie's usually dour face now beamed. On the overhead speakers Burl Ives was singing, "Have a holly-jolly Christmas ..."

"Katie," I said, looking her straight in the eye, "if you're still not planning to go into the ministry, what *are* you doing after you graduate this spring?"

She caught my drift. "Dr. Dunwoody'll blow a gasket," she said.

"Well, the university would have to have a full professor like myself act as academic chair, but we'd need an administrative director. Let's face it—you've got all the knowledge and skill ... you'd be the cofounder of an academic department if we can pull this off!"

Katie's smile, like the Cheshire cat's, almost eclipsed her face.

"Listen, I know it's a long shot," I said, "but if we put our minds to it, I think we could sell this to the university. They need it. *We* need it! What do you think?"

Squinting a little as if summoning a stray thought, she quoted: "'We are only as strong as we are united, and as weak as we are divided.'"

"Nietzsche?" I asked.

"No. Dumbledore."

So, with all the assiduity of a beaver colony on a tight schedule, we set to work. After obtaining and completing the necessary paperwork, not a small task, by the way, and talking with the department's potential faculty members, the next item on the agenda was to arrange a meeting with Dennis Kinealy, a solemn, stately Irish Catholic with a hook nose, who, were he not already the university provost, could have had a career as a somewhat haughty archbishop in a Victorian novel. He agreed to meet with us over the holidays.

Rumor had it that a certain *froideur* existed between the provost and Dr. Dunwoody, precipitated no doubt by Dunwoody's aforementioned imperiousness, and I hoped this might work to our advantage. I was right. No sooner had Katie and I outlined our plan than a hint of a smile crossed Kinealy's thin face. With his pencil he tapped the papers on his desk.

As we sat on the squeaky leather chairs in his drab but tidy office on that overcast December afternoon, the provost glanced down at our forms and requisition. He perused our list of nearly two dozen professors who had committed to teach one or more courses in the new department. "Hmm," he murmured, "Mears and Fredericks ... Rojas, Fields, Lambert ... Park in Biology, Evans from Drama, Fouchee ... and I see you list a couple of recommended adjuncts from the community ... like Rabbi Rachel Zeller." He tapped his pencil on the papers again. Without looking up, he said, "Quite, quite impressive, but ... no one from the seminary ..."

I waited till he caught my eye. I pursed my lips and shook my head. He understood.

"Well, I'll be frank ...," he said, "I like it. The university's tried in the past to establish an undergraduate department of religious studies, but we've always met with resistance from a certain quarter. But your approach is fresh, imaginative, nontraditional. Its core mission doesn't overlap with that of any other department, not even the seminary's. You're drawing from existing faculty—interdisciplinary—a broad spectrum, which is good, and anyway, it's the only way the university could afford it. Obtaining the course releases shouldn't be difficult. And I like it because I believe this was the university founders' original intention way back in the 1830s—a down-to-earth, every-person's approach to religious education. And this comes at a good time because we've recently received several endowments earmarked for the undergraduate school, and one donor even specified 'spiritual enrichment.' So, funding for an administrator and the extra courses should be no problem. I think we're covered."

Katie and I could hardly restrain our joy.

Kinealy then outlined the process, which was more byzantine than I'd anticipated. First, he would have to consult with his vice provost and the Provost's Council, who would in turn present a recommendation, with any emendations, to the Faculty Senate and the Academic Program Committee for discussion. Assuming no red flags were raised, Kinealy would then seek formal approval from the academic dean and the Dean's Council, the Executive Officers' Board, and then, finally, the University Council. If they all approved, the Finance Office would review everything and, if Fortune favored the bold, allocate the required funds. Then President Costa would rubber-stamp the proposal and draft a formal letter of declaration.

"But know *this*, however"—there was a sudden, distressing chill in Kinealy's voice, as when a messenger in a Shakespeare play enters from stage right to announce the king's death—"before any of that can happen, I'll have to meet in person with the heads of all the affected departments to obtain signoffs ..."

And we knew what that meant.

IN THE DAYS that followed I had forebodings of the unpleasant tête-à-tête that I knew was in the offing. Katie had heard through the grapevine (that is, Ms. Adams, the seminary's secretary, had told Dolly De Angeli, the English Department's secretary, who told Ms. Lambert in the library, who told Katie and me) that just after Provost Kinealy had left Dunwoody's third-floor office in Erickson Hall, a distinct thumping could be heard within. Dunwoody was either beating his desk in frustration or practicing to be a Japanese taiko drummer.

As I worked late that same evening, Cornelius Dunwoody materialized suddenly in the doorway of my office and, unbudging, like Samson between his pillars, seemed to be weighing the pros and cons of bringing venerable Beetham Hall down upon our heads.

"Have a seat," I said. "We'll talk."

"Start explaining, Bonham—*now!*"

"Well, ... you see," I began, "I was walking across North Quad this past September ...," and I related the whole story, beginning with Katie and her triple espresso and concluding with how happy the provost thought the founders would be. To his credit, Dunwoody listened to the end, though not without a fair amount of grunting and goggling of eyes as though he were swallowing hard-boiled eggs.

"Do any of these professor friends of yours have theological training?" he asked at last.

"Well, you see, that's the point ... they're all highly qualified in their own—"

"Yes, yes, I'm sure, but what gives them the right?" he said, pinning me with the look of the basilisk. "What right do they have to teach *religion?* Do any of them know Hebrew or Greek? Have they studied theology or exegesis? How do we know they can interpret the Bible correctly? And who's going to check them for orthodoxy? *You?* And how do we know they're even Christians?"

"Well ... frankly, several of them aren't. There's Dr. Naazim el-Atar in sociology and—"

He made a noise that sounded like a spit take in a comedy routine. "This is outrageous, Bonham. Your moronic course on the English mystics was bad enough, but an entire department! ... What were you thinking? It's like beginners' night at the bowling alley—all of you, amateurs with no business meddling in any of this ... And *Theophily*! What nonsense! And what makes you think ..."

He was on a roll, so I decided to sit it out, as if I were waiting for a long freight train to pass. If I'd had a radio, I would have flipped it on.

A few minutes later he was still talking: "... and why should the university trust the likes of you to teach its students anything about religion? It's irresponsible. It's untrained people like you who've always made a mess of things—"

I interrupted. "As if you so-called professionals have fared any better. Do you know how many dozens of denominations there are, each with its own school of theology, and each convinced the others are wrong and—?" I stopped. He little "deserved the compliment of rational opposition," as Jane Austen once wrote.

"And what stupid notions are you filling Ms. Westcott's head with?" he said. "If she was having doubts, why didn't she talk to *me*?" I flashed back to Katie's eyeroll when I asked her that same question. He continued, "She was one of the most promising students I've ever taught; I considered her my protégé, and now *you've* ruined her career—"

"She'll be a great administrator—maybe even our department chair someday." Then I added, "And *she* knows Greek and Hebrew." I meant it to sting.

"You're a lunatic, Bonham. You've never published so much as an article in the field of religious studies—"

"Actually, I compiled an annotated anthology of fifteenth-century religious poetry—"

"That's the point! You're an English professor, a poetry scholar, a *grammarian* ... not a theologian. You can't teach religion by virtue of being a master of ... of ... the subjunctive!"

"Oh," I mumbled, "would that I were!"

"And it takes more than leather elbow patches to make a scholar!" A low blow. He folded his arms across his chest and glared at me, as if expecting a response. "Do you know what you are? A dreamer—a bona fide, pie-in-the-sky, wild-eyed dreamer."

"Well, I do my best thinking in my sleep—"

"I'll tell you this," he said, pulling himself up to his full height, which was still nothing to brag about, "I will do everything in my power to make sure President Costa doesn't sign off on this moronic idea. You haven't heard the end of it, I promise." And with that he turned and stalked back down the dark hallway.

Again I was reminded of Poe: "Deep into that darkness peering, long I stood there, wondering, fearing ..."

A shout echoed from the far end, "And you're an idiot!" A distant door slammed.

"But a well-meaning one," I said to myself. "And yes, I'm sure I haven't heard the end of it."

CHAPTER 2
THE FORUM ON FAITH

Our good Lord answered to all the questions
and doubts that I might make, saying full comfortably,
"... Thou shall see thyself that
all manner of thing shall be well."
—*Julian of Norwich, 1342–1416*

When I was nine or ten years old, I had the great privilege of being beaten up by Roger Schroder, one of the neighborhood's preeminent bullies and a fellow whom one couldn't help but pity—if only because Fate was clearly grooming him for long-term incarceration. When he was done beating me up, he looked down at me with a kindly expression and said, "Just to show you there are no hard feelings ..."—and he beat me up again.

So, in hindsight, I should have been wary on that bright, chilly February morning when Cornelius Dunwoody cornered me—literally, in a glassed-in right angle of the library entrance—and spoke those words.

At the time, Katie and I were waiting for President Costa to make a crucial decision regarding our proposal. The heads of all the affected departments had signed off with their blessing —except, of course, Dr. Dunwoody. The Provost's Council had recommended, in their turn, that his veto *not* be considered since our department would draw its staff from the undergraduate college and local clergy rather than the graduate Seminary and School of Theology, but President Costa, needing to maintain good relations with the seminary, wanted time to weigh things. So the process was stalled on her desk.

Ever since the confrontation in my office more than a month earlier, Dunwoody had remained as silent as stout Cortez upon a peak in Darien. Until today.

"Listen, I know I came on a little strong before," he said. "I apologize. Just to show you there are no hard feelings"—(the very words)—"I'd like to bury the hatchet and make you an offer."

"An offer?" I repeated. The Roman poet Virgil had dire things to say about Greeks bearing gifts, but I briefly wondered whether the admonition might also apply to professors of New Testament Greek.

"Yes," he replied. "As you know, next month is the Forum on Faith, and I was hoping you'd take part."

"Take part?" I was beginning to sound like a parrot.

"As a favor to me. You see, we have an empty chair on one of the panels. Nothing out of your depth, Bonham ... just a general discussion on 'New Directions in Faith in the Twenty-First Century.' Sort of freewheeling ... open ended. Very *Theophily*, if you know what I mean. Right up your alley, don't you think, eh?"

"Who are the other panelists?"

"Generalists like yourself—there's an Episcopal priest from

the city and some popular inspirational writer. Easy-peasy. No prep required."

I can do that, I thought—answer a few questions, offer sage advice, smile, and look important. And it might demonstrate to President Costa that I'm a team player, diving into the spirit of things, so to speak, and perhaps this was an indication that Dunwoody was beginning to reconsider his objection to the new department. I liked the way he said, "Very *Theophily!*" So, relieved that our little contretemps seemed to be over, I responded, "Sign me up!"

"With pleasure," said Dunwoody. "I'll owe you one."

An unmistakable herald of spring is the appearance of posters stuck to every vertical surface, announcing the Cupperton University Forum on Faith. The event, sponsored by the Seminary and School of Theology, takes place at the end of March every year and is a chance for students and the public alike to hear what current authors and scholars in the field of religion have to say. For a long weekend, panel discussions and workshops are offered throughout the mornings and afternoons, and lectures and concerts take place every evening.

Early in the year, ambitious seminarians start vying for seats in the various cars scheduled to make trips to the airport to pick up the distinguished speakers, more than an hour's drive to the city each way. I cannot imagine what special kind of hell it must be for those unsuspecting dignitaries to be stranded in the backseat of a compact sedan with an overzealous graduate student giving a dramatic recitation of his or her dissertation-in-progress. I've heard that some seminarians go so far as to ensure that the child safety locks are activated to prevent escape.

In the past, I'd attended sessions at the Forum, but this was the first time I'd been asked to participate. I was flattered and rather excited. Still, when I told Katie the next morning at the CupperTea, she glared at me. "Let me get this straight, M.B."—she'd taken to calling me *M.B.* recently—"*Dunwoody* asked *you?*"

"That's right."

"Hmm" was all she said.

KATIE'S *HMM* stuck to me like a tick until the week of the Forum. On the morning of the panel, to relieve my anxiety, I staked out Phipps Auditorium an hour early, scanning the cavernous echoing space and watching as the tech staff checked the lighting and the sound system. They handed me a small pocket receiver with a wireless microphone to clip to my lapel. I paced the stage and brooded.

Soon, others began to stroll through the entrance, including my co-panelists. As we shuffled over to our chairs on stage, I introduced myself. The Reverend Joseph Clark, the Episcopal priest, was a bulky, bright-eyed, gregarious fellow, whose smile seemed permanently affixed; he was dressed in his clerical collar and sported a pin on his black tunic that read, "JESUS IS COMING (LOOK BUSY)." Renata Baker, the other panelist, was a perfectly coiffed, vivacious thirty-something writer of inspirational nonfiction for like-minded thirty-somethings. She was, as Katie informed me, a *New York Times* bestselling author, a fabulously popular blogger, and a master of social media—but "an intellectual lightweight" nonetheless, in Katie's overeducated opinion.

As the three of us chatted, I watched the attendees enter, singly and in groups—there were backpacked undergraduates studying their smartphones; seminarians talking volubly about *ideas*, no doubt; and faculty members and townspeople who were there for no other reasons than enjoyment and edification. And, of course, Katie, my personal claque, took a seat in the front row.

Finally, bringing up the rear were President Costa and Provost Kinealy, who found seats near the back. Just as the lights dimmed and the moderator stepped to the podium, I saw Dunwoody squeeze his way, unapologetically, past a half dozen attendees to claim the empty seat next to President Costa. I thought of Katie's *hmm*.

The moderator was, like Katie, a third-year seminarian, and she too had once attended my mystics seminars. She smiled and raised her hands to silence the happy rumble of conversation. As we panelists sat in the hazy glare of the spotlights, she thanked everyone for coming and introduced the three of us, whom she characterized as "a priest, a popular writer, and a prof." After delivering a short exposition on the morning's topic, "New Directions in Faith in the Twenty-First Century," she opened the discussion by pointing to a young woman in the front row, two seats over from Katie, who directed her question to Ms. Baker: "Thank you. Ms. Baker, it's an honor to have you here at Cupperton. I've read all your books. I'd like to ask about your prayer life. How do you pray, and how does your prayer life affect your writing, and how is prayer even relevant in the modern world?"

I didn't listen to her answer because I was too busy taking in the surroundings and thinking how I would have answered the question myself, though I can't imagine anyone wanting to know about my prayer life, such as it is.

The next question was for Reverend Clark. A young seminary student asked, "What is your greatest challenge as an urban pastor?"

"Mostly getting out of bed in the morning ...," he quipped. When the laughter died down, the affable priest continued his response as I again gazed out over the fresh young faces.

A few minutes later, the moderator pointed to one of those fresh faces. "Yes, you. Second row."

The young man was a seminarian whom I'd seen on campus. I think his name was Jason. He said, "I'd like to ask Dr. Bonham who his favorite theologian is."

I reflected for a moment and answered with what I thought was a charming twinkle in my eye, "Certainly ... Charlie Brown."

The auditorium erupted in laughter. I caught Katie's eye. She smiled. Pleased with myself, I continued, "I think the late Charles Schulz, in his classic *Peanuts* cartoons, hit upon almost every modern spiritual dilemma we face—depression, insecurity, doubt, alienation, little red-haired girls ..." More chuckles. *This is fun*, I thought.

"But Dr. Bonham," the student persisted, "in times like ours, don't you think we need *strong* theological guidance? Seriously, with so many conflicting voices out there, I would like to know which contemporary theological writers you read and would recommend to the rest of us."

Everything got quiet. A basic rule of repartee, which this student had obviously never learned, is not to step on someone else's punchline unless you have a better one of your own. It's undignified.

"Well, I *am* being serious," I said, "but I can't say I read contemporary theology. It's not my field of study."

Unbelievably, the student wouldn't quit. In a shaming voice, he added, "But shouldn't it be *every* Christian's field of study?"

His words, of course, were an answer disguised as a question, so I let it go by shrugging and glancing back at the moderator.

Reverend Clark stuck a plump finger into the air. "If I may ..."

"Yes, Reverend Clark ...," said the moderator.

"I have a couple of recommendations." He turned to the seminarian. "Being of the Anglican persuasion"—chuckles throughout the auditorium—"I'm quite fond of Alister McGrath. Have you read him? He writes on a wide range of topics. Quite accessible. Also, check out Christopher Hall on the historical church, or perhaps Rosemary Radford Ruether or Phyllis Trible if your bent is feminist theology, and if you're looking for apologetics, be sure to read Richard Swinburne. Top notch."

"Thank you, Reverend Clark," said the moderator. As I sat there, I could feel my face flush the color of pickled beets.

Then the moderator pointed to a woman who asked Ms. Baker if she had any tips for young writers. Again, I didn't listen. I was too shaken.

Several minutes later, another question came to me from another seminarian, a young man named Rowan whom I'd often seen with Katie: "This is for Dr. Bonham. Could you, as the academic on the panel, talk about the importance of the biblical languages in our time ... and how they've shaped your faith?"

I was conscious of furrowing my brow, which I realized made me look either miffed or dimwitted. I said, "I'm afraid I don't *know* the biblical languages ... but as a professor of Middle English literature, I can attest to the rugged beauty of Wycliffe's translation—"

"But the Bible is the founding document of our faith! How can any Christian *not* be curious about learning the *original* languages?" Another answer parading as a question.

"Well, I didn't say I wasn't curious, but I just ... it's not my field." I floundered.

I fully expected Reverend Clark's pesky finger to prod the air again, but the moderator, in the conversational equivalent of a mercy killing, broke in, "All right ... who else has a question?"

But before anyone could respond, Ms. Baker oh-so-helpfully raised her hand. "Excuse me ..."

"Yes, Ms. Baker," said the moderator.

"I can't claim to be a scholar like these gentlemen, but I did take one semester of New Testament Greek in college, and it changed my life. I still have a Greek interlinear on hand for my personal Bible study. I encourage everyone to study at least a little Greek."

I stared at her.

Then I glanced down at Katie. In her distress, her glasses were starting to steam up, making her look like Little Orphan Annie in the old cartoons.

I have no idea what transpired in the next twenty minutes except that the questions were directed to Reverend Clark and Ms. Baker. I was in a daze. What, I wondered, was going on? I felt a gnawing ache in the pit of my stomach—

I was awakened from my trance by titters from the audience. The moderator was talking. "Dr. Bonham, did you hear? Someone has a question."

"Oh ... yes ... I'm sorry," I said. "Of course."

"Right," said yet another bright-eyed seminarian, this one female, "I have two questions. First, perhaps the most important issue regarding faith in the twenty-first century is how we should balance tradition, experience, and general revelation in our spiritual lives. I would like to know your opinion. Also, I'd be interested to know whether you think Teilhard de Chardin's concept of a teleologically unfolding cosmos has become even more relevant in our time."

For a moment I thought it was a joke, the punchline of which had sailed over my head. But no one was laughing, though I heard a tiny whistle of disbelief escape Reverend Clark's lips. With all eyes fixed on me, I glanced at Dunwoody in the back row. He shrugged and made that funny little frowny shape with his mouth the way people do when they're impressed with something, as if he were saying, "Hmm. Good question. Wish I'd thought of that."

Then it hit me ... he *had* thought of that. This was all a setup.

Feeling the bile coursing through my veins, I croaked, "I'm afraid I'll have to defer. I've not read Teilhard de Chardin, nor do I have strong feelings about general revelation."

Uncomfortable laughter echoed throughout the hall. I felt sweaty and hot all over.

I don't know how much longer the panel lasted, but when the lights came on, seemingly days later, the attendees offered up a polite round of applause, then shuffled off to their next session. Reverend Clark, beaming, shook my hand vigorously and told me what a magnificent job I'd done—"Really, really terrific," he insisted; "this was great, wasn't it? Just great!"—and a crowd of young admirers gathered around Ms. Baker, with books in their hands for her to sign. I looked up and saw Dunwoody talking animatedly to President Costa at the back as they exited the auditorium. My heart sank.

I couldn't move. Katie dashed up onto the stage, where I was still seated.

Defeated, I bellowed, "Jesus, Mary, and Joseph!" forgetting, of course, that my microphone was still on. Those who hadn't yet left the auditorium looked in my direction with alarm.

When they saw that I was still conscious and breathing, they continued on their way.

I fumbled for the mic switch and said to Katie, "Did I come off as badly as I think I did?"

"Yes," she said.

"I was the intellectual lightweight on the panel, wasn't I?"

"Yes."

"I wish you'd been in my place. You could have answered those questions ..."

"Yes," she said, giving me a pat on the shoulder, "but none of that matters." Then in a stony voice she added, "Dunwoody's behind this ... and I think I'm gonna have to have a talk with Rowan—like right now," and off she sprinted.

In the days that followed, it became clear that our proposal was on life-support. When Katie and I asked Provost Kinealy where things stood, he shook his head and said, "It's still on the president's desk; she wants another couple of weeks, but I'm afraid it doesn't look good. And"—he peered intently at me—"your performance at the Forum didn't help."

ABOUT A WEEK LATER, as I was going up the steps of Beetham on my way to teach Mystics 402, Katie seemed to emerge from nowhere (I believe she's part genie) and handed me a scrap of paper. "Call this number, M.B.," she said, "like immediately. I'll go to class and keep everyone in line till you get back. Just call."

I knew Katie well enough by now to trust her with my life, to say nothing of mysterious phone calls, so, having left my phone at home as usual, I popped into the English Department office and asked Dolly De Angeli, the departmental secretary, if I might use her desk phone. I punched in the number and soon understood Katie's urgency, for the call gave me a glimmer of hope.

After 402, I jogged over to Erickson Hall, mounted the three flights of steps, and rapped on the doorframe of Dunwoody's office. He looked up from his stacks upon stacks of papers (he was, I knew, on a committee that was producing a new Bible translation). "Humph. It's you." He looked back down at his work. I've had warmer greetings from traffic lights, which are, at least, green on occasion.

Out of breath, I said, "So sorry ... can't stay to chitchat, but I'm afraid I need to beg a favor. I hesitate even asking, but here's the scoop. You see, Ms. Westcott received a call today from another school. A student delegation is visiting campus on Thursday, and they're hoping to connect with someone to confer with them about philosophy and theology and the Bible and what not. And yes, I confess, I knew I'd be *way* out of my depth. So, here I am, metaphorical hat in hand, to ask if you'd consider talking to them. It wouldn't take more than an hour, and I suspect a few of them might even be good candidates for the seminary. And, if you remember, you *did* say you'd 'owe me one' for volunteering at the Forum."

He looked at me indulgently. "So, you admit to limitations, do you, Bonham? Well, that's a promising sign. Of course I'll help." I'm sure his gracious condescension was the consequence of knowing that the Department of Theophily was all but kaput.

THE FOLLOWING THURSDAY MORNING, Katie and I welcomed the visiting scholars to my classroom in Beetham. We talked, exchanged stories about our respective academic institutions, and waited for the chairman to arrive. Eventually, over the din of conversation, I could faintly hear the main door slam far off and footsteps tromping up the echoing tiles of the hallway.

No sooner had Dunwoody set foot in the classroom than he stopped short as if he'd been greeted by an overeager Boston cream pie. He couldn't have looked more stunned if he'd walked into a faculty meeting of leprechauns.

Being the empathic soul that I am, I immediately intuited the source of his stupefaction and realized, furthermore, that I was in part responsible. Somehow, I must have neglected to inform him that the visiting students with theological questions were first and second graders from the local Christian elementary school. How I could have been so absentminded, I don't know, but there it is. Things happen. And the irony of it all is that I'd long known from any number of sources that Dunwoody had never been what is called "good with children." One of my informants had even used the phrase *chronic, acute pedophobia.*

There were about thirty girls and boys chattering loudly and having a hard time keeping their hands to themselves. Their teacher, Ms. Amanda Niles, was the one with whom Katie and I had spoken on the phone, and she had indeed told us that her precocious charges were starting to ask tough questions about God, faith, and the Bible, questions that she and her colleagues at the school couldn't answer. So, she thought, why not make a field trip to the university out of it? They could talk to a real theologian, ask their questions, then have pizza and chocolate milk at the cafeteria. After that, they'd been promised an hour's playtime in the arboretum where they were looking forward to dashing around our lovely eleven-circuit labyrinth, something I myself enjoy doing, though at a more meditative pace.

The classroom was in an uproar until Ms. Niles, sounding like Moses addressing the querulous Israelites, shouted: "Hey!

Everyone! Settle down!" When the settling down had for the most part been accomplished, she regained her composure and said, "All right, then. Thank you, Dr. Bonham, for inviting us to your classroom. We've been so excited to talk to someone about our questions. Class, I'd like you to meet Dr. Cornelius Dunwoody, who's in charge of the Seminary and School of Theology here at Cupperton—and who Dr. Bonham says is one of the smartest people at the university. He's been kind enough to take time out of his busy day to talk with you. Do you all remember what you wanted to ask? Who wants to start?"

Small hands shot up everywhere—and Dunwoody stood there, pale and clammy, like a pillar of salt on an especially humid day. I wondered whether I should check his vitals.

"Avery," said Ms. Niles, pointing to a red-haired girl in the front row who not only raised her hand but waved it vigorously, like a hyperactive Hermione Granger.

Avery pinned Dunwoody with a hard, accusing glare and said, "Why did God let my cat die?" She sounded threatening, as though she held Dunwoody personally responsible. "I prayed and prayed, but he still died. His name's Boots and—"

Other voices shouted out, "My dog died," "Arlo did too ..." "My parakeet ..." "My hamster ..." It felt as if a riot were about to break out.

Ms. Niles waved her hands as though she were flagging down a train. "Children ... children! One at a time! Avery, go ahead."

"My mother said God needed a cat more than we did, but I think she's making it up. Will I see Boots in heaven? I *want* to see Boots!"

Dunwoody stood there, working his mouth open and closed the way a goldfish does. At length he spoke. "Well ... animals in heaven, um, I'm sorry to say ... well ... there are differing opinions. On the negative side, I believe it was ... uh ... Basil of Caesarea who wrote ..."

I was standing by the window, and Dunwoody glanced over at me. I shook my head and shut my eyes briefly as if to say, "Nope, don't go there."

"Or ... or ... well, no, I mean, on the positive side, Tertullian somewhere in his *Treatise on the Soul* ... no, wait, I think he was negative too ... um ..."

An awkward silence followed as the frantic little search engine in Dunwoody's brain clicked through his mental files. We all waited.

Hoping to ease his distress, Ms. Niles interjected, "Professor, how about the Bible—does it say anything about animals in heaven?"

Dunwoody looked at her as if she were daft. But then, oddly, he brightened up. An idea had occurred to him. He made a gracious gesture in my direction and said, "Do you know who we should ask, boys and girls? Dr. Bonham here knows more about these kinds of things than just about anybody; don't you, Bonham? He'll explain it all to us." His sarcasm dripped.

He thought he had me over the theological barrel, and that the barrel was about to go over Niagara Falls ... except he didn't know that these were questions I'd been pondering ever since, well, since first grade.

"Those are great questions, Avery," I began, "and thank you, Ms. Niles, for bringing such bright, inquisitive students to see us! As far as I'm concerned, the Bible *does* talk about that. Think about Noah's ark. Did God save just Noah and his family? No. He saved the animals too. In Psalm 36 it says, 'Man and beast Thou savest,' which to me means that God takes care of all his creatures, people and animals. He made them, right? Why would they *not* go to heaven? And I like it when Paul says —you've heard about the apostle Paul in Sunday school I bet—

well, he says that 'God will unite *all* things.' That is, God will bring them all together in the end, and I can't help but feel that *all things* includes pets. What do you think?"

There were smiles and even a couple of cheers among the young theologians.

"Now, I've got a question for all of you," I said. "Do you know C. S. Lewis? He wrote the Narnia books ... your parents have read those to you, right? Well, he thought it was quite possible that there will be tame animals in heaven—all those animals that were loved by people on earth. But he also wondered this: do you think God will let mosquitos in?"

There was laughter and yells of "No way!"

"There would be a lot of them, for sure," I said. "So, here's what Lewis thought: maybe God will send mosquitos to that *other* place, and that will be *their* heaven!"

Laughter erupted. One boy said, "Nobody likes snakes either!" though one of the girls objected, "I like snakes!"

"Of course, we won't know till we get to heaven, will we?" I said.

After a short pause, Ms. Niles asked, "What other questions do you have for Dr. Dunwoody?"

A boy in the back raised his hand. "My grandfather uses bad words and doesn't go to church. Will he go to heaven?"

Dunwoody, who was starting to reprise his goldfish impersonation, turned in my direction again and snarled, "Be my guest, Bonham."

I asked the boy, "What's your name?"

"Dan."

"Here's a question, Dan. You love your grandfather?"

He nodded.

"Is he good to you?"

Nod.

"What do you like about him?"

"He takes me fishing. He talks to me about stuff. And he's really, really funny."

"I bet he loves you a lot. And I would also bet that God loves him for all the ways he loves you. Don't you think?"

Nod.

"Well, that's a good sign, isn't it? The Bible says that God *is* love, so there has to be a little piece of God in your grandfather, right?"

From the far corner of the room, a girl asked, "What's heaven like?"

By this point, I'd worked my way to the front of the room, while Dunwoody had taken my place by the window.

"Well," I said, "who here likes Christmas?"

Shouts and yells.

"So, do you know what's in all those packages before you open them?"

A lot of animated chatter ensued.

"That's right. You *don't*. Not until Christmas morning. But you know they're going to be wonderful! You know it because the people giving them to you love you so much. Well, to me, that's heaven. We don't know what's inside it, but we *know* it's going to be special because the one who gives it to us loves us even more than our families do."

The students nodded and smiled.

Someone asked, "Why do bad things happen? My friend's house burned down."

"Wow! That's a big question," I said, "and I don't know, and I'm not sure anybody does, but I've got a story that helps me think about that. In my English classes I teach about a woman named Julian who lived hundreds of years ago in a place called Norwich, and she loved God a lot. But she was upset about bad things happening as well. She had a lot of questions she wished she could ask God. So, one time, when she was really sick, she had a dream. In that dream, she saw Jesus and decided to ask him some of those questions. Jesus answered her, saying basically, 'Julian, the truth is that bad things will happen, and people will suffer, but I can promise you this: all shall be well.' Then Jesus repeated it, just so she'd understand: 'All shall be well ... and all manner of thing shall be well.' It wasn't the answer Julian had expected. Instead, Jesus was saying that at some point, maybe sooner, maybe later, everything would be all right again."

I let that sink in for a moment. Then I said, "That's what I love about Julian's dream. We don't always get the answers we want or expect. But you know what? Our questions and doubts —all these things we deeply, desperately want to understand but don't—well, they're all ways of showing God how much we care. Think of that: all these questions you have right now are ways of showing how much you love God! And I suspect Jesus loves us *especially* for those hard questions because they're a chance for him to comfort us. So keep asking, keep wondering, even if you don't get the answers ... because Jesus is always there, saying, 'All shall be well.'"

From the back of the room, Katie gave me a double thumbs-up.

AT THE END of the hour, Dunwoody, his bald head suffused with crimson, collared me and hissed under his breath, "You're so smug, Bonham! You tricked me. And you know as well as I do that everything you said was bunk ... I wish I could—" He was about to say more, but Ms. Niles approached to thank us.

"Dr. Dunwoody," I said, "I'd like to introduce you to Ms. Amanda Niles." Curtly, he shook her hand. Then, after a dramatic pause, I added, "Amanda *Costa* Niles."

"*Costa?*" Dunwoody's expression turned from restrained rage to bewilderment. "You're related to President Costa ...?"

"I'm her daughter," said the teacher. "My mother has told me *so* much about you and Dr. Bonham. In fact, she was the one who suggested I call Dr. Bonham to arrange all this ..."

I smiled at Ms. Niles and said, "Please tell your mother what a great help Dr. Dunwoody was this morning. I don't know what we'd have done without him."

Dunwoody shot me a nasty look, then flashed an insincere smile at Ms. Niles, shook her hand again, and left abruptly.

A few minutes later, as Katie and I were halfway down the front steps of Beetham, someone grabbed my arm from behind and swung me around. Dunwoody glared at me. "You think you're so clever, Bonham, you prig! You set me up!"

"Not at all," I said. "Not at all. After the panel at the Forum, I just wanted to return the favor ... and to show you ... there are no hard feelings."

TWO DAYS LATER, Provost Kinealy called to say that the logjam in the president's office had broken. She had overruled Dunwoody's objection to the new department, and the proposal was now moving on to the next stage. Kinealy even added that the president was giving our project her "most enthusiastic support" and that she could see more clearly than ever why Cupperton needed a Department of Theophily. By the end of April, the rest of the signoffs were obtained from the various committees and the Finance Office.

The day after we received the letter of declaration that our proposal had been approved, Katie, as was her habit, materialized in my office and said, "I've done it!"

I looked at her quizzically.

"I promised myself I'd do it if we got the department, but I wasn't sure what I wanted it to say until the first graders came."

Again, I gave her a puzzled look. She rolled up the sleeve of her black T-shirt, and there on her right deltoid was a tattoo.

A red rose, under which the florid script read, "All shall be well."

CHAPTER 3

THE BANQUET

If, my Lord, a kiss signifies peace,
why should not our souls ask it of Thee?
What more can I beg of Thee than ...
that Thou wilt kiss me with the kiss of Thy mouth?
—*Teresa of Ávila, 1515–1582*

"**M**arteen, you look sad."

From my tree-shaded bench in North Quad, I looked up and saw Dr. Graciela Rojas with a concerned look on her face. It was a bright mid-August afternoon, warm and restlessly breezy, and the campus was abuzz with preparations for freshman orientation. The new students and their parents were due to arrive the following day. Now that the Department of Theophily was about to hang out its shingle and declare itself open for business, you would think that I, like David in his linen ephod, would be dancing before the Lord with all my might, but instead, my mind was filled with dark ruminations.

Graciela sat down next to me, leaned in, and said softly, "Tell me, Marteen, what is the trouble?"

WHEN I CONSIDER the many advantages of age, I realize that few things in life make me wish I were twenty-seven again, but Graciela Echeveria Rojas is one of them. I experience a gentle, almost imperceptible tremor whenever she addresses me in her beautiful, rich Mexican accent as "Marteen." Paul Verlaine's phrase *l'extase langoureuse*, "languorous ecstasy," comes closest to describing that feeling. And while I know it's futile to grouse about Time's wingèd chariot, I often find myself repeating that wistful line by the Italian poet Moro: "Were the river but a cup less quick ..."

When Graciela first arrived on campus as an associate professor two years earlier, I was her designated faculty mentor. She had recently received her doctorate in Hispanic Literature and Cultures from the University of Arizona, having written her dissertation on "Teresa of Ávila's Dialectical Feminism," which soon found an interested publisher. It's a brilliant piece of scholarship in which she weighs, as if in a balance, the great Spanish saint's own somewhat harsh misogyny on one hand with her energetic advocacy of women's expanded roles in the church on the other. Since Graciela and I share a fascination for the mystics, we became fast friends.

So fast, in fact, that I became something of an avuncular confidant. Not only was she still grieving her father, who had died the previous summer, but in January of her first year of teaching at Cupperton, she disclosed to me the details of her recently broken engagement. Her longtime boyfriend from her undergraduate years at Santa Clara had been drafted into the NFL, but she had come to realize that fame—and product sponsorships—had gone to his head. He was a ruggedly photogenic middle linebacker whom the television sportscasters had dubbed "Roadblock." His team was having an exceptional season, but, as Graciela put it, he was far more interested in Super Bowl rings than wedding rings—and a certain cheerleader's name was mentioned as well. So Graciela broke off the engagement before her first Christmas at Cupperton. To crown the former boyfriend's well-earned misfortunes, his team lost in the first round of the playoffs, and he tore his ACL.

Graciela was now dating a somewhat unimposing young man of normal proportions whom she'd met at the Catholic Newman Center on campus. He was in charge of Cupperton's Information Technology Center, and I'd known him only as "the Computer Guy" because he was always on hand when the toner in the English Department's printer ran low (what *is* toner?) or when I accidentally erased an entire semester's grades. His real name, I learned, was Nate, and he had a master's in computational engineering from MIT; he designed computer games and knew several languages, Spanish among them. He was clearly brilliant, and I grudgingly grew to like him, largely because he and Graciela seemed so blissful together. They had chemistry, and I sensed that some jubilant knot-tying was inevitable. I was hopeful, however, that her feminism would steer her away from adopting his surname; Señora Graciela Rojas Herkenroeder does not exactly skip trippingly on the tongue.

Much later, when I asked Katie why computer geeks seemed to have all the luck, she answered, "Because they're the new superheroes, M.B. Get used to it."

WHEN GRACIELA FOUND me on the bench that sunny Sunday afternoon, I was brooding ... not over Time's wingèd chariot nor the Ascendency of the Geeks, but over some distressing news that Katie had reported to me that morning. Dark forces were stirring in Mordor.

Now that the Department of Theophily was about to become a thriving concern, the university had provided funding for a celebratory banquet the following weekend—an initiatory rite, so to speak—just before the start of classes. Invitations had gone out to the faculty and administrators, and most had RSVP-ed in the affirmative. Katie and I were greeted on campus daily with smiles and congratulatory handshakes. Among the invitees were the faculty of the School of Theology, and that, as so often before, was the source of my disquietude.

According to the banquet's bill of fare, I was scheduled to address the teeming masses at the conclusion of dinner, with the intention of outlining the new department's philosophy and introducing its participating faculty, Graciela among them. But Ms. Adams, Katie's mole in the seminary, had leaked to Katie that a conspiracy was afoot: Dunwoody and his accomplices—more than a dozen individuals—were organizing a protest. After indulging in our free meal (your choice of Salisbury steak, crusted tilapia, or vegetarian platter), the theology staff intended to walk out en masse the moment I reached the podium. A figurative poke in the eye as a way of expressing their displeasure.

After I related all this to Graciela, she said, "That is so childish. Let them walk out. It just makes them look petty."

"It's sophomoric, I know," I said. "The mature thing would be to ignore it, but it'll be such a blot on an otherwise glorious evening—on Katie's evening and yours—on everyone's evening. They have no right."

"Have you confronted him?"

"Dunwoody's unconfrontable," I replied. "I've tried in the past. No doubt he'd deny the whole thing ... and then thank me for giving him the idea."

As we continued to chat, I spied half a dozen young women approaching from the other side of the quad, between the Sheeres Museum and Phipps Auditorium. One of them carried a folded piece of fabric, and as soon as they spotted Graciela, they headed in our direction.

"Señorita Rojas!" one of them shouted.

"Hola, Señorita Griffith," Graciela shouted back. When the students reached us, Graciela said to them, "You know Dr. Bonham ... a dear friend. How can we help you?"

The young Ms. Griffith was one of Graciela's Spanish students, but it was not for academics that the group had sought her out. Graciela was also the faculty advisor for the CWA, the Cupperton Women's Association, and these upper-classwomen before me were, I perceived, the group's inner circle, its *conseil militant*, who had arrived on campus early to rouse the rabble and mount the barricades during freshman orientation.

Carefully they unfolded a banner that must have been ten feet long, and they held it up. Its giant silk-screened Helvetica caps read:

WELCOME, FRESHWOMEN! GET WOKE!
LEARN ABOUT GENDER ISSUES AT CUPPERTON—JOIN THE WOMEN'S
ASSOCIATION

"We've got a question," said Ms. Griffith. "We want to hang it on the iron gate over the west entrance so the new students will see it as they drive onto campus tomorrow. But someone said it's not allowed. We checked, and there's no rule; but someone else said it's too 'in-your-face,' that it wouldn't be fair to all the other groups on campus."

Graciela thought for a moment as the women refolded the banner. With a sly smile, she said, "Well, we would never want the CWA to be too *'in-your-face,'* now, would we?" She pinned them with a meaningful look.

The women hesitated, then caught her drift. "Oh, okay then," said Ms. Griffith, "we'll do it."

They turned, and as they marched off in the direction of the West Gate, Graciela called after them, "If anyone tries to stop you, pay no attention and tell them to call *me!*"

They waved and disappeared down the hill.

"You're not afraid of anyone, are you?" I asked admiringly.

"Only God, Marteen."

We sat in silence for a few moments, listening to the high whine of the summer locusts and watching a maintenance crew putter past in their golf cart. Somewhere in the distance, conveyed faintly on the breeze, were the strains of the university orchestra rehearsing for the orientation ceremony.

Then Graciela said, "So, you plan to speak at this dinner, and then they walk out, yes?"

"Yes."

"What if someone else spoke? What if I spoke instead?"

"Well, you'd be putting yourself on the firing line ..."

"I think I know how to keep them from leaving."

"You've got a plan?"

"Maybe. Like Señorita Griffith ... perhaps we need to be a little 'in-your-face.' Who was invited? You have a list?"

"Katie'll get it to you."

"How many seminary people?"

"About fourteen, all faculty."

"Then trust me. I think I know what to do."

"I could never *not* trust you, Graciela."

MONDAY AND TUESDAY, the first two days of Freshman Orientation Week, are set aside for the Activities Fair, held outdoors in the CUSS, at which the various departments and campus organizations introduce themselves to the incoming students. Ms. Griffith and the CWA set up an information table in an effort to win callow young hearts and minds. The Quidditch Team, the Cheese Appreciation Society, and the Intramural Flag Football Club were represented, as was the university's literary magazine, *The Flyting*, of which I am the faculty sponsor. One of my favorites is the Sasquatch Club, which claims to investigate elusive, oversized fauna but is actually an excuse for heading into the woods once a month, rain or shine, with beer. The campus Republicans ostentatiously smoked cigars at their table, while the Democrats earnestly handed out voter-registration cards. The Nihilist Society's table, amusingly, was empty for the entire two days.

Katie and I unfolded our own modest card table and taped a poster across the front that read, in Katie's neat script, "Ask us what Theophily is." We were surprised by how many students and parents did just that.

My mood had improved due to Graciela's sanguine influence, and now, seeing how effervescent Katie had become while speaking with the new students, I felt positively boomps-a-daisy. Katie, like a carnival barker with a good bedside manner, had a knack for compelling, persuasive rhetoric, and I caught a glimpse of what a wonderful minister she would have become. I was grateful that Theophily was now her passion. One young woman named Kyeesha must have talked with Katie for half an hour and became so excited that she declared to us both, "Well, I'm planning to study music, but I think I'll do a double-major with Theophily now!"

In the last hour of the Activities Fair, however, the needle swung back toward the foreboding end of the dial when I spied Dunwoody at the opposite end of the CUSS. He gave me one of those odd little two-finger salutes and nodded grimly. Then, like the moving finger having writ, he moved on.

On the Saturday of the banquet I discovered that my old tuxedo (admittedly a hideous getup with wide velvet lapels) no longer fit like a glove, but more like a wetsuit—tight in all the wrong places. Even the cummerbund seemed to have shrunk. So I reverted, as always, to my customary tweed coat and baggy corduroys, which are, I suppose, the aged professor's equivalent of the fashionable woman's little black dress, suitable for all occasions.

Late in the afternoon, I strolled over to the Banquet Hall next to the Admin Building to find that Graciela and Nate were already at the entrance, waiting to greet the guests. Speaking of fashionable women, Graciela was wearing a stunning royal-blue dress with a deep drop back and loose, lacy sleeves, and Nate, with uncombed hair, was wearing a too-short knit tie, faded jeans, and sneakers. I was reminded of a college roommate of mine named Dudley who once formulated what he called Dudley's Law: "The best-dressed women go with the goofiest-looking guys." Still, I couldn't help but notice how gleeful they seemed, and from Graciela's impish smile, it was obvious that she had something up her sleeve, loose and lacy though it was.

Inside the hall, the catering staff was smoothing table-cloths onto the round tables and pouring water into glasses by the trayful. Katie was a blur of activity. She too was elegantly attired: black leggings and plain black jumper—

sleeveless, so that everyone might see her rose tattoo. Her short black hair, newly buzz-cut in a few places, had been moussed at a tight, dramatic angle, as if styled by a Cubist with OCD. She ran back and forth from the kitchen to the hall, directing the servers, lighting candles, ordering the caterers around, and making sure everything was ready, which made me think of Gandalf before the Battle of Helm's Deep—a comparison that would have made her blush, I'm sure.

I soon realized that Katie had a young man in tow. Smiling and amused by the bustle around him, he'd obviously been told to sit on one side of the banquet hall so that Hurricane Katie would be free to career through the room as needed. I introduced myself. His name was Tyrell, and he told me he was on the worship staff at a local church. Not wanting to be an obstacle myself, I settled in next to Tyrell, and together we chatted and watched Katie dash back and forth, which was not unlike watching a one-person tennis match.

Soon, the guests began filing in, including Dunwoody and his holy hooligans. After everyone had mingled for a time, Dr. Alice Mears, chair of the Psychology Department, clinked a spoon on a water glass and directed everyone to find their seats. Graciela and Nate, Katie and Tyrell, a few select Theophily faculty, and I found our chairs at the two long tables on the raised platform at the front. A speaker's podium with a microphone stood between them. Anxiety gripped me as I took my seat. After Dr. Mears recited a short blessing, the servers started dealing out the salad plates like a band of croupiers.

As I looked around, I had the uneasy feeling that the eminent professors of theology were staring at me, though glancing away as soon as we locked eyes. It was unnerving. I felt self-conscious. I leaned toward Katie to my right. "Do I look all right?"

"Like Einstein in a wind tunnel," she said, "but yes, you're fine."

I RECALL little of the meal itself, except I think I had the tilapia. Since Katie was occupied with Tyrell to her right, I chatted with Dr. Mears to my left, though in hindsight I must have seemed somewhat overwrought because I remember asking her several times, in a hopeful tone, if she was the kind of psychologist who could prescribe medications. She thought I was joking.

As the meal neared completion, I sensed the moment had come. I looked down toward the other table, caught Graciela's eye, and nodded.

She pushed back her chair, rose, and strode to the podium. She is the kind of person who commands attention without even trying, and this evening, in the flickering candlelight of the hall, she looked sensuous and regal, as if she had just stepped out of a Pre-Raphaelite painting. (Have I already mentioned that she was wearing a stunning royal-blue dress with a deep drop back?) The room grew quiet. All eyes were on her. As she stared out over the gathering, she paused. The waitstaff bustled in and out, clearing the dessert plates.

It was clear that Dunwoody and his crew had expected me to open the proceedings, so, somewhat unsure about the timing, Dunwoody sat there momentarily, staring at Graciela. He shifted his gaze in my direction, and, in return for his greeting to me a few days earlier, I gave him one of those two-finger salutes. Piqued, he gave a quick, covert nod in every direction of the compass, and slowly, more than a dozen professors—all men—scooted back their chairs to stand.

That was the moment Graciela had been waiting for. As

everyone's eyes sparkled in the candlelight, she said, more loudly and more drawn out than you would have expected, *"You!"*

I jumped. It was like a clap of thunder, after which you notice how silent everything becomes.

Those who were preparing to leave turned to look, each thinking he himself was the object of Graciela's untamed, barbaric yawp. Her timing was perfection. Frozen in place, many were still hovering bent-kneed above their chairs. The distant sound of a shattering water glass could be heard from the kitchen. The blood thumped in my ears.

Then, in her soft, dark, elegant voice, she said, almost like a purred invitation, "Will you *disrobe* me with your stares?"

In books, usually courtroom dramas, you often encounter the phrase *an audible gasp ran through the crowd*, but I had never actually experienced it before. After just such a gasp ran through this particular crowd, everyone stared at Graciela in disbelief, certain that they must have misunderstood.

Graciela continued,

> *O for your kiss! For your love*
> *More enticing than wine,*
> *For your scent and sweet name—*
> *For all this they love you ...*

It was passionate, riveting. It was one of the most astonishing moments of my life, and I wished it could have lasted forever. One by one, those who were standing—too embarrassed, or perhaps too curious, to leave—lowered themselves back onto their chairs, hoping no one had noticed.

She paused, and with her dark eyes glistening, she looked out over the faces that were all staring, unblinking, back at her. Her body language loosened, and she smiled warmly. "Welcome, everyone, *bienvenidos*. I am Graciela Rojas, and I am so proud to say I will be teaching a class in the new Department of Theophily this fall—on 'The Wisdom of the Spanish Mystics.' We hope you enjoyed your meal. We are glad you are here."

I saw Dunwoody trying to catch the eyes of his coconspirators, but they had all reseated themselves and were giving their full attention to the woman at the podium.

She continued, "Now, I'm sure you all recognized my text for this evening ... from Canticles, though you may call it the Song of Solomon, or the Song of Songs. I quote from poet Marcia Falk's translation, though my first exposure to those beautiful lines was from the Spanish Bible I grew up with—the great Reina-Valera, which is something like your King James. In Spanish it reads, *'Oh si él me besara con ósculos de su boca! Porque mejores son tus amores que el vino.'*

"So why Canticles? Isn't it an earthy book about erotic love? Yes. It is. Isn't it about the Lover's passion for his Beloved? Yes, of course. But for me it's also a book about God's all-encompassing love, and I believe no book is more appropriate for this evening than that one ... this evening on which we celebrate Cupperton's newest interdisciplinary program, the Department of Theophily ... the department of the love of God.

"Centuries ago, the men in charge of choosing the canon of Scripture arranged everything in more or less chronological order—from Creation to the new heaven and earth. For them, Scripture was a great epic story that takes place through time. But for me, the Bible is a portrait of a great passion, a passion far beyond time. If I had been asked to arrange those same books, I think I would have put Canticles first, for is it not the book that talks about God's love in the most explicit, intimate, generative terms? And did not that love exist even before creation itself? Perhaps it was even the reason for creation."

She paused and scanned the faces again. No one made a sound.

"Now, I'd like to ask, how many of you were approached by Señorita Westcott and Dr. Bonham last fall with their questions: 'Can you honestly say you love God with all your heart, mind, soul, and strength?' and 'When do you most feel like you love God?' Raise your hand ..."

Dozens of hands shot up. I had forgotten that Katie and I had talked to so many people, though it was clear, if anyone had ever doubted it, that we hadn't talked to a single seminary professor.

"And how many of you took those questions seriously and thought about them long after you were asked?"

The same people raised their hands.

"When I was asked," Graciela continued, "I was stunned. I told Katie that just knowing God loves me is enough, and it is, but I knew there was more to it than that. And that same day, something inside me whispered that it was time to reread Canticles.

"What strikes me about that book is this: *we* are the Beloved. We are the object of a great and passionate love. That seems simple, yes? But there is something else—we are *not* the Lover and never can be. Even if we were capable of loving God with all our heart and mind and soul and strength every second of every day, our love would still not amount to a drop in the ocean of how much we are loved. Our vineyards, in the language of Canticles, are in disarray, and the little foxes have spoiled them. We know that even on our best days, we are not all that lovable, and being loved in spite of that makes us uncomfortable. But until we learn how to be comfortable with being loved, we have no chance at all of loving in return.

"Never have I heard a priest deliver a homily on Canticles. Not once. It is, perhaps, too sexual, too passionate. I have, though, heard people warn us sternly that we must be careful to distinguish among the various kinds of love: *agape*, *eros*, *storge*, *philia*, *ludus*, and so on. But why? What are we afraid of? Canticles, I believe, tells us that God is greater than all our categories. Love is love, and God is love no matter what kind it is or what name you give to it ... as long as it's truly love.

"One person who was not afraid to let all those loves flow together like great waters was my personal heroine, Santa Teresa of Ávila, and she even wrote a powerful commentary on Canticles. In it, she goes so far as to beg a kiss straight from the mouth of the divine Lover, just as the Beloved does in Canticles. And what is that kiss? She calls it peace, which for her is, I think, that state of fullness, of maturity, when we are finally comfortable with being loved despite our inadequacy, our inability, and our impatience with our own failings.

"I was speaking with our friend and colleague Dr. Naazim el-Atar two days ago," she looked to her left where he was seated at the high table, "and he told me about the Theophily class he's teaching this fall, about the poetry of the Sufis. He told me about another great spiritual writer who also wrote about this divine kiss. The thirteenth-century Muslim poet Rumi asks if he might kiss God, but the poet knows that just that one kiss will cost him his whole life. With incredible joy, his soul tells him to make the purchase anyway because, at that price, it's a great, great bargain. One's whole life for a kiss!

"Our challenge is not so much to love God more—although even wanting to love God more *is* loving God more—as it is to accept that we are the Beloved. Until we can rest in that peace, we will find it hard to love God or other people or even ourselves.

"God shows us love every day, whether we realize it or not

... through the caring we receive from others, through the food we eat and the air we breathe, through the sunshine and through Nature, beauty of all kinds, through art and literature, through the great saints of the past, through all our opportunities to help and serve others ... and, for those who believe, most especially through the love Christ showed for us on the cross.

"For Jesus is there in Canticles too, I believe, in the beautiful line that I have taken as my life verse: in the Reina-Valera it says, '*Porque fuerte es como la muerte el amor ... Sus brasas, brasas de fuego, Fuerte llama*'—'For love is as strong as death. ... It burns like a burning fire, a powerful flame.' Jesus is that burning fire whose love is as strong as death ... was stronger than death. Once we understand the truth of that, we will experience that peace and know we have been kissed by God.

"And so, Katie"—Graciela turned in our direction—"I tell you this. Knowing that God loves me *is* enough. It is a promise that day by day, whether we are aware of it or not, we learn to love God just a little more in return. That is what the Department of Theophily is about. We are all beginners—hardly even infants—in this spiritual life no matter how mature we might think we are.

"On this special evening, I want to thank Marteen and Katie ... thank you both for your inspiration, for your questions, and for your vision and persistence. And thank you too to all the professors who have agreed to teach in the Department of Theophily. Each of you, in your own way, understands the promise of that commandment, and, like Santa Teresa, you encourage us to open all our senses to love, to find that peace.

"Thank you, everyone. Thank you for being here, and good night."

IN HINDSIGHT, my recollections of the rest of that evening are a jumble, a happy mist of scenes "no more yielding but a dream." I remember the guests chatting, thanking us, shaking our hands, and filing out as the catering staff stacked chairs and folded tables. I remember the five of us—Graciela and Nate, Katie and Tyrell, and me—standing in a tight circle outside afterward, in the cool air, beneath a thousand sparkling stars, feeling jubilant and relieved.

And here's an irony. I don't remember seeing Dr. Dunwoody or, for that matter, any of the seminary staff leave the hall. Had the enmity abated? Had it vanished like the dew? All those who had planned to exit with a bang ended up exiting with a whimper. And here is something even more ironic ... I felt sorry because what else could I do? I now saw them in a different light, that they were every bit as vulnerable and needy as I was. Like all of us, they were weak people whose own vineyards needed tending. And it made me love them somehow.

Perhaps it was the glow of the evening, Graciela's words, or the warmth of something I can't explain, but I felt that whatever petty resentments Dunwoody might still harbor toward me and the Department of Theophily, they were negligible in the vast scope of the universe. Our conflicts had been nothing more than a marvelously silly drama that was itself part of a larger, marvelously intentional love.

And that was all right. For that evening, at least, I knew that all things were unfolding as they should. "Trust God," as Graciela once quoted Teresa of Ávila to me, "for you are exactly where you are meant to be."

CHAPTER 4
A MINISTRY OF PROFANITY

These ministers make religion a cold
and flinty-hearted thing,
having neither principles of right action,
nor bowels of compassion.
They strip the love of God of its beauty.
—*Frederick Douglass, 1818–1895*

I can almost hear some of you whispering, "But what of Katie Westcott? Is it well with her soul?" The answer is, like Ms. Westcott herself, complex. The dust of the department's celebratory banquet had hardly settled before she commissioned the local Sailor Jerry to tattoo "Beloved" over a Valentine heart on her left shoulder, but I wish that were sufficient to report that peace like a river now attended her way. Life is seldom so neat.

And you'd be most justified in inquiring after her soul if you'd seen her, as I had, at the reception following the first official guest lecture sponsored by the Department of Theophily. Our guest speaker that Saturday evening in mid-November was the Reverend Oday Jefferson Walker of Gibsonville, North Carolina, and his subject, as the posters around campus declared, was "Moses and the Burning Bush: A Prophetic Call to Free the People."

He began his talk by quoting Isaiah 61: "The Lord hath anointed me to preach good tidings unto the meek; he hath sent me to bind up the brokenhearted, to proclaim liberty to the captives, and the opening of the prisons to them that are bound." His theme was that we love God by both freeing ourselves from our internal oppressors—to become our truest selves in Christ—and then looking outward to come alongside those who are engaged in freeing themselves from their internal and external oppressors, whether those oppressors are addiction, illness, poverty, racism, sexism, violence, and so much more. That is the essence of our prophetic calling, as he defined it—a Moses-like calling. Reverend Walker punctuated his talk with quotations from Sojourner Truth, Frederick Douglass, and Dr. Martin Luther King Jr. He ended the evening by reading, in his booming voice, another passage from Isaiah that describes what is expected of God's people: "'To loose the bands of wickedness, to undo the heavy burdens, and to let the oppressed go free, and that ye break every yoke,'" and the reverend concluded, "I can think of few more powerful or urgent biblical commands than those."

The talk was well attended, and, to my surprise, even the Rev. Dr. Dunwoody deigned to make an appearance and acknowledged that our visitor had impressed even him, though he couldn't resist observing that the Department of Theophily had procured someone with a *seminary* degree to be its first official guest speaker.

As was her custom for visiting lecturers, President Costa, at her stately Georgian-style home, held a reception afterward, which included a special vocal performance by Kyeesha Reed.

(You will remember her as the incoming freshman music student who, during orientation three months earlier, had declared her intention of becoming a music and Theophily double major.) With Tyrell, Katie's boyfriend, on piano, Kyeesha delivered a soaring rendition of "Peace in the Valley," the high notes of which were enough to put goosebumps on your goosebumps.

Prone to trafficking in clichés as I am, I later said to Tyrell, "Kyeesha sings like an angel," to which he responded, "No, I think the angels sing like Kyeesha." No one who attended the president's soirée, I'm sure, will soon forget the power and charm of that performance.

I was mindful of the fact, however, that one person had avoided it—conspicuous by her absence: Katie Westcott. When I sought her out, I found her lurking in the kitchen, assisting the caterers in washing and drying the president's china.

What, you might ask, could have induced her to abscond in that way? If you guessed that she was jealous of Kyeesha and Tyrell, you could not be farther off the mark. Allow me to explain, for on the subject of Katie Westcott, I'm one of the few who is *au courant*.

Katie is the kind of person who is so aware of each passing moment, analyzing every circumstance with what is sometimes called "a lazar-like focus," that I suspect even Sherlock Holmes would have felt uneasy in her presence. She is able to absorb information quickly and grasp difficult concepts with the ease of a mechanical engineer of above-average intelligence stacking toy blocks.

The drawback is that she objectifies her inner life in much the same way, which results in what professors of physics refer to as the *observer effect*—the object under scrutiny is altered by being scrutinized. In its crudest form, it is not unlike those zealous witch hunters centuries ago who managed to drown any number of respectable women on the assumption that, had they been witches, they would not have drowned. Scrutiny can be lethal, and Katie, by testing her emotions, drowned them, leading her to conclude that they didn't exist in the first place and that she was incapable of loving God.

A small chink in her armor appeared at this time, due to the munificent influence of Tyrell Robson, and yet, that chink had little to do with romance. Her approach to romantic love was much the same as her approach to everything else—it was a curious existential phenomenon like any other.

Tyrell, in his turn, accepted this quirk in her character and even found it endearing, even amusing at times. His emotions, by contrast, were at once both deep and completely on display, and he adored Katie for the mysterious, intriguing character that she was. The more intense she became—whether complaining about people who peek at their phones during a conversation or squabbling with seminarians about antinomianism—the more admiring Tyrell grew. He would smile, captivated by her precociousness like a doting parent at a Christmas pageant.

No, it was not love that pierced her shell. It was music. Tyrell was the assistant choral director at the Bethel AME Zion Church not far from campus. He was a pianist, a singer with an extraordinary voice, a songwriter, and a choir conductor of unusual charisma. It was gospel music—not the smarmy praise songs Katie grew up with, but hardcore, gut-punching gospel music—that pried open the lid of her soul, even if only a millimeter. No matter how much she analyzed it, she couldn't objectify the agitation that stirred within her as she listened, helpless and overwhelmed, to a mass choir singing at full rafter-shaking volume "You Are Welcome in This Place." Tyrell told me she would sometimes weep. She felt the music reverberating in her chest with an almost painful kind of joy, jarring her body like a San Andreas temblor. To her, Tyrell was a magician, and as much as she hoped to discover the secret behind his tricks, she knew in her heart that no trickery was involved. It was real magic.

And that is why Katie was hiding among the kitchen staff at the reception for Reverend Walker. She knew she would not be able to handle the inexplicable emotions stirred by something as simple as Kyeesha singing "Peace in the Valley." She was drawn to, as well as terrified by, these experiences of "deep calling unto deep," as the psalmist so aptly put it.

The rest of the time Katie was Katie—systematic, direct, analytical. As the Department of Theophily's administrative director, she proved wondrously efficient, resolving every sort of crisis—from trapping a terrified squirrel in a waste basket in biology professor Soo-jin Park's classroom (during her "God in Nature" Theophily class no less) to hand-correcting fifty silk-screened posters from the art department that advertised Reverend Walker's talk as "Mooses and the Burning Bush." She squiggled the two o's together to look like a flame—a burning bush. She's clever that way.

She had, in fact, arranged his entire visit. A month and a half earlier, while gazing out my office window in Beetham Hall, I heard an abrupt "Hey, M.B." behind me that nearly made me fall off my chair. I swiveled around to see Katie, who, as usual, had materialized out of nowhere as if beamed down from the Starship Enterprise. Tyrell was at her side.

"Relax," she said. "Listen. Tyrell and I have an idea. We need to make a splash around here—as a department, I mean. How about a visiting lecturer? Every other department does it. You know, the seminary's got the former archbishop of Canterbury coming later in the semester, and that's going to be big, but I think we can steal some of their thunder. And we know just the person." And they proceeded to take turns telling me about the Reverend Oday Walker, who, as an AME pastor, had been part of Bishop William Barber's inner circle on the Poor People's Campaign. Tyrell had met Reverend Walker at some conference the week before, and he was willing, able, and even eager to speak at Cupperton on short notice.

I had hardly said more than, "Uh ... sure," than Katie had arranged the entire event. She secured the funding, made the flight reservations, ordered the posters (misspelled through no fault of her own), reserved Murphy Chapel, and helped President Costa plan the reception.

When I asked her how she could be so efficient, she said, "You gotta learn to multitask, M.B.," to which I replied, "The closest I get to multitasking is reading in the bathtub."

But ... all this is prelude to the events that occurred the morning after the lecture.

ON ANY OTHER Sunday at Cupperton, Reverend Walker would have attended Bethel AME with Tyrell, Katie, and Kyeesha; in fact, I suspect he would have been asked to preach. But since his afternoon flight was scheduled for one o'clock, and since the Bethel service didn't even start until eleven that morning, the reverend suggested that we all go to a ten o'clock service at a church he'd heard about in the somewhat distant town of Baldwin, which was just a few miles from the airport. That way, we could deliver him directly to his flight afterward. The church was called the Caring Zone. The name alone seemed promising.

Tyrell, who excused himself from his duties at Bethel that morning, even managed to commandeer his church's minivan so that he, Katie, Kyeesha, and I could accompany Reverend

Walker to church and to the airport immediately afterward. After an early meal of coffee and bagels at the CupperTea, we headed out. Tyrell was at the wheel.

No sooner had we zipped through the university's West Gate than Reverend Walker, in the passenger seat, asked Tyrell if he was familiar with some song or other, which led to the two of them trading old gospel songs, singing snatches, and gleefully one-upping each other, while Kyeesha, beaming like bright Phoebus in the back seat between Katie and me, filled in the harmonies. I glanced over at Katie from time to time; she stared out the window with a fixed expression, trying hard not to have her own deep called unto that other, deeper deep.

At one point, all of us, except for Katie, of course, attempted a four-part harmony on "Take My Hand, Precious Lord." Although I suspect I was a discordant link in the sonorous chain, I sang with gusto. As someone once told me, my singing is, if nothing else, well-intended. Still, it was a joyous road trip. Had Jack Kerouac gotten religion and driven cross-country with the Blind Boys of Alabama, he could not have had a more epic journey than ours.

But it was all too short. After an hour of obeying the little voice on Katie's phone, we found Baldwin and turned off the highway onto a local frontage road. Two minutes later, we arrived.

I was taken aback. Although the sign read "The Caring Zone," it was clear, as we pulled into the nearly empty parking lot, a bit earlier than we'd estimated, that aesthetics were not high on the list of things they cared about. Abashed by my snobbery, I reminded myself that the Creator delights in being worshiped anywhere, even in the most sterile, paint-peeled, barn-like structures—wherever two or three are gathered. Then again, you'd think that the church staff would at least make things minimally inviting for those two or three. The

grounds were characteristic of the strip-mall school of land-
scape architecture—a couple of crow-topped light poles and a
few scrawny saplings held up by wires. At one end of the pot-
holed parking area stood a large pile of gravel, with rakes and
shovels poking out at odd angles.

I soon realized we were being watched. A small group of
men, ushers no doubt, stood unsmiling at the entrance, scrutinizing the words *Bethel AME Zion* displayed on our van. They
followed our movements with heavy expressions as we
debarked, and, as we approached and greeted them, they shot
us quick, wordless nods, which made me wonder whether
humans were high on the list of things the church cared about.
One of them gave me the kind of look that makes you feel as if
you'd forgotten to put your pants on that morning. I was
tempted to check.

Skirting the gravel pile, we entered the wide double doors
of the sanctuary. We introduced ourselves, and one of the
ushers directed us to the very last row of the as yet vacant
sanctuary. I asked if it might be possible to sit closer to the
front, to which he responded, "This row is for special guests." I
noted how he put a slight backspin on the word *special* and
how the other ushers stared at Reverend Walker and Kyeesha.
And they seemed especially aware of Tyrell and Katie, who
were at that moment holding hands—though more out of
apprehension than affection. It also didn't help that Katie was
going through a deep-purple-lipstick and pink-tipped-hair
stage of life.

But from that remote vantage point, we were at least able
to study the congregants as they began filing into the hall,
chatting in clumps among themselves and finding their seats,
although as soon as they spotted us, they tended to glance
away, and their conversations grew less animated. No one
nodded in our direction, let alone greeted us.

As the sanctuary filled, Reverend Walker leaned toward me. "The kids," he whispered, "look at the kids." At least half of the teenagers were hunched forward on the edges of their folding chairs, looking down, some with their faces in their hands as if in training to be professional mourners. They spoke to no one, and no one spoke to them.

At ten o'clock sharp, the pianist, on an out-of-tune upright, launched into a galumphing rendition of "We Gather Together."

Our next premonition of things to come was when the minister, a sixty-something man with Marine-style buzz-cut hair, starched white shirt with rolled-up sleeves, and a ragged Bible in hand, stepped to the lectern. He opened with announcements. "I've just been informed that we're two people short in the nursery ... would some of you ladies"—again, there was that little backspin, this time on the word *ladies*—"please volunteer to help out?" A couple of women exited stage left. "Also, you'll notice that the gravel for our parking lot was delivered, so I need some of you *men* to volunteer. We have plenty of rakes and shovels, so pitch in after the service. The Lord bless you."

Someone in the front row muttered something to the minister.

"Oh yes, of course," the minister continued, "I also need to remind the youth that evangelist Myron Buford Spragg will be speaking right here from this podium next Friday, Saturday, and Sunday nights for our Teen Revival Weekend. His topic will be 'The Sins of Youth.'" After a dramatic pause, he added, "So you *know* you'll want to hear what *he* has to say!"

I wondered how many decades it had been since parents inflicted names like *Myron* and *Buford* on innocent progeny. It would now probably constitute abuse.

While we had previously noted that half the teenagers had

buried their faces in their hands, now every last one, male and female alike, seemed to be participating in a bomb drill, ducking and covering being the only means of surviving in this barren, brightly lit chasm of shame.

Not content merely to inform, the minister, addressing the tops of the teenagers' heads, felt obliged to exhort as well: "... And I expect every one of you young people to be there. I'm sure you can drag yourselves away from your phones and your skating boards and your video games for three hours each night to attend—I see you hanging out at the hamburger shack and lining up at the picture show"—I also wondered how many decades it had been since I'd heard someone say the words *picture show*—"so I know you're not busy. Things were bad in my day, but I can't imagine how much worse they are now. So, no excuses. Be there, or the deacons'll be talking to your parents, I promise you that! Amen. The life Jesus saves may be your own!" He smirked unpleasantly, pleased with this final bon mot.

The tinny piano lumbered into "Oh, for a Thousand Tongues to Sing," and the congregation sang the words projected on the back wall. Tyrell and Kyeesha, despite having beautiful voices, barely mumbled, afraid to stand out. Reverend Walker, by contrast, sang out boldly, which caused some of the congregants in our section to stop singing altogether, as though embarrassed.

After a short prayer, the pastor began his sermon. It was titled, according to the bulletin, "What's with Mr. Herod?" The minister painted a vivid portrait of the evil king, manipulated into killing John the Baptist and indulging himself in "the lusts of the flesh." Although the minister dwelt somewhat heavily on the indulging and lusting bits, his sermon began as a straightforward rendering of the gospel story. Unobjectionable. Then, at its paroxysm, the pastor asked the title question, "So, just what *was* with Mr. Herod?"

The gist of his answer was this: "My friends, I am here to tell you what was wrong with him—he was *feminized!*" There was no backspin on that word; it was a full double backflip. "That's right! *Feminized!* Satan wormed his way into Herod's soul through the *women* in his life! His wife and stepdaughter led him around by the nose so that he grew fat and lazy. He was sissified. I bet he even talked in a high voice. Maybe he even lisped! Instead of being the absolute head of his family, as the Lord calls us men to be, he was scared of his women and did whatever they wanted. He might as well have neutered himself right then and there."

I winced and felt slightly sick.

The minister's spiritual takeaway a few minutes later was more of the same: "Men, this is God's clear message for you today: if you don't want to be like that fat sissy Herod, don't let yourself be *feminized!* You are the head of your families; so you wear the pants and answer only to God. Amen and amen."

And the people (to my astonishment) said, "Amen."

Feeling my face flush, I stared straight down at the linoleum tiles at my feet during the lengthy prayer that followed. I hardly listened. I could sense that Katie, Tyrell, Kyeesha, and Reverend Walker were staring straight down as well.

After the prayer, the minister gestured in our direction. "I see we have some visitors with us today ... the Caring Zone welcomes you. Would you be so kind as to introduce yourselves and tell us what brings you here?"

I looked at Katie. We'd planned for her to make any necessary introductions if we were so called upon. Fearless, she stood. "Yes, thank you, we're from—"

"I'm sorry, young lady," the minister cut in, "but we're a

full-gospel church here, and in 1 Corinthians 14:34 the apostle Paul clearly commands, 'Let your women keep silence in the churches: for it is not permitted unto them to speak.' Anyone raised in the faith knows this to be the true word of the Lord. Amen. So, would one of you *gentlemen* please tell us about yourselves?"

Even before I could absorb what had just happened, Reverend Walker stood slowly and calmly. "Thank you, pastor," he said in his gracious, Southern way. "I am Reverend Oday Walker from North Carolina, and I've been visiting my dear friends at Cupperton University. You mentioned the youth revival, and we all know how important the youth are. It's the same in my church. Might I encourage your young people with a brief word from the Lord?"

The minister nodded somewhat hesitantly.

Up to this point, Reverend Walker's deep voice had been slow and cordial, but now his tone changed, and his words came flying through the air like an avalanche. "Listen, you young people! Don't pay attention to that jackass at the front! What the hell kind of church is this, making women feel all trashy and making black folks sit in the back row? Listen, you teenagers, soon's you get old enough, you get as far away from this place as you can—but hear me now, I can tell you from experience, Jesus is real, my brothers and sisters, more real than this damn church is ever gonna let on. He's a miracle! He's magic and he's alive and he loves you so much, and God's love is all around you, caring for you, wanting your best ..."

Needless to say, pandemonium erupted. Halfway through the outburst, the minister began urging, "Ushers, get that man out of here ...," and when he realized that Reverend Walker was not about to stop, he yelled, "Someone, call the police! Call 911!" Right and left I could see phones lighting up. The teenagers too seemed to light up, snapping their heads upright, wide-eyed in surprise, and giving the reverend their full attention.

Reverend Walker was in the spirit. He had the kind of bull-horn voice that could be heard above just about any sort of din. "I been in jail five times for bearing witness to the Truth—so you just ask your revival man next week how many times *he's* been in jail for Jesus. Listen, these bastards here are lying to you, trying to make you feel small. Don't let 'em do it! You're valuable and loved, you're good people. So you get the hell out of here as soon as you can—and remember, Jesus is a miracle, he's real, and he loves you the way you are. Look for him ... you'll find him ... don't give up, he's out there ... waiting for you ..."

By that time, several of the ushers had made their way down our row, two or three from each side. Quickly, the reverend said aside to the four of us, "Don't resist. Let 'em lead us out."

Confronted with a man the size of Oday Walker, the ushers proceeded with trepidation. "Please, come with us ... please, quiet down ... outside, this way ..." In the background there was frantic conversation, and the minister was still shouting and had started to approach us. Some of the male congregants had thrown off their jackets, far more willing to engage in physical coercion than the ushers were, and the teenagers, delighted with the whole scene, smiled and laughed. All the while, Reverend Walker was still shouting over his shoulder, "Get the hell out of here and look for Jesus—he's alive—he loves you!"

Per the reverend's instructions, we let the ushers lead us out, though not without a bit of jostling and shoving. Once in the parking lot, we made a frantic dash for the van and piled in —all except Reverend Walker, that is, who sort of sauntered calmly to the van as though he was, well ... as though he was leaving church on a Sunday morning.

In old movies—or *picture shows* as the minister called them —you sometimes see scenes of angry townspeople waving torches and pitchforks as they chivvy Frankenstein's monster from their midst. At that moment, when I glanced out the rear window, I knew how the monster felt. A half dozen men had grabbed the rakes and shovels from the gravel pile and were shaking them in our direction. Only the torches were lacking.

With tires squealing and gravel flying, Tyrell pulled the van out onto the frontage road, and we sped away with all the vigor that six cylinders could muster. Within a minute, two police cars, their lights flashing, shrieked past us in the opposite direction—heading toward the Caring Zone.

A mile or two farther on, feeling anxious and breathless, we merged onto the bypass toward the city and into the safety of the morning traffic. We exhaled. No one had spoken yet.

Finally, placing my hand on the reverend's shoulder in front of me, I articulated what the rest of us were thinking: "What happened back there, Rev?"

He turned in his seat, looked me straight in the eye, and, with the brightest of bright smiles, said, "Prophecy, my brother, prophecy!"

Immediately, the mood lightened. Katie, Tyrell, and Kyeesha all started talking at once. They laughed, recounted their thoughts and feelings, compared notes, and laughed some more.

"That was incredible," said Tyrell. "Did you see how they looked at Katie and me? It was like they'd never seen an interracial couple before! I was so nervous, I couldn't even sing. Reverend, you really sang out on those hymns."

"Well," said the reverend, "nobody doesn't love 'Oh, for a Thousand Tongues.'"

"I was so scared," said Kyeesha. "One woman in the back kept looking at me. Every time I turned, she was staring. And I was sure that guy in the biker bandana was gonna hurt somebody."

Tyrell added, "Did you see that pickup truck with the Confederate flag? And there was a bumper sticker near the exit: 'Heavily armed; easily pissed.' Do you think they had guns?"

Katie said, "We didn't even make it to the offertory! I was going to leave a note in the collection plate that said, 'Help! I'm a teenager in this church!'"

I said, "I would never have had the nerve to do what you did, Rev."

"And it's illegal," added Tyrell, "to disrupt a church service in this state."

"Well, it was risky, I know," said the reverend. "I'm sorry if I put you all in danger ... but I couldn't help it. It's a faith thing. You all heard my talk last night. We're called 'to loose the bands of wickedness, to undo the heavy burdens.' If I hadn't spoken up, I'd be a hypocrite, now, wouldn't I? If we're going to free the people, then we got to speak the truth—"

"That wasn't exactly speaking in the truth in *love*, though, was it?" asked Katie in her matter-of-fact way.

The reverend said, "Oh, Katie, let me tell you something— I'd hate to have you hear me when I'm *not* speaking the truth in love."

Kyeesha asked, "What about all the profanity? How could you do that in church?"

"Listen, you all," he said, "you saw how miserable those young people were. It broke my heart. I didn't know how long I'd be able to preach, so I had to spice things up a little to get their attention. Wake 'em up, you know. You see, those kids are gonna remember this morning the rest of their lives. They'll be telling their grandchildren about it fifty years from now, all about how this crazy preacher started preaching from the back row. Now, listen. This might have been the *only* chance *any* of them would have to see a different side of the gospel, to know the Lord's looking out for them. And you know something? Every time they tell the story, they'll say, 'That man kept saying, "Jesus is real; he's a miracle."' They'll be preaching it themselves, you see. That's why I had to use those words. They need to remember it the rest of their days! Might be their only hope."

After a pause, he added, "It's like what Paul wrote in Galatians, you know, that verse about all those people preaching a 'contrary gospel.' He said, '*Anathema esto!*'—and that doesn't mean 'bless their tiny little hearts'! You see, so many people wake up in the morning and see only enmity and distrust toward anyone who's not like them, people of color and gays and women, other religions, and even fellow Christians. That's what their faith's about; they think that whatever disrespect they can muster toward those people must be how they can best serve God. It's sad."

"Tell me, Rev," I said a few moments later as we exited onto the ramp toward the airport, "where did you hear about the Caring Zone anyway?"

"Oh, now, that's another story. I'm thinking I must have misunderstood," he said. "Someone at the reception last night ... kind of a small fellow ... bald ... got talking; don't think he introduced himself ... a professor maybe. I told him about not having time to go to Bethel before my flight this morning, and he said I might want to try this Caring Zone church ... it's right near the airport, he said, 'I think you'd like it.' But now, with all the noise at the reception, I'm thinking maybe he was telling me not to go there. I don't know."

I looked over at Katie. With her jaw firmly set and her eyes nearly shooting flames, we exchanged a meaningful glance.

TEN MINUTES LATER, in the middle of the cavernous, bustling airport concourse, the five of us wrapped ourselves in a tight group hug. We stood there, amid the flow of travelers, like an island in the stream. Kyeesha, for whom the emotions of the morning had finally kicked in, cried, which caused me to mist up as well.

At the entrance to the security gate, the reverend said, "Thank you all for your hospitality. I promise I'll pray for you all, and you do the same for me. And say, Kyeesha, could I ask you a favor? Would you just sing that chorus ... you know the one ... just sing it with me one time before I go?" And he and Kyeesha began to sing "Peace in the Valley" at full voice and unashamed, right there in the airport.

But suddenly, a soft, Cindy-Lou Who kind of voice joined in with them. I could tell from Tyrell's expression that he was as shocked as I was. It was Katie.

> *There'll be peace in the valley for me someday,*
> *There'll be peace in the valley for me, O Lord, I*
> > *pray;*
> *No more sorrow and sadness or trouble will be;*
> *There'll be peace in the valley for me.*

Then the reverend said, "Let's all sing it again, together—even you, Martin." And we did.

A few minutes later, after hugging the reverend one last time, the rest of us climbed the stairs to the observation deck and waved goodbye to his plane. We could just make out the reverend's face filling one of those tiny windows as he waved back.

Later, with her phone's help, Katie found us an alternate route back to the university, one that didn't take us through Baldwin. Just in case.

THE NEXT DAY, I was back in my office, with my feet up on the desk. Still shaken by the previous day's events, I was trying to distract myself with the latest issue of *Renaissance Studies* when the object of my ire, Dr. Dunwoody himself, appeared in the doorway. He seemed cheerful—which is one of his least attractive moods.

"So, did Reverend Walker enjoy his visit?" he asked.

"He did. He certainly did. And I know he'd like to come back."

"Good, good ... so, did you take him to church?"

I let the question hang in the air as I studied Dunwoody's unctuous smile. I asked, "You recommended that church to him, didn't you? And here I thought our little feud was over."

"Well, now, let me think ... we talked about a number of things, but I don't remember if the subject of churches came up at all. No ... I don't remember. So ... how was it?"

"Quite honestly," I said, "it was the most powerful, most beautiful, most moving service I've ever been to. The reverend even got to preach, and he received an overwhelming response from the congregation. He enjoyed it immensely. We all did."

Dunwoody's smug expression changed to one of bafflement. "Now, hold it. You went to the Caring Zone ... in Baldwin ... right?" he asked, not caring that he'd just given himself away.

I nodded.

"You're kidding," he said. "I've heard about that place. How can that be?"

I smiled and replied, "Prophecy, my brother, prophecy."

CHAPTER 5

A VISIT FROM THE ARCHBISHOP

At last we hapless men
Know all our haplessness all through. Come, then,
Endure undreamed humility: Lord of Heaven,
Come to our ignorant hearts and be forgiven.
—*Alice Meynell, 1847–1922*

"Excuse me, sir ... are you done? ... Sir?"

I snapped out of my reverie to find myself at a noisy, crowded soirée, being addressed by a young woman in a white serving apron. She was bearing a large tray of crudités, and I seemed to be holding, in one hand, a small plate piled much too high with baby carrots and, in the other, a pair of silver vegetable tongs. I was momentarily flummoxed.

Seeing the tongs, however, which I returned to the tray, I was at least able to reconstruct the route that my runaway train of thought had taken.

It had begun, as you probably guessed, with Saint Dunstan.

If you're like me, you can never grasp a pair of tongs without thinking of that intrepid tenth-century archbishop of

Canterbury who is said to have seized the devil by the nose with a pair of red-hot blacksmith's tongs, called wolf jaws. You'll recall this ditty:

> *A tale, I know, has gone about*
> *That Dunstan twinged him by the snout*
> *With pincers hot and glowing ...*

But what had arrested my attention was not the tongs so much as the implausibility of the maneuver, for not only would "pincers hot and glowing" be unwieldy, most likely requiring the use of both hands as well as considerable dexterity, but surely the devil would have bolted, or at least ducked as soon as he saw such an incandescent object veering face-ward. It's a mystery. And a nose is a relatively small target, though I suppose it's possible that the devil's is larger than average, hanging down, perhaps, like a zucchini or an extra limb.

Anyway, I'd been pondering Dunstan's stratagem for no other reason than this: the nose of Cornelius Dunwoody, which is of only average size, was a mere ten feet away from where I stood, and if anyone would have been justified in seizing it with vegetable tongs, 'twas I. I would have thought that after the scurvy trick he'd played on Reverend Walker and the rest of us, Dunwoody would have retired from acting on his baser instincts. But no.

It was at this point in my ruminations that the young caterer had startled me back to reality.

The occasion was the gala reception at President Costa's house to honor the university's current visiting lecturer, the Most Reverend Nigel H. Townsend, who, like Dunstan a thousand years before him, was an esteemed former archbishop of Canterbury, and who, earlier that evening, had received an honorary doctorate from Cupperton. As the author of several noted books of theology, he had also been awarded the Jeremy Taylor Prize for Excellence in Religious Writing, though I missed that portion of the festivities, as you will see.

Though I'd been deeply humiliated by the day's events, a friend had convinced me to put in an appearance at the reception anyway, if only to show Dunwoody that he had *not* gotten the better of me—and to ask forgiveness of the former archbishop for my transgression, though the actual blame lay elsewhere.

As at Reverend Walker's reception two weeks earlier, Kyeesha Reed was called upon to perform. Once again, Tyrell accompanied her on piano, though this time, to my surprise, Katie Westcott had been recruited to sing a harmony. Though proud of her, I was distracted, and during the opening strains of their rendition of "O Love That Will Not Let Me Go," I couldn't help but think of Sun Tzu's remark from *The Art of War,* which, for obvious reasons, I'd been reading of late: "Opportunities increase only as they are seized." Sadly, I'd already relinquished the silver tongs.

But none of this, I know, makes sense without a few essential details, for this story begins much earlier—on the morning of that same fateful day.

THAT CHILLY, overcast Friday in late November had begun with a hot chai and a breakfast bagel at the CupperTea. As I walked across North Quad a few minutes later, gingerly dodging students scurrying to their eight o'clock classes, a voice hailed me from behind. It was Katie. Out of breath, she huffed, "Hey, M.B.—Dolly—she's looking for you, like *right now.*"

The news alarmed me, for to refuse an audience with Dolly De Angeli is among the more consequential missteps one can make in life, on a par with shooting an albatross with a crossbow or pocketing a bishop's silver candlesticks. So, as fleetly as a gazelle, I hoofed it over to Beetham Hall.

Ms. De Angeli has been secretary to no-one-knows-how-many English Department chairs and has outlasted every university president, except the current one, of course, since the Nixon administration. Although her given name is Dolores, she goes by Dolly, and she's as autocratic a character as you're likely to meet this side of imperial Rome, though endearing in her own way, with a Brooklyn accent and a manner of address that would shame a buccaneer. I've never seen her not chewing gum, which makes me wonder whether she's ever replaced it.

As I entered her office, she swiveled in her chair. With her elbows on the armrests and her fingers intertwined, she looked a bit like Don Corleone—if Don Corleone had been an older woman with preternaturally red hair and too much rouge. "Hey, sweetie," she said in what writers of crime-noir fiction refer to as a whiskey voice, "you got my message. Good. Here's the thing, hon. You're gonna do me a favor is what."

"You name it, Dolly," I said.

"It's like this—some hooligan's been chucking eggs at windows all over campus—"

"Yes, I've noticed," I said. "Do you suppose the Easter bunny's gone postal?"

"Huh?" she snapped.

Since humor can be a dicey proposition with Dolly, I just said, "Nothing. Sorry."

"Look," she said, cracking her knuckles, "our windows got hit good last night, and since this bishop guy's coming and all, you gotta wash 'em. Could you do that, doll? Won't take a minute. The brush and bucket's in the janitor's closet."

Gallantly I responded, "Uh ... why can't Bert do it?"

"He's over at Phipps with the other maintenance guys, getting ready for tonight. Some kinda problem with the lights or something. Bert's good with that stuff. So it's up to you. You gotta spiff the place up—before that bishop guy gets here. Right?"

So my assignment was clear. Had the pope himself ordered me to do it, I'd have demurred, but since the directive came from Dolly, I leaped to it like a hare. I'm a sucker for brassy older women who use cheeky endearments.

Five minutes later, I was outside Beetham in the near-freezing air, lathering the first-floor windows with a long-handled brush, whistling jauntily as I scrubbed, and shivering as I bedewed myself with sudsy water in the process. Absorbed in my task, I failed to hear footsteps approaching, though I soon detected an intentional throat-clearing somewhere abaft.

I turned. There stood Dunwoody, looking as smug as someone's uncle after bowling a strike. "Bonham, so here you are," he said, and then, pointing to my brush, he added, "and it appears I need to congratulate you on finally having risen to your level of competence."

I chafed inwardly. He was flanked by a dozen seminary professors and students, some of whom snickered. Just as two wolves howling at slightly different pitches can sound like an entire wolf pack, so too a couple of seminarians snickering can sound unpleasantly like an entire third-year symposium. They were accompanied, as I'm sure you foresaw, by a rosy-cheeked, baronial-looking gentleman in a clerical collar.

"Reverend Townsend," said Dunwoody, "I would like you to meet Dr. Martin Bonham."

With the brush still in my left hand, I reached out my right to the former archbishop. Since I'd checked *Debrett's Handbook of British Style* the day before, I knew that Dunwoody had muffed his introduction. Upon leaving the archbishopric, a retiring archbishop becomes a regular bishop and may be introduced as either "bishop/right reverend" or "archbishop/most reverend," but never just "reverend." Bowing politely and opting for the more formal honorific, I responded, "It's a pleasure to make the acquaintance of the *Most* Reverend Nigel Townsend."

Now it was Dunwoody's turn to chafe inwardly. He grumbled, "Your Grace, in addition to his interest in the custodial arts, Dr. Bonham teaches English in his spare time, and he's the chair of our new Department of Theophily."

The archbishop looked quizzically from Dunwoody to me. "*Theophily*? ... As in 'love of God'? That sounds interesting."

Before I could open my mouth, Dunwoody replied, "Yes, it's our amateur religion department ... for undergraduates. Anyone from *any* discipline is allowed to hold forth on whatever vague notions they have about faith."

"Still, that seems quite promising," said the archbishop.

"But as you can imagine," said Dunwoody, "it creates some tension between the seminary and the college, resulting in a bit of collegial rivalry, but all in good fun. While the department has its adherents in the administration, the whole thing reminds me of that old saying 'It's dull and makes everyone else dull too.'" More snickers from the third-year symposium. "But we muddle through, don't we, Bonham, eh?"

"Boswell," I snarled in a low voice, dragging out the word. The archbishop grinned.

"Excuse me?" said Dunwoody, offended.

"It was James Boswell ... *The Life of Samuel Johnson*—a friend of his says of someone, 'He is not only dull himself, he is the cause of dullness in others.'"

Before Dunwoody could formulate a retort, the archbishop turned to me and asked, "Are you, by any chance, *the* Martin Bonham who compiled *Religious Poets of the Fifteenth Century*?"

"Why ... why, yes, I am. How did you ...?"

The bishop reached out his hand a second time and said, "What an honor! It's one of my favorites; in fact, I often travel with it to read on the plane—passes the time delightfully ... I've memorized so many of the poems—but I'm afraid I left my carry-on bag in London by mistake, so I'm not only lacking your book but basic toiletries as well. Dr. Dunwoody said he'd provide those for me later. But now I wish I had that volume. I'd so love to have you sign it."

"Well, I could provide you with a fresh copy," I said. "I have some in my office."

"Would you? How wonderful! I'd be most appreciative. Mine is positively dog-eared—and please, do me the honor of inscribing it 'For Nigel.' None of this *Most Reverend* nonsense." He smiled again. "My favorite is 'I Sing of a Maid That Is Matchless.' You know, the part about 'The King of Kings, her son,' ... and ... what's the bit about April?"

"'All so still He came ...,'" I prompted.

"Yes, that's it," and he recited:

And all so still He came to where she was,
as dew in April falleth on the grass;
and all so still He came to her bower,
as dew in April falleth on the flower.

"Oh, that's lovely!" He turned to Dunwoody's horde. "You've read the professor's anthology, I'm sure ..." There were blank looks and a shuffling of feet. "Oh, you should. It's charming!" Then turning to me: "You'll be there tonight, I hope?" he said.

"With bells on, and I'll bring the book."

"Brilliant. You know, I'd love to get a photo, but I left my mobile in my carry-on. Maybe"—he turned to the seminarians

—"one of you would be willing to snap a picture and text it to me?"

So, with long-handled brush in hand, I had my picture taken, arm and arm, with the Most Reverend Nigel H. Townsend, with whom I was now on a first-name basis. (I keep a framed copy on my desk to this day.)

Dunwoody, clearly miffed by my newfound status as a celebrity among the former archbishops of the world, was suddenly eager to continue their tour, and so, after a few gruff pleasantries, he pivoted, and the group shuffled off.

Musing pleasantly as I watched them disappear through the doors of Sheeres Art Museum across the quad, I was startled by yet more chuckling, this time from above. Dolly had just popped her carrot-topped head out of one of the upper windows.

"Hey, I got it!" she said.

"Got what?" I asked.

"That thing about the Easter bunny. That's a good one. But look, sweetie, you better get a move on. No telling when that Cranberry guy's gonna be here."

THAT EVENING, no one was more surprised than I to find myself not just in attendance at the event honoring "that Cranberry guy," but actually seated on stage, shoulder to shoulder with a half dozen specially invited dignitaries. The former archbishop's talk, sponsored by the Seminary and School of Theology, was the major cultural event of the fall semester, and as I looked out over the people slowly filing into Phipps Auditorium, I thought of that line from one of Shakespeare's *Henry VIs*: "Now am I seated as my soul delights."

I had none other than Bishop Townsend himself to thank

for my presence on stage, for Dunwoody would most certainly have preferred me to be elsewhere. Earlier in the day, after Mystics 401, when I'd returned to my office to retrieve a copy of *Religious Poets of the Fifteenth Century* for the bishop, Katie popped out from behind the door, again in her role as special envoy. "Hey, M.B., looks like you got in good with the bish."

"Oh?"

"Yeah, Ms. Adams sent me. She said a bunch of muckety-mucks are going to be on stage tonight with the archbishop, and he wants *you* there as well—asked for you by name! It'll be great for the Theophily Department to be represented, don't you think? ... sort of makes a statement. Is that lit or what?" Yes, I agreed, it was lit.

Though my chair on stage was at the far end, obviously tagged on at the last minute, I was thrilled to be part of the proceedings. To my right, from St. David's City Church, was the Reverend Joseph Clark, one of my co-panelists at the Forum on Faith the previous spring, as you'll recall. This time he had a pin on his black tunic that read "PRESS HERE TO ACTIVATE SERMON." He leaned over and crooned in my ear, "What a smashing time we had at the Forum, didn't we? Here on this very stage!" A moment later, he pointed to my book and chuckled in his affable way, "Planning on some heavy reading? ... Nothing like the fifteenth century for religious poets, eh?"

Not knowing whether he was being facetious, I sort of rotated my head noncommittally.

Next to him sat the Very Reverend Alexandra Hobson, who beamed beatifically in every direction and made little waving gestures—wavelets—toward any number of individuals in the audience. As bishop, she oversaw the local Episcopal diocese and according to the program would later present the former archbishop with the Jeremy Taylor Prize.

Beyond these two cheery Episcopalians sat Drs. Bigelow

and Barnes, both considerably less cheery, being, as they were, from the seminary, and farther down the row were Provost Kinealy and President Costa. Two seats on stage were as yet unoccupied: one in the center for the former archbishop and one on the opposite end for Dunwoody.

My indispensable claque Katie was not in the audience, for she'd gone to President Costa's house to rehearse with Tyrell and Kyeesha for their performance at the reception later. Still, I was cheered by the presence of several other compatriots: theatre professor Carl Evans (my closest male friend); our librarian Ms. Lambert (my closest female friend); Graciela and Nate; as well as Tom Fouchee from the Art Department. And front and center sat Dolly De Angeli with her implausibly red hair and red high-top tennis shoes.

Just then, someone tapped me on the shoulder. It was Dunwoody. "Bonham, I seem to have arrived before the group that's escorting our guest. They should've been here by now ... anyway, that puts me in a jam. Do you think, right after the ceremony, you could give him this?" He plopped a small cloth sack in my lap. "It's all the things he needed—toothbrush, razor, comb ... Just give it to him when you give him your book. I'd do it, but I need to slip out early to pick up some things for the reception, and he wants to go back to the lodge before then to freshen up." As Dunwoody dashed off to his seat, I tucked the sack, along with my book, under the chair.

Reverend Clark leaned toward me and said, "Dunwoody's a good man, eh?" in a tone that seemed to say, "God's in his heaven and all's right with the world." Again, I nodded vaguely.

At that point, the archbishop was escorted onto the stage by a pert seminarian. The house lights dimmed, the audience hushed, and Dunwoody approached the podium.

He began, "Good evening, Archbishop Townsend, Bishop

Hobson, President Costa, honored guests, ladies and gentlemen. As I stand here tonight, somewhat nervously, looking out over this distinguished sea of faces"—I cringed. How can a sea be distinguished? And a room full of human heads looks nothing like the sea, more like a pumpkin patch—"I am reminded of something John Calvin wrote in his *Institutes of Christian Religion*: 'We lose our ability to speak well when we stop speaking with God.' In a few minutes, we will hear from a man who has spent a career speaking with God and then speaking about it, articulately, to the rest of us.

"But first, allow me to introduce our guests ..."

Starting with President Costa, he introduced those of us seated on stage, and in each case, he made some memorable quip, sometimes touching, sometimes amusing. Of President Costa, he said, "As president of this institution, 'She openeth her mouth with wisdom; and in her tongue is the law of kindness.'" Of Reverend Clark he said, "If it's true, as Solomon says, that 'a man's wisdom maketh his face to shine,' then be forewarned: if you go to St. David's to spend time with Reverend Clark, you'll need to apply sunscreen." Laughter ensued.

Dunwoody's introduction of me was as follows: "And finally, on the far end, Dr. Martin Bonham, professor of English, sometime window washer"—he cut a glance in my direction and smiled charmingly—"and chair of our new Department of Theophily. Although we've had our differences, I must say that among all my acquaintances here at Cupperton, he is the one who most reminds me of Saint Paul." The compliment took me off guard. I was touched. There was a pause, and then he added, "And if you've ever been to Saint Paul, you know what a boring city it is." Another laugh ensued, this one uproarious. I mustered a wan smile.

Finally, Dunwoody, with much fanfare and more inapt metaphors, introduced our speaker. When he was done,

Bishop Townsend rose and stepped to the podium, with his steely gray hair shining in the spotlight and his eyebrows flaring upward, Tolkien-like, at the ends. Robustly built, but not heavy, he had a demeanor that was both warm and imposing at the same time. Seeing him stand there, I understood what must have possessed the ancient Romans to coin the word *gravitas*. He thanked the chairman, the audience, and the dignitaries, paying a special compliment to President Costa. Then placing his hands firmly on either side of the podium, he looked out over the crowd.

"Tonight, I have but two words for you. They are the soul of my address, the heart of my homily for this evening, though were I to speak from now till next All Saints Day, I could not even begin to plumb their depths. The saints have exemplified them with their lives; the great writers have parsed them with their tomes; and when we stand before the Judgment Seat, we will speak them from the very core of our being. I had planned to speak on a different topic tonight, but in meeting and mingling with so many of you wonderful people today, I felt that Cupperton, like the rest of the world, is in special need of those two words. They are ... *forgive me.*"

He paused. Whoever first devised that bit about hearing a pin drop knew what he or she was talking about. Every eye was on the archbishop.

"In our churches we often hear exhortations to forgive others; it's a central command of the Christian life. Unless we forgive, Jesus tells us, we cannot be forgiven. No spiritual equation is more foundational.

"We are often tempted, however, to forgive others almost with an attitude of noblesse oblige, assuming a kind of superiority over the person we are forgiving; as Oscar Wilde said, 'Always forgive your enemies; nothing annoys them so much.'" The audience laughed. "Other times we forgive as a kind of object lesson in how good we think we are, how patient and understanding. And sometimes, when the intensity of the offense fades, we think we've forgiven when we've merely forgotten. But even when the forgiveness is sincere, we're prone to lose track of the other, harder part of that spiritual equation—asking others to forgive us."

I swallowed hard. I had the feeling that some heavy convicting was on the way.

"Someone once defined a neurotic as a person who says, 'I'm sorry' all the time. We tend to apologize perfunctorily so that others will like us and think we're a decent sort after all. We often say it as casually as 'Good morning.' But 'forgive me' goes deeper, requires more from us.

"When it comes to genuine, heartfelt forgiveness, I do not turn to the theologians and the philosophers—who can make sense of them anyway?—but to the poets. They tend to speak most eloquently on the subject. I think of George Herbert, Henry Vaughan, Emily Dickinson ... someday someone should compile an anthology on just that subject." He glanced in my direction, then continued, "How many of you recall from your school days the poem by Victorian poet and priest Gerard Manley Hopkins—called 'Felix Randal'?"

I had to resist the impulse to shoot my hand into the air like a Bingo winner. I also had to resist the temptation to glance down the row to see how Dunwoody, at the other end, had reacted to the archbishop's disparagement of theologians.

"That poem is a portrait, an elegy really, of one of Hopkins's late parishioners, a farrier, a person who shoed horses for a living. The poet is candid about Felix's coarse ways and spiritual doubts. Still, Hopkins prays, 'God rest him all road ever he offended.' It's a lovely line. The phrase *all road* was a common country idiom at the time, meaning 'everything.' In other words, 'God, forgive every one of Felix's offenses.' But

Hopkins gives it a clever twist. The shoes that Felix put on the horses' hooves would have pounded down half the roads in Ireland, far and near, so the poet is, in a sense, asking the roads themselves to forgive the farrier. And now, in my own times of prayer, I pray that line: 'God, forgive me all road ever I offended'—both the roads I'm aware of and those I'm not.

"Think for a moment. Are there people in your life from whom you should ask forgiveness, someone with whom you've shared a deep animosity or even just a … *collegial rivalry*?"—he was referencing the conversation with Dunwoody that morning—"Perhaps, instead of waiting for the other person to ask for forgiveness, it's time for you to look into your own soul and say to that person, 'Forgive *me* all road ever I offended.'

"Another poet, less familiar, speaks to me just as profoundly. Alice Meynell, a contemporary of Hopkins, is probably best remembered by you literature majors as the person who discovered Francis Thompson and first published his famous poem 'The Hound of Heaven.'

"Meynell wrote a poem called 'Veni Creator'—'Creator, Come'—in which she ponders all the indignities that God, through Jesus, suffered here on earth, being tempted in all ways just as we are. But then she asks, did Jesus *really* experience *every* humiliation? 'Left'st Thou a path of lowliness untrod?' she asks.

"And she answers her own question in a surprising way. Since Jesus was perfect, he never committed a sin. And since he never committed a sin, then he never experienced the humbling act of asking someone for forgiveness. He forgave others—even from the cross—but nowhere do we find him asking another to forgive him. So Meynell boldly suggests—only the poets have this kind of audacity!—that Jesus's experience on earth was not quite complete. How could he have carried all our burdens to the cross if the experience of asking for forgiveness and being forgiven was not included? 'Give heed,' Meynell says to God, 'Look at the mournful world Thou has decreed. The time has come.'

"It is time, she says, for Jesus to dwell within her own heart, and within the hearts of everyone who stands in need of being forgiven, so that God might learn, might feel what that last bit of being human is like. She ends the poem with these words: 'Come, then, / Endure undreamed humility: Lord of Heaven, / Come to our ignorant hearts and be forgiven.'

"So, I ask you again, from whom do you need to ask forgiveness? Does it seem too hard, too humiliating? Then perhaps the time has come for you to ask Jesus to enter your heart and to allow him to experience that forgiveness along with you. Only in that way can he fulfill the last portion of his mission on earth. It is not just a way of showing love to the person from whom we're asking forgiveness, it's a way of showing our love for God by allowing God to know firsthand that small, remaining piece of humanity. It's time to say, 'Creator, come.'"

He paused and scanned the pumpkin patch of faces before him. Then he said, "Let us pray ... Dear Lord, you know our thoughts, and you know those from whom we need to ask forgiveness. If we do not have the strength to do that, please come into our ignorant hearts and be forgiven with us. And, dear Lord, forgive us all road ever we offended. Amen."

The place was silent for several seconds until a voice in the back repeated, "Amen," which was followed by applause.

So, there it was. The bishop's message had been directed in large part at Dunwoody and me, and the message hit home. I bore the weight of my own animosity toward Dunwoody, a weight that seemed to grow more ponderous with each passing month, and the only way to get past that simmering acrimony would be to take the bishop's advice ... to seek forgiveness. There had been moments, I admit, when I loathed the chairman. Now it was time to stop.

President Costa approached the podium. "Thank you, Bishop Townsend. Let's have another round of applause."

Lost as I was in my penitential mood, I was somewhat oblivious to the next portion of the evening, which was the presentation of the bishop's honorary doctoral degree from the university. As foretold, Dr. Dunwoody had slipped out of the auditorium during the previous round of applause, but I had already planned to catch him at the reception. We needed to talk.

President Costa read a lengthy commendation, recounting the former archbishop's accomplishments and citing the many reasons for granting him the honorary degree. She handed him a certificate in a leather binder, but just after she had draped the navy and gold doctoral stole of the university over Bishop Townsend's silver head, a phone rang—obviously belonging to one of the dignitaries on stage—and the ringtone could not have been more beastly. It was the opening phrases of "Baby Elephant Walk" done in a sort of quacking flatulence, as if performed by a choir of whoopee cushions. The audience began to stir, then to giggle. Were the occasion not so solemn, I would have laughed aloud, though I felt embarrassed for whoever sitting near me had such a relentless device lurking in their coat pocket—or in their tunic pocket, in the case of the cheery Episcopalians, whom I suspected of being in possession of the infernal machine.

As the jingle continued, I decided to glance down the row of dignitaries to my right, discreetly, to see who the culprit might be. But here's the odd thing: every one of them was glancing back at me. It was unnerving. Reverend Clark sort of motioned downward with his eyes, giving me a hint of some kind, and then, between musical iterations, he whispered, "I think it's yours," which was preposterous, of course, because I'd left my phone at home, and anyway, my ringtone is a thoroughly meditative "Für Elise."

Then I felt a cold rush of dread. The sound was coming from beneath my chair, from the bag of sundries that Dunwoody had given me to relay to Bishop Townsend. Frantic, I picked it up and tried to stifle "Baby Elephant Walk" by putting it under my arm inside my tweed jacket. It helped only marginally, and by then, laughter had spread throughout the auditorium.

Things seemed to move in a jerky sort of accelerated motion, as though I were in an old Buster Keaton film. I clutched the sack to my chest and ran to the wings. A smattering of applause broke out as I exited, and, as I dashed for the rear door, I tried to untie the drawstring, but I found it was tightly knotted. Eventually, as I stood outside in the cold, the baby elephant drew its last breath.

FOR WHAT SEEMED LIKE AN ETERNITY, shivering and shaken, I sat on the long concrete wall by the loading dock behind Phipps, the evil sack still in my hand. It was all too clear who was responsible for the mayhem. Soon I could hear the voices of the crowd dispersing around the front of the auditorium, the evening with the former archbishop having just ended, and much laughter could be overheard. All thoughts of asking for forgiveness vanished like the March Hare down his hole.

When I felt that the coast was clear, I sneaked back through the metal fire door to retrieve my overcoat and *Religious Poets of the Fifteenth Century* from under my chair. As I stepped across the now-dim stage, members of the maintenance crew were pacing back and forth across the aisles, collecting discarded programs and lost mittens and scarves. Although my friends appeared to have abandoned me, no doubt on their way to the reception for the archbishop, one shadowy figure seemed aware of my presence, for that figure was bolting up the steps at the side of the stage and hurtling in my direction.

It was Dolly. She stopped in front of me and in her pugnaciously empathic way asked, "Hey, doll, what the hell? I been looking for ya."

Touched by the fact that she alone among my acquaintances had sought me out after my recent discomposure, I said, "Dolly, you are too, too kind ... you live up to your namesake; you are truly of the angels ..."

"Huh?"

"You know, De Angeli—*of the angels.*"

"Oh, yeah. Right. Well, I'll tell ya, I really felt for ya. Y'okay?"

"I think so." I gave her an awkward hug, and she hugged me back rather vigorously. I should have known better than to risk such a public display of affection, for, with her bright eyes shining, she pondered for several seconds, then asked, "Say, hon ... you got a girlfriend?"

Though flattered by the hint, I thought it best to move on as quickly as possible. "What a day this has been ... it's like this ..." So, sitting in the dark, on the chairs previously occupied by the cheery Episcopalians, I unfolded my tale of Dunwoody planting the booby-trapped phone on my unsuspecting person.

"Wow," she said, "he really slipped you a mickey, didn't he?"

"I can't show my face at the reception now," I said. "Maybe you'd do me a favor and give my book to the archbishop—"

"Naw, you go anyway," she said. "You can't let him take

you for a patsy. Show 'em you're not afraid. If you don't stand up to mugs like that, they getcha every time ... I should tell ya about my third husband sometime ..."

"Yes, I suppose I should take the high road," I said.

"Hey, I said go to the reception, but forget about the high road. That just means you got farther to fall. Ya know? No, you gotta get him back. You *get him back*, doll, you understand?"

Except for the intermittent smacking of Dolly's gum, all was quiet in the cavernous auditorium. The cleaning crew had gone. Then Dolly leaned in close and said in a low voice as if imparting a secret, "Say, hon, you want I should ... uh ... make life hard for this Dunwoody? I got friends in the seminary, if ya know what I mean."

At that moment, I found myself just a little more terrified than usual of this red-haired octogenarian in high-tops. No telling to what extremes she would go to help a friend in need. Life is best lived, I realized, by staying on the good side of the formidable Dolly De Angeli.

"Thank you," I said, "but no. I should handle this myself."

"So, whatcha gonna do?"

"I don't know," I said. "I just don't know, but I'll think of something."

CHAPTER 6

SHOULDER ANGELS

The angel of righteousness is delicate
and modest and meek and gentle.
... The angel of wickedness is ill-tempered
and bitter and foolish and his deeds are evil.
... You have, therefore, the workings of both angels.
—*The Shepherd of Hermas*, c. 150 CE

N ever have I experienced even the slightest inclination to own a firearm—which I account a great blessing. The Deity, no doubt with the benefit of omniscience, knows that I would shoot myself in the literal foot at the first opportunity. I can't even hammer a nail without hitting my thumb. Milton could well have been referring to me in *Paradise Lost* when he wrote of Satan that his "devillish Engine back recoiles / Upon himself."

My ill-luck with "devillish Engines" was borne in upon me with particular force in the days that followed Bishop Townsend's visit, when, spurred on by the indomitable Dolly De Angeli, I found myself possessed of dire and retaliatory thoughts. According to Katie Westcott, someone in the audience had even videoed my confused leave-taking from the stage and posted it on TikTok with the title "Baby Elephant Dash." It had gone viral.

"Good," I replied, "everyone will see I was the victim of a cruel prank."

Katie just said, "Nah, doesn't work that way, M.B."

Dunwoody's prank was not just malicious toward me but also rude to the former archbishop ... and far below the ethical standards of someone who professes to be a Christian. As a result, I felt justified in lowering my own ethical standards in return, if only temporarily and solely in the interests of justice, of course, as I'll explain shortly.

I remember a time in my youth when I found a five-dollar bill wafting down the street, and since no one was nearby to claim it, I claimed it myself. At once, the urge overcame me to spend it frivolously, or, as my mother said, the money was "burning a hole in my pocket." Now, in the aftermath of the evening with the archbishop, I felt as though I were in possession of a free "Pay Dunwoody Back" coupon that was burning a hole in my pocket, if not my soul.

What transpired was this: a few days after Bishop Townsend's departure, I was in the Student Stores in search of a comb as well as the latest issue of *The Chaucer Quarterly*, which I'd heard contained a controversial article on the pronunciation of terminal *e*'s in *The Canterbury Tales*. (If you're interested, track down my vehement letter of response to the editor in the Spring issue.) And there in the store, in a basket marked "Special Sale," were a number of items left over from the summer: inflatable beach balls, swimming goggles, and foam noodles—items now unwanted in the depths of December. But the item that most intrigued me was a small package labeled "Water Balloons—Aerodynamically Designed for Perfect Throwing."

In a sort of Hegelian synthesis, I placed the theoretical concept of water balloons alongside the hard fact that Dr. Cornelius C. Dunwoody, almost daily, walked directly beneath my third-floor office window on the way to his lair in Erickson Hall. Once I had juxtaposed those two ideas, a third seemed to emerge on its own, the gist of which you can readily imagine. As Oscar Wilde once wrote: "An idea that is not dangerous is unworthy of being called an idea at all."

My reasoning was incontrovertible.

I realize that the notion of dousing aging seminary professors with water bombs in the middle of winter may seem juvenile, but consider the many advantages. First, it is relatively harmless, what the French call *une farce d'écolier*, "a schoolboy prank." Compared to the premeditation and malice aforethought exhibited by Dunwoody when triggering phone grenades in cloth pouches and suckering innocent lambs into attending armed-and-dangerous religious establishments, water ballooning seemed innocuous. Second, it is efficacious. In college, friends of mine often performed this act, so I knew it to be simple in conception, execution, and outcome. The victim is amusingly surprised, and the attacker pleasantly invigorated and gratified. Third, the public at large, in my experience, tends to regard the perpetrators of such acts as wits and bon vivants. And fourth, Dunwoody deserved it.

You see, incontrovertible.

So, the next day, I rose early to await the passing of Dunwoody. Knowing that he taught an eight-o'clock Hebrew class, I arrived at my office by seven to set the springs of my snare. I extracted six balloons from the plastic packaging and filled them in the restroom sink at the other end of the hall. When fully loaded, they were about the size of softballs and of the same shape, which is obviously what was meant by "aero-dynamically designed." I knew that "perfect throwing" would be unnecessary since I intended to allow them to drop straight down, two at a time, one pair quickly after another. While gravity was clearly on my side, timing would be the main challenge. Still, I reasoned, even if I missed a direct hit, any ordinance landing in close proximity would not only startle the target but soak its pant legs and shoes.

As I raised the window sash in my office, the freezing wind scattered a stack of loose final exams from my desk to the floor, but there was no time to collect them now. The clock was ticking. The old steam radiator beneath the window clanged into overdrive. Bracing myself against the cold blast, I lifted my six grenades from the box in which I'd transported them and gently laid them on the sill ... and waited.

Soon, by leaning out the window, I could see Dunwoody, afar off, as he trudged across the faculty parking lot behind Beetham Hall, wrapped in his scarf and crowned with a white polar cap with large, fleecy-white earflaps. The cap made him look as though his head were composed of the internal organs of a feather pillow. Such a large target would be impossible to miss. It wouldn't be long now.

But I'd made a vital miscalculation. During the heat and humidity of summer, my office window is sticky and difficult to raise and lower, but in the dry, cold air of winter, as I only half-consciously noticed, it slid upward with surprising ease. What hadn't occurred to me was that it might just as easily slide down of its own volition—which is exactly what it did. Gravity was clearly on the window's side as well.

The balloons, of course, were in the direct path of the window's descent. The immediate lateral geyser created by the convergence of the twain managed to inundate the front of my trousers as well as the floor, and it made a violent hissing sound as it splattered across the radiator. My "devillish Engine" had indeed "back recoiled" upon myself.

One of my munitions managed to survive the guillotining, but it must have been damaged somehow, for as soon as I lifted the sash and tried to extract it, it burst in my hand with a muffled sploosh.

I then glanced down to see the top of Dunwoody's furry cap drifting past. Unless he detected a few drops of water dripping from the third-floor ledge, he would have had no hint of the ambuscade he had narrowly escaped. I reflected bitterly on the unfairness of life.

Though taken aback, I am stoic in such situations. Reversals are to be expected, or, as Chaucer reminds us, "Thus doth Fortune turn her wheel." But when I saw the water had also doused my six-volume set of the works of seventeenth-century cleric and mystic Thomas Traherne—which had been stacked on the floor for months due to lack of shelf space—that is when I let rip a ferocious, stentorian expletive.

Pulling myself together, I assessed the situation. First, I did what I could to save my Trahernes from damage, though it was too little too late for two of the volumes. Next, realizing the extent of my own dousing, I removed my corduroy pants and draped them over the radiator to dry. As I stood there in my wingtip Oxfords and boxer briefs, I contemplated my next move, which I determined was to take my unused "Engines" and toss them resolutely into the trashcan.

I didn't have time to consider my next, next move, however, because the office door cracked open and a sort of disembodied head sporting a red beret appeared in the interval.

"You okay?" It was Carl Evans, whose office was at the other end of the hall, near the restrooms. He stepped into my office and shut the door behind him.

"Reasonably," I said.

"I heard a shout," he said. Then, noticing my state of *deshabille*, he added, "Am I catching you at a, uh ... bad time ...?"

"The worst," I said. "Have a seat."

So, I explained everything, beginning with the free "Pay Dunwoody Back" coupon burning a hole in my pocket and ending with the water-logged Trahernes.

BEFORE CONTINUING, however, I must introduce you to Carl Mason Evans, who, upon having just entered my office, now takes center stage in this drama. As chair of the Theater Arts Department, he directs the Cupperton Players as well as the Lab Theater, and he wears the sock and buskin in any number of local theatricals. He's also my closest male friend and confidant. I was relieved that it was his head that appeared at my door and not some other, for Carl is a man of discretion and sagacity. A fine actor, singer, director, mime, and juggler, he is himself a noted prankster on campus, so I knew he would lend a sympathetic ear, especially since he had witnessed my ignominious retreat during the archbishop's ceremony. Carl is married to Sara, a brilliant and talented woman whom he met in an off-Broadway production when Carl was earning his MFA at Columbia. They have two daughters, Celia and Rosalind.

My first experience of Carl had been at a faculty soirée that he and Sara had thrown several winters earlier when they were new on campus, and I use the word *experience* advisedly, for one doesn't simply meet Carl Evans. One experiences him the way one experiences a sudden rainstorm or the *1812 Overture* with cannon.

At this party, for instance, he was prevailed upon to perform "Let Me Entertain You" from *Gypsy*, a hilariously extended version, complete, as I recall, with someone's woolen scarf in place of the feather boa. He began by descending the stairs from the second floor, in vamp-like fashion with high kicks—I believe both shoes flew off—and completed the number by returning the same way. Though he sang it a cappella, one would have sworn he had accompaniment, for Carl is, as Chesterton said of Walt Whitman, an orchestra unto himself.

Needless to say, his bigger-than-life persona makes him one of the most popular and beloved professors on campus. Seldom is he seen without a gaggle of theater majors clustering about him as he holds forth like Socrates doing stand-up in the Agora.

I would seem to be an unlikely candidate to befriend such a sought-after individual, more than two decades my junior, but I won his heart later at that same soirée when I performed a dramatic reading of Stanley Holloway's old dancehall routine "Albert and the Lion," which is always a crowd pleaser. It is the only recitation I know (apart from the prologue to *The Canterbury Tales*). Still, it was one recitation more than any of the other professors at the party knew—drab lot that we are—so I have since become a regular at Carl and Sara's dinner table. Celia and Rosalind refer to me as Uncle Bon and often ask me to reprise "Albert and the Lion."

As an Episcopalian of fairly radical stripe, Carl, along with Graciela, was among the first to agree to teach a class for the Department of Theophily—two classes, actually, one on "Performance as Worship" (*not* "Worship as Performance," mind you) and a half-credit seminar on the "The Actor in Search of God."

UPON HEARING MY "DEVILLISH ENGINES" story, Carl thought for a moment, then said, somewhat sententiously, "'Heat not a furnace for your foe so hot that it do singe yourself.'"

After weighing his comment in the depths of my soul, I replied—"*What?*" I had expected applause for my initiative and cheers for my aplomb, not Shakespeare.

"What do you mean *what?*" he said. "It's *Henry VIII*—"

"I *know* it's *Henry VIII*—but what do you *mean?*"

"Well ... frankly, what I mean is that vengeance is beneath you. Do you need more quotes to convince you? There's the 'croaking raven' bit in *Hamlet*—"

"*Vengeance?* You make it sound so dastardly," I said. "It wasn't vengeance! It was more like a ... like a rejoinder, a clever riposte. It's like this a big chess match Dunwoody and I are engaged in, and it was my move."

He looked at me with a baleful expression.

Raising my voice, I continued, "I mean, really, *revenge*! You make me feel as if I'm carpooling into the Ninth Circle of Hell with Count Ugolino."

Carl executed a classic dramatic pause, raised an eyebrow, pinned me with a pointed look, then said, "I appear to have hit a nerve."

"You have *not* hit a nerve!" I thundered, which, of course, only proved his point.

"Okay," he said, "calm down. You call it a riposte, but it's also an assault ... even if a sort of *baptismal* assault. I hate to get all moralizing on you, but what if Dunwoody'd had a heart attack or fallen and broken his leg? What if *you'd* fallen out the window? Or what if he'd had you arrested for assault and the school fired you? Where would the Department of Theophily be then? It could happen. You'd be hauled before the Faculty Disciplinary Committee at the very least. I mean ... you and Dunwoody ... look, this is how wars start, right?"

"Oh, come on, it happens all the time on campus—"

"Among frat boys who've had too much Coors Light."

I sat there, my cheeks flushed with shame.

Then, adding the final nail, he said, "And what, pray tell—just *what* would Celia and Rosalind think of their Uncle Bon if I were to tell them? I mean, really!"

I pouted like a spoiled child. "You're no fun." I took a deep breath. We were silent for a long time. He sat with his elbows on the arms of the chair, hands clasped under his chin, tapping his index fingers together and waiting for me to respond. "Well, in the end, it failed," I finally said, "and there was no harm done, and ... I ... you're right. I know, I know. It was a dumb idea. I was angry and got carried away. You saw what happened at the archbishop's talk. What else can I say?"

"Uh ... pants."

"*What?*" I said.

"Your pants ... I think your pockets really *are* burning." He pointed.

I thought I'd detected an acrid smell a few moments before, and when I turned, my corduroy pants were smoldering as they lay draped over the radiator behind me.

I briskly snatched them off and held them up. Dark scorch marks ran laterally across the legs. I waved them to disperse the smoke and said, "Look, I'm sorry. We won't talk about it again. But promise me one thing—please, please, *don't* tell Ms. Westcott, all right?"

At which point, Katie popped her head in the door, sniffed the air, and said, "Hey, M.B., what's with the pants?"

I'M sure there are humiliations worse than sitting in your skivvies while being shamed by MDiv's less than half your age as well as bombastic drama professors in red berets, but at that moment I couldn't imagine what they might be.

Naturally, Carl felt obliged to tell Katie all about the whole incident (he thought himself particularly droll when he said he needed to "brief" her on the situation), and worse yet, as I sat there with my singed pants draped across my legs, they proceeded to talk about my moral failings as though I weren't present.

"It's strange," Katie said to Carl, "that he considered such an act. It's so out-of-character, like he needs a vibe-check. It's like he's not fully self-aware."

"Hmm, not self-aware at all," said Carl. "I wonder if he can even recognize himself in a mirror. And *most* people develop a conscience at some point in their lives, the ability to know right from wrong."

"*Most* people," repeated Katie, "but not all ... sociopaths and such."

Carl said, "I rather like the image of Shoulder Angels. I find that helpful ... you know, one on each shoulder—"

"Like in the *New Yorker* cartoons," she said.

"Exactly. I remember one in which the Good Shoulder Angel says to the Bad Shoulder Angel, 'Stop calling me *holier-than-thou*! I *am* holier than thou!'"

Katie laughed.

I rolled my eyes.

Carl continued, "But seriously, it's a good metaphor. You know Marlowe's *Doctor Faustus*, right? We did it in Lab year before last. As Faustus weighs the idea of selling his soul to Mephistopheles, a Good Angel and a Bad Angel appear on stage and try to persuade Faustus one way and the other. Of course, the Bad Angel wins. Near the end, as the Good Angel exits in despair, he says to Faustus, 'And now, poor soul, must thy good angel leave thee; the jaws of hell are open to receive thee.' It's chilling. Then there's *The Castle of Perseverance*—a morality play two centuries before Marlowe. In the prologue, Mankynde, a sort of Everyman, is caught between his Good Angel, who tries to 'teach him goodness,' and his Bad Angel, who is full of 'false enticing'"—with his fingers Carl made a villainous little clawing gesture in my direction—"The Bad Angel tempts Mankynde with three enemies: 'the world, the Devil, and the foul flesh.' Here's a question, Katie: which of those do you think covers water balloons? Anyway, Mankynde finds shelter in the Castle of Perseverance. That one ends better than the Marlowe."

Addressing Carl, Katie interjected, "Here's one for you. You ever read *The Shepherd of Hermas*? Greek, second century. As far as I know, the book contains the first reference to Good and Bad Angels, and here's the cool thing: it says they live inside us. That's a powerful concept. Our struggle with evil isn't external. It's internal ... like Paul in Romans when he says, 'That which I should do, I don't. And that which I shouldn't do, I do.'"

"Nope, haven't heard of that book," said Carl, "but the Book of Common Prayer echoes Paul where it says, 'We have erred and strayed from thy ways like lost sheep ... And we have done those things which we ought not to have done; and there is no health in us.' How about you, Martin, have you ever read *The Shepherd of Hermas?*" But before I could submit to the embarrassment of admitting that, no, I hadn't read it either, Carl continued, "You know, Katie, come to think of it, there's a hint of that in Greek drama. The chorus sometimes acts as a character's conscience, weighing the good and bad among various options. The choral odes often contain two parts, the *strophe* and the *antistrophe*, the thesis and the antithesis."

Katie said, "You know, this would all make a terrific Theophily class: 'Shoulder Angels: Loving God by Making Right Choices.' In seminary, we called it orthopraxy. Maybe

Martin should teach that one. He might learn something in the process."

Carl said, "It's basic, isn't it? Yeah, a real Theophily concept."

Katie said, "What do you think, M.B.?"

Just as I was about to open my mouth for the first time, the nine-o'clock buzzer rang, and Carl intoned dramatically, "Alas, alas, I'm late for class," and he dashed out.

Katie stood up, threw me a tiny wave, and said, "Gotta go."

MIDWAY through my following week's journey (to paraphrase Dante), I found myself in a darkened theater.

I was seated in the front row of the Lab Theatre's annual Christmas production of *The Second Shepherd's Play*. (Ordinarily, I would inform you that it's an anonymous English play from the late fifteenth century, part of the Wakefield Cycle of so-called mystery plays, but I don't want to sound pedantic.) Carl directs the play every year in association with the nearby St. Timothy's Episcopal Church, and this year, Carl's daughters, Celia and Rosalind, ages five and seven, respectively, were making their stage debuts—playing sheep, of course.

Fortunately, Katie and Carl were no longer pillorying me. We'd talked, I'd been absolved, and the foolish balloon episode, like the balloons themselves, had been relegated to the rubbish heap of history. The teasing had ended. And now, along with other friends and faculty, I sat expectantly in the dim theatre. After the performance, I'd been invited to Carl and Sara's house for a Christmas party and our annual gift exchange.

One odd thing about that Sunday matinee, however, was that Carl acted as though it alone was to be my Christmas present. Just a few days earlier, he'd dropped by my office, plopped a ticket on my desk, and said, "Merry Christmas from the girls and me." It seemed odd because he knew I was planning to attend the performance anyway, and with the faculty discount, the expense was negligible. I confess to being miffed because I'd already purchased his gift, a rather expensive volume that I found at the Agèd Page Used Bookshop in Ware. In any case, I thanked him and said I was looking forward to the event, as I did every year.

The opening of *The Second Shepherd's Play*, as you know, introduces three shepherds—Coll, Gyb, and Daw—who walk onto the stage, one at a time, to keep watch over their flocks by night and to complain in comic terms about the weather, the local landlords, and their spouses. In this production, about a dozen children, including Celia and Rosalind, were dressed in fluffy sheep-style headgear and with black-painted noses, milling about the stage and bleating intermittently, to the amusement of the adoring parents.

Eventually, a local shady character named Mak enters to kibitz with the other three. More jokes and complaints are exchanged until the entire company decides they are tired and need to lie down for a nap. As soon as the shepherds are comically snoring, Mak leaps up, looks left and right, twirls a nonexistent mustache in vaudeville fashion, then steals one of the plump sheep (in this case, Celia Evans), which Mak transports home to his wife, Gill.

At first, Gill is panicked that the theft will be discovered, but the prospect of a mutton dinner persuades her to be an accomplice. So, they decide that if the shepherds come searching for the lost sheep, they will hide it in the crib in the corner and explain that Gill has just given birth. Then, with a pillow stuffed beneath her apron, she will pretend to be in labor with the fake baby's twin. Surely, the sight and sound of a woman in labor will deter the shepherds from searching their hut. That decided, Mak returns to the field and pretends to be asleep with the others so he won't be suspected of the theft.

When the shepherds awake, they discover that a sheep is missing and begin a frantic search. The house lights go up, and, as Mak skulks away, Coll, Gyb, and Daw, ad-libbing all the while, steal out into the audience in search of their sheep. They look under the chairs and deep inside people's hats and backpacks. Every year, the audience loves this part of the play, and it's sure to get laughs.

From somewhere off-stage, a crew member inexplicably shouts, "All set," to the actors, and as the lights go down again, Gyb then pivots to the door at the back of the stage. Lab Theatre, I should explain, is a makeshift auditorium on the third floor of the Cramer Building, and the door to which Gyb has just pointed leads to the fire escape landing.

He turns with a grand gesture and exclaims, "There's one place we haven't looked ...," and he opens the door. There, as if on cue, stands Cornelius Dunwoody, wide-eyed and flabbergasted, like a deer caught in the headlights, or, in this case, the spotlights. What is even more amazing is that he looks sheeplike in his ever-present fleecy polar hat.

Not even Samson could do a better job of bringing down the house. The audience roars into laughter. Dunwoody, sheepishly, you might say, looks left, then right, then makes a hasty exit down the fire escape.

Gyb turns to the audience and, mugging a little, ad-libs, "Nope, I don't think that was one of ours!"

Another peel of laughter.

How such a thing could have happened, I have no idea. Then it occurred to me—perhaps *that* was Carl's Christmas gift. But how?

The rest of the play proceeded smoothly. As soon as the

shepherds suspect who it was who has stolen their sheep, they rush to Mak's hut to confront him and Gill. At first, the shepherds are deceived by the newborn-baby ruse, but the jig is up as soon as the sheep bleats loudly from the crib—"Ba-aa-ah!" Celia delivers her one line brilliantly.

But then, amid the hilarity, comes the moment in the play that always catches one's breath. In a flash of brilliant light and color and smoke, a majestic angel appears on the raised platform to the left—this year, the angel is played by none other than Kyeesha Reed, and in her deep contralto, she begins to sing, "Go tell it on the mountain, over the hills and everywhere ..." She then instructs the shepherds to go to Bethlehem, where they will find a real baby, a holy king, who has just been born. It's a dazzling, beautiful moment.

When the shepherds arrive at the manger, they kneel by the crib of the baby Jesus and offer their modest gifts—cherries, a bird, and from Daw, a ball so the baby can, as he says, "go to the tennis," a line that always gets a laugh. But all the while, I couldn't get out of my mind the image of the wide-eyed Dunwoody in the doorway.

At the Evanses' party that evening, the usual crowd was in attendance: Katie and Tyrell, Graciela and Nate, among many others, and most surprising of all, Cornelius Dunwoody in the flesh, who, to his credit, seemed to have accepted his moment in the spotlight with relative good humor, though when I arrived, he was interrogating Carl about some details of his performance.

"So you're saying Bonham had nothing to do with this? He didn't put you up to it?"

"Not in the least, trust me," said Carl.

"You're *sure?*"

"I'm sure." Then turning to me as I approached, Carl said, "Here, ask him yourself."

"No," I said to Dunwoody, "I promise you. I was as surprised as anyone."

"You're a good sport, though, Dr. Dunwoody, and that's a fact," said Carl. "A lesser man would have been upset. You see, Martin"—Carl turned to me—"every year, as you know, it's a tradition that we draw at least one unsuspecting audience member into the action. Usually we just pull someone from the seats and either make them help look for the lost sheep or have an actor turn their coat inside out—or go through their purse item by item or whatnot. One year we had a pizza delivery guy walk into the action. In fact, we got Martin up on stage a couple of years ago, didn't we?" I nodded. "It's all in fun, so thank you, Dr. Dunwoody, for going along with it. I'll be sure you get free admission to the spring productions. And I must say, you're a natural-born actor. Your expression was priceless."

Dunwoody, not knowing quite what to say to such fulsomeness, looked at me and snapped, "Don't gloat, Bonham! You enjoyed every second of it! ... And now, if you'll excuse me, I'm going to get some canapés." He stalked off.

"So, how in the world did you pull that off?" I asked Carl in a quiet voice.

"It was easier than I expected. I invited him personally but told him the play started a half hour later than it actually did. Then, I had one of the crew direct him to the back stairs, telling him to wait till the lights dimmed so it would be safe for him to find his seat without interrupting the play. He thought it was the door to the balcony! The lights went down, and there he was."

"So, you weren't taking revenge ... on my behalf?"

"What? Of course not. Some of us are *above* revenge."

"Should I feel guilty that I laughed?"

"Not at all. Like I said, it's tradition. I have no beef with Dunwoody whatsoever, but after I saw him in his fuzzy cap on campus last week—it was just too tempting ... so theatrical! I like to think of the performance as sort of a *Dunwoody ex machina!*" Carl then glanced into the living room. "And now," he said, "if you'll excuse me, I've been called upon to entertain."

Sara was waiting at the piano, and together they led everyone in singing a combination of Cole Porter tunes and Christmas songs.

LATER, after the company had dwindled somewhat, Katie, Carl, and I stood in the kitchen, preparing to exchange our Christmas gifts.

"First," I said to Carl, "thank you for my present. It was perfect ... and far better than the replacement Trahernes I'd been hoping for—volumes five and six, by the way ... for future reference."

I then extracted a package from the inner pocket of my winter coat and gave it to Carl. He opened it. It was a facsimile edition of Oscar Wilde's handwritten manuscript of *De Profundis*, and I could not have chosen a more perfect gift. He was euphoric.

As far as Katie, she's the only person I know who, upon being given a copy of Spinoza's *Ethics* in Latin, would let out a little squeal and give me a warm hug.

When she handed me her package, I squeezed it and looked at her suspiciously. She smiled and said, "You've already got every book under the sun, M.B., so I went with *wearable* this year.'" I tore it open to find a new pair of brown corduroy trousers.

"It's perfect," I said and gave her another hug.

As fate would have it, Dunwoody entered the kitchen at that moment in search of more canapés. He did a double take. "Pants?" he said.

"Yes, from Katie."

"That's an odd sort of gift," he said.

I said, "Well, a hole got burned in the pocket of my previous pair."

Dunwoody just shook his head and walked off mumbling something about me being an idiot.

"Merry Christmas," I called after him.

"Hmmph," he said.

I didn't disagree.

CHAPTER 7
MS. WESTCOTT'S STORY

God, kindle Thou in my heart within
A flame of love to my neighbor,
To my foe, to my friend, to my kindred all,
To the brave, to the knave, to the thrall.
—Gaelic "Blessing of the Kindling"

Hi. This is Katie Westcott.

Do you remember way back last spring when Dr. Bonham and I were trying to get the Theophily Department together and I was in my last semester of seminary? Well, M.B. asked me to tell you about how I managed to graduate with my MDiv while Dr. Dunwoody was breathing down our necks and everything, sort of from my perspective. So here goes.

As you know, Dr. Dunwoody was really ticked off about the whole Department of Theophily thing, so he did his best to make my life miserable for my last semester, and you already know how miserable Dr. Dunwoody can make people when he wants to. He was really miffed when the Department of Theophily got approved (just after he and M.B. talked to those first and second graders), so the weapon he chose to get back at me was one of my best friends: Rowan.

Rowan and I had started at Cupperton together, two and a half years earlier. I first met him in the CUSS on orientation day while we were waiting in line for our seminary welcome packets, and the first thing I said to myself when I saw him was ... *elbows*. He was gawky and kind of angular ... asymmetrical somehow. Later that day, we got coffee at the CupperTea, and we bonded over espresso, biblical Greek, and the fact that we were both pretty geeky. He had dark, scraggly hair, was tall and skinny, and his voice still had that middle-school crack in it, even though he was in his early twenties.

He was one of the most insecure people I've ever known. He hated himself for the way he looked and talked, and, as he told me that day over coffee, his decision in the ninth grade to become the world's greatest biblical philologist someday didn't exactly help him get dates.

And then there was his name. It was *Rowan Wayrich*. "Try saying it five times fast," he said. I tried, and I saw his point. He told me that when he was growing up, his teachers, year after year, stumbled over it during roll call, calling him *Rowan Rayrich* or *Roarin' Wayrich* or whatever, which always made the other kids crack up. Eventually they called him *Wo-Wo*. And it didn't help that even he, until he was about five years old, could only manage *Wowan Waywicks*. I thought of Elmer Fudd in the Bugs Bunny cartoons saying, "Be vewy, vewy quiet! We're hunting wabbits!"

"So, what's your middle name?" I asked. "Maybe you could use that."

"... *Warren*" was his glum response.

I was about to say, "See, that's not so bad—*Rowan Warren*

Wayrich," but I knew I'd screw it up. It made my tongue swell up just thinking about it. So I just said, "Oh ..."

More importantly, he was also one of the most brilliant people I've ever known, something of a language prodigy. He'd majored in German at Oberlin (his pastor father was from Berlin, so Rowan grew up with the language)—he loved the German philosophers and theologians—but like me, he also had a second major in Greek. He managed to learn basic Hebrew as an undergraduate, and since I didn't start Hebrew until I got to Cupperton, Rowan was willing to tutor me, and in return, I coached him in Latin, which had been my minor at Carleton. I shared with him my passion for the early Church Fathers and the creeds. So it was a good trade-off. Throughout our first year, we studied together in the seminary library almost every night until it closed at eleven o'clock, and we became best friends.

By the middle of second semester, it was clear that we were almost complete pariahs in the seminary, mostly because we had very few friends and were two of the top students in our class. A lot of the others were jealous.

One day during our first spring semester, Rowan and I were having lunch in the cafeteria when one of our few friends, Jason Albright, who was pretty geeky himself, plopped his tray down at our table. "Well," he said, "I bet you guys didn't get tapped by the Eleven-Nineteens either."

We looked at him blankly.

"Yeah," he said, "invitations went out last week. I guess I'm not cool enough. Either of you get invited? Although I suppose if you did, you couldn't say."

"Eleven-Nineteens?" I asked.

"You don't know?" Jason sat down and moved in conspiratorially. "Yeah, it's this really exclusive secret society for seminary students and a few select undergrads. Invitation only. No one even knows what the name means ... they have initiation rites and everything."

"Eleven-Nineteens, huh?" I said. I thought for a moment. "Well, if it's a secret society, that'd make sense ... the year 1119 was when the Knights Templar was founded"—which I knew because I'd just read Umberto Eco's *Foucault's Pendulum*. I was into postmodernism, conspiracy theories, and semiotics at the time.

Now it was Jason's turn to look blank.

"You know ... the Crusades," I said. "The Knights Templar was this secret organization that raised money and built forts for the crusaders. Some people claim they're still around in some weird form or other and all mixed up with the Illuminati and the Freemasons and one-world-government stuff ... creepy." Jason shook his head, so I added, "Like in *The Da Vinci Code* and *Indiana Jones and the Last Crusade*—you remember those movies, right?"

"Vaguely," said Jason.

"Katie," Rowan interrupted, "you're overthinking it. I'm sure they're not that bright. Here's my theory. What if I were to do this ..."—he took his empty water glass, pretended to guzzle it, and rolled his eyes like he was drunk—"or what if I said, 'They could just as easily have called themselves the 'Seven-Thirty-Fours'? ... Think about it ... Gospels ...'"

"Oh, of course!" I said. "That's it. How juvenile! I mean, really!" Jason still looked baffled. I said to him, "Don't you see? It's Matthew 11:19 and Luke 7:34. In both verses Jesus says people accuse him of being a glutton and a winebibber. The Eleven-Nineteens is just the 'gluttons and winebibbers' club— you know, tongue-in-cheek. They probably go out drinking on weekends. Who cares?"

"Oh my gosh," said Jason, "that must be it ... though still, they have a bad reputation ... vandalism and stuff ... all sorts of pranks around campus. Egging windows is their calling card."

"Really? That's pretty dimwitted," I said, "I'd expect that of undergrads—but not seminarians."

"You'd be surprised," said Jason.

"I guess so," I said.

"Well, we're well out of it then," said Rowan, "and I couldn't care less."

BUT THINGS CHANGE. After our first year at Cupperton, Rowan went back to Ohio to work at his parents' church (they're copastors of a big Lutheran congregation near Dayton), and I spent the summer at Cupperton, taking advanced Hebrew as well as shelving books in the undergrad library and doing odd jobs for Ms. Lambert, the head librarian, like dog-sitting for her bullmastiff, Belle, while she vacationed in Australia.

In the fall, Rowan and I started our second year, but something happened that kind of put a damper on our relationship. Late one night in December, with stars sparkling everywhere overhead, we had just left the library after studying for finals and were walking past the big painted boulder in North Quad (I can still remember we were talking about Greek versus Hebrew ablatives—morphological cases and prepositional particles) when he stopped. It was cold, we could see our breath, and all I wanted was to get back to my dorm and go to sleep.

"Katie," he said. He sounded serious. His voice didn't crack.

I turned. Staring, he leaned toward me. Awkwardly. For a kiss. I stood ramrod straight, terrified for some reason, and (I blush when I think about it even now—I'm so ashamed) my involuntary response—I swear it was involuntary—was to shudder. Head to toe. Maybe I could say it was just the cold, but I couldn't bring myself to kiss him back. I could see the hurt in his eyes.

So, then and there, sitting on a bench in North Quad, shivering like crazy, my voice shaking so I could hardly talk, I explained to him that I wasn't interested in him "in that way," that it wasn't his fault, that I was worried I wasn't even capable of feeling love, that I wasn't sure I even loved God, that I liked him as a friend, and on and on. In other words, it was awful.

Though we continued to be friends, from that point on our relationship changed. We also became rivals. As the top two students in our class, we became competitors. We still studied together, out of habit more than anything, but we were guarded. If I did extra-credit work, I didn't tell him because I didn't want him to do extra work as well. While it spurred us both to excel, it took a toll. By the time we left for summer break after our second year, we were in full combat mode. His last words to me that June were a dark "Don't study too hard."

"You neither," I replied. I didn't tell him I'd signed up for one of Dr. Dunwoody's summer seminars.

DR. BONHAM HAS ALREADY TOLD you about my taking his Mystics 401 seminar as an elective at the beginning of my third year, something that Rowan mocked me for ... "Ooo, the great English nitwits," he'd say. I explained to Rowan that I didn't know what I'd have done without M.B. and all the friends we were making that semester, that I was in a bad way, and that the possibility of creating a Department of Theophily kind of saved my life. "What a waste" was all he said. We continued to drift apart.

The Forum on Faith took place the following spring, while M.B. and I were waiting to hear from the administration about our proposal. As you know, Dr. Dunwoody planted seminary students, including Jason and Rowan, in the audience to embarrass M.B., and Rowan was the one who asked the question about biblical languages (what else?).

Right after the Forum that day, I was furious with Rowan and determined to confront him. In a sort of foggy rage, I searched all over campus, tearing from Phipps to Erickson, from the arboretum to the library, all the while muttering under my breath, "We're hunting *wabbits*; we're hunting *wabbits* ..."

I found him with Jason and some other seminarians in front of their dorm. As I approached, I heard someone say, "Oh God, the Theophily queen!" and someone else, mocking my haircut, said, "Look, it's Katie Wedgecut!" Another made a cawing noise, no doubt because of my black clothes. Hysterical. When I walked up, they stopped talking and looked at me with smirks on their faces.

Then, shaking, standing nose-to-nose with Rowan, I was about to start yelling when I realized something. "Oh my gosh," I said to him calmly, "you're in the Eleven-Nineteens now, aren't you? And these are all your little winebibber buddies—"

It was a well-placed hit. He was expecting shouts and insults, but not that. Suddenly embarrassed, he pulled me around the side of the dorm.

"You're all jerks," I yelled over my shoulder as Rowan directed me down the sidewalk, pulling on my arm. "Get your hands off me!" I roared. "You're worse than all of them!"

"Shh, Katie, don't." His voice cracked.

"How could you do that? How could you embarrass Dr.

Bonham that way? You *know* how much the Theophily Department means to me. We've worked so hard—"

"Look, I'm sorry I didn't tell you about the Eleven-Nine-teens; we're not supposed to," he said.

"Well, *sorry* doesn't cut it! You sabotaged us. On purpose!"

He was quiet for a long time. "Katie, I can't explain now, but I did what I had to."

"What does *that* mean? Did Dunwoody put you up to it?"

He shook his head and walked away. "I didn't mean to hurt you."

"You're a jackass!" I stomped off.

A FEW WEEKS LATER, after M.B. and I found out that the Department of Theophily had been officially approved, I knew Dr. Dunwoody would find a way to get back at me. It didn't take long. Through Ms. Adams, the department secretary, he sent a message that he wanted to see me in his office. When I arrived, he was polite, praised the nice weather, offered me tea, and asked if I wanted to borrow any books. It was odd and awkward. I said no.

"Well, Miss Westcott, I'll get to the point," he said. "Late last semester I informed you that you were on track to be top of your class, which meant you'd be receiving the Founders' Prize at graduation and giving the address that goes with it. Well, I'm sorry to say, depending on final grades, of course, you're likely to be edged out."

"What? By who?"

"Rowan Raywich."

"Wayrich," I corrected.

"Right, Owen Wayrich."

I gave up.

"Yes, after checking the transcripts," he continued, "I've found that though you both have straight A's, he's a half credit ahead of you, which means that he's actually first in the class. You're still number two, however, so you should feel proud of that. You and Mr. … uh, you and Rowan … are two of the finest students we've ever had at Cupperton."

"That's not possible. I know for a fact I've taken more classes."

"Not according to the transcripts."

Never before had I noticed how much Dr. Dunwoody looked like a short, bald Severus Snape.

"No," I said through my teeth, "I attended summer sessions the last two years, one full-credit class each summer— including yours on Greek pseudepigrapha last summer. And right now I'm taking Dr. Bonham's Mystics 402 as an elective, which is another whole credit."

"I'm afraid that's not enough," he said.

"But I *know* I took as many classes as Rowan during the school year—and he spent *both* his summers working at his parents' church."

"Yes, precisely, but he received independent-study credit for that work—"

"What?" I was stunned. "All he did was help paint the nave and build a playground."

"Be that as it may, it was a valuable learning experience. He got full credit."

"But he's not even going into ministry," I said. "He's gonna teach—and where'd he get that extra *half* credit anyway? I want to see the records."

"You know I can't show you Mr. Waywich's wecords —*records*—they're confidential. You're a brilliant student, Miss Westcott," he said, "but it's time for you to learn to deal with disappointment."

I turned and left his office in a huff. I could hear my heart pounding in my ears.

As I was going down the front steps of Erickson, it hit me. Rowan had sold his soul. That's what he meant by "I did what I had to." In exchange for agreeing to hassle Dr. Bonham at the Forum on Faith—and betraying me, his friend of two years—Rowan must have been promised he'd get top ranking in the class.

So, I tromped back up the steps, into the lobby, and took a sharp left into Ms. Adams's office on the first floor. Years before, when I'd left for college, my father had just one piece of advice: "Make friends with *all* the secretaries; they're the *most* important people on campus. You'll see." I'd tried to do that, and now I was hoping it would pay off. Taking a deep breath, and as calmly as I could, I asked, "Ms. Adams, would it be possible for me to take a quick peek at Rowan Wayrich's transcript?"

From the way she hesitated, I could tell she knew what was going on. She looked at me warmly for a short time, thinking, then she said, "I would, Katie, but you know the chairman would be furious. It's against policy. And anyway, I gave him the file yesterday morning." She then gave me an odd little smile and added, "It's on his desk ... in a red folder ... right side, I think it's underneath a novel he's reading."

I took the hint.

After leaving her office, I walked across the lobby to the seminary library, which takes up half of the first floor of Erickson, and I tried to focus on studying for my Moral Issues III exam. I worked there the rest of the day, distracted and hurt. Before long, I knew what I had to do. Late that evening, just before maintenance locked up the hall for the night, I quietly unlatched the rear window that looked out over the trash-loading area behind the building. I then walked over to the CupperTea and drank espresso until well after midnight.

When I felt the time was right, I walked back to Erickson, then slipped behind the big green Dumpster in the loading area. When I was sure no one was around, I crept up to the building, and, with the help-up of an overturned trashcan, I lifted the window and climbed through. I closed the window behind me.

When I turned around, I gasped. Someone was standing there, a shimmering ghost at the other end of the library, spreading its arms open as if inviting me. Then ... realizing it was only the way the moonlight was hitting the oversized globe near the opposite window, I plopped to the floor, panting. After sitting in the musty dark for a few minutes to calm myself, I was surprised by how bold I began to feel—no pounding heart, no nervous anxiety, just a concentrated rage. The espresso was kicking in.

Since Ms. Adams had once confided to me that a motion-detecting alarm had been installed in the main lobby, I knew I'd have to go up the back service stairs, the door to which was not far from the rear window. Step by step, I made my way up the cramped, bad-smelling stairwell to the third floor, to the academic offices, and tiptoed down the hall. Dr. Dunwoody's door was unlocked.

I stepped over to his desk and rummaged through the piles of books and papers. On top of one pile, I was surprised to find a somewhat lurid-looking novel called *An Assassin in the Stacks: An Academic Mystery Romance* by Mina M. Rathbone. I picked it up and scanned the back cover—something about a college professor who has a steamy affair with a beautiful young visiting lecturer who turns out to be an international spy. *Trashy*, I thought, but at least it showed that the chairman has a human side. And then I saw it ... the red folder.

But at that exact moment, just as I was reaching for the transcript, I heard a muffled commotion, a shuffling of feet somewhere on the main stairway. Peeking out the door, I heard more scuffling. It grew louder. Someone—more than one person—was coming up the stairs ... and fast. There were hushed voices. I rushed out the door and looked down the hall in both directions. I knew I could never make it all the way to the back stairs before the intruders got to the third floor. Since I suspected the chairman's office just might be the target of whoever was hurrying up the steps, my only option was to dash into the men's room two doors down. Just as the door closed behind me, I heard voices at the top of the main stairs.

I jumped into one of the stalls, shut the door, and listened.

Outside the restroom, a male voice hissed in a harsh whisper, "Really ... this door, I swear I saw it close."

"You're crazy."

"I'm checking."

"Just don't touch the lights. Security'll see it. I'm gonna go mess up you-know-who's office."

Panicked, I scrambled up onto the toilet, one foot on each side, so that my feet couldn't be seen under the stall door. With luck, the person who was about to come in wouldn't open it.

The restroom door creaked open. Footsteps shuffled across the tiles, moving here and there, and then stopped in front of my stall. A faint shadow shifted under the door, paused, then moved on. My heart pounded so hard that I was sure whoever was out there could hear it. My only hope was that his heart was pounding just as loudly.

When I heard the footsteps fade in the direction of the exit, I exhaled. But just when I thought it was safe, my foot slipped, and I came crashing down to the side of the toilet. My glasses went flying.

"Who's there?" a voice barked—Rowan's, of course. That

crack in his voice! What were the chances? (Later, I remembered a quotation from Aristotle that sort of defined that moment: "It is probable that improbable things will happen." You see, Dr. Bonham's not the only one who can quote old books!)

"Dammit, Rowan, it's me—help me up." Every muscle in my body felt bruised.

He opened the stall door. We could barely see each other in the dark. "Katie? What the hell are you doing here?"

"I should ask you the same question."

"Shh. They'll hear us."

"This is an Eleven-Nineteens thing, isn't it? What's going on?" On my hands and knees, I rummaged around on the tiles for my glasses.

"None of your business," he said. "And why are you here? This is so bizarre ... Over there ... glasses ... next stall."

"Jeez, Rowan, I can't believe how you've changed ... you used to be, like, a really nice guy. This isn't like you. You're just ... disgusting." I found my glasses and staggered to my feet.

"Yeah, like you should talk," he said. "Look at you ... with your creepy tattoo and spiky hair and Theophily stuff ... Dr. Bonham and his English nitwits. At least I have *friends*—"

It was a nasty jab, but we didn't have time to argue because someone—I think it was Jason—ran down the hallway, thumped his fist on the door once, saying in a muffled sort of yelp, "Cops! Cops! Rowan, get out!"

More shuffling in the hallway, heading toward the main stairs. Muted panic from below.

"Oh, great," said Rowan, "now I'll get expelled a month before graduation."

"Yeah, well, you should've thought of that before joining your little boys' club."

He glared at me, then feebly said, "Katie, I can explain—"

"Shut up!" I snapped. "We gotta get out of here." Everything in the hallway went silent for a moment. "Okay, follow me," I said. We crept out of the men's room and down the hall toward the back stairwell.

Behind us, from the main stairs, we could hear shouting from two floors down: "Stop! Stop right there!" ... no doubt a police officer in the lobby. And footsteps charging up the main stairway.

Rowan and I rushed down the back stairs, jostling each other as quietly as we could, and when we got to the library, blue lights were flashing everywhere outside. Through the glass doors between the library and the lobby we could see campus security and police corralling students left and right. Jason was one of them. We crouched low, then started crawling.

"This way," I said. Reaching the wall nearby, I raised the window.

We climbed out onto the trashcan. I closed the window behind us and set the can upright. No sooner had we ducked behind the Dumpster in the loading area than a police officer came running around the back of Erickson with his flashlight panning in every direction.

Not hesitating a moment, I threw my arms around Rowan's neck and kissed him on the mouth. His body went stiff as a brick wall. I hissed in his ear, "Kiss me back, you idiot, like you *mean* it." He caught on.

Just then, the officer rounded the back of the Dumpster and shone his flashlight in our faces. We pretended to be startled and embarrassed, and the officer said, "Oh, sorry. There's been some trouble here tonight. You two better go home ... or, uh, find someplace else."

"Oh, my," I said in my best innocent-coed voice. "Thank you, officer. We will."

When we were safely back in North Quad, out of breath and still shaking, Rowan kind of cooed, "Katie, you're wonderful; I don't know how to thank you—"

"Then don't, you jackass," I said. "I'll never forgive you—for any of this!" And I stomped off.

STILL FUMING THE NEXT DAY, I went to see M.B. at his office in Beetham. He jumped as usual. I always seem to startle him.

"Did you hear about Erickson last night?" I asked.

"Indeed. The rumor mill has been churning in the break room all morning," he said. "It's astonishing how a little shaving cream, toilet paper, and a few eggs bring out the Picasso in some people. Some suspensions are pending, I hear … one Jason Albright and one or two others."

"Yeah, well … I was there."

His eyes popped open wide. So I told him the whole story, from meeting Rowan at orientation our first year to fake-necking with him behind the Dumpster the night before.

When I told him I'd "stooped to theft" to find the transcripts and failed, he said, "*Stooped to theft*—Ms. Westcott, what a degrading phrase. In truth, you weren't planning on *stealing* anything. Just peeking. I think something like *resorted to skullduggery* has a more romantic ring to it, don't you? Or how about *engaged in chicanery*? So much depends on how we phrase things—"

"M.B.! You're not listening!" I was irritated.

"Of course I'm listening," he said, "and the solution to your transcript problem could not be simpler. Recently, I've been beset with queries from that dashing fellow in the computer department—you know … uh, what's his name? … the Computer Guy. Apparently, he discovered that I'm *mejores amigos* with Dr. Rojas, and like the courtly lover in *The Romance of the Rose*, he's in pursuit of the object of his adoration, the Rose, or, in this case, Dr. Rojas. And I can't say I blame him— I'd have done the same at his age. Have you ever read *The Romance of the Rose*? It's lovely, a bit breathy in spots ... C. S. Lewis discusses it in his *Allegory of Love*—"

"M.B.—*focus!*"

"I *always* focus," he said huffily, "just not on what everyone else wants me to. Anyway, I provided him with much useful information, and in gratitude he said to me, in essence, 'Unto half my kingdom is yours.' So I suspect a surreptitious online inspection of the aforementioned transcript would qualify as such. I shall make inquiries. In case of irregularities, I shall instruct him to bring it to the attention of the authorities."

Two DAYS LATER, Dr. Dunwoody passed me on the steps of Erickson and snarled, "There was a mistake. You're first after all," and he slithered off.

Amazed, I rushed to M.B.'s office once again to find out what happened.

"Quite simple," he said. "The Computer Guy—his name is Nathan Herkenroeder, by the way, though just *Nate* to his intimates—checked, and as you suspected, he found that you are most assuredly first in your class, an honest half credit ahead of Master Wayrich ... not the other way around. So he informed the registrar of the mistake, and the registrar, along with Provost Kinealy and President Costa, who suspected a conspiracy was afoot, considering the source, swung into action and demanded that Dunwoody rectify the error. Simple." Then he added, "You'd better start preparing your address."

BUT I DIDN'T PREPARE an address. And I didn't receive the Founders' Prize. Here's why.

As I lay wide awake in bed that night, I started thinking. Why was it so important to me to be first in the class? Was it just to spite Rowan? Was it vanity? My job as the Theophily Department's administrative director in the fall was secure. It was a dream come true. But Rowan planned to take a year off to work and save money in hopes of applying to Yale or Princeton or Duke Divinity for his doctorate. He still wanted to be the world's greatest biblical philologist, and first-rank status, along with the cash and prestige of the prize, would mean a lot to him, far more than they did to me. And though he was still a jackass, I couldn't blame him for needing friends, for wanting approval and acceptance after so many years of feeling lonely and rejected—even if those friends were Eleven-Nineteens. He was lucky that he hadn't been expelled. He'd done his share of stupid things, but who hasn't?

So the next morning, I went back to Dr. Bonham's office, startled him again, and said, "M.B., I'd like to change my Mystics 402 status from 'for credit' to 'audit.'"

"But," he said, "you'll lose a full credit, which will mean that your friend Rowan will be a half point ahead ..." He paused. "Oh ... of course, yes, I see ..." He folded his arms across his chest, tilted his head at a funny angle, and smiled. "Let me tell you something, Ms. Westcott. You are a remarkable young woman, a saint among seminarians, which is a rarity, I think. You have no idea how honored I am to be working with you. May I treat you to an espresso?"

GRADUATION, as always, took place in Phipps Auditorium. I don't remember much of Rowan's Founders' Address. It was pretty conventional—hallowed halls, fond memories, late nights of study, endless coffee, and so on. Except for the last part—which was about ... well, it was about me.

Standing at the lectern in his purple gown, Rowan said, "But the greatest thing I learned during these three years had nothing to do with academics. Rather, I learned the importance of grace. So much grace has been shown to me that I'm ashamed I didn't show more of it to others. In fact, I'm only standing here today because of the gracious, unexpected, and unearned sacrifice of one of my dearest friends. She knows who she is.

"Recently, I was telling a professor that I thought that next to love, grace was the most important thing in life for those of us who follow Jesus, and he said, 'Well, most people would say it's obedience, but I guess it's like a pendulum. First, everyone says obedience is the important thing; then the pendulum swings back over to the grace side, and everyone says that's the important thing. Back and forth.'

"It didn't occur to me then, but I now realize he was wrong. Obedience and grace aren't opposites, they are the same thing. Obedience is nothing more than showing other people the same grace that God has shown us. We show our love to God not by living with some hard, grim attitude of obedience—the kind Kierkegaard says Abraham must have had, an unquestioned obligation, stark and trudging—but by simply and joyfully sharing God's grace with others.

"Today, I'm grateful to God, my parents, my teachers, my fellow students, and to the person who taught me this valuable lesson. I don't deserve to be here. I didn't deserve anyone's sacrifice, and I could never begin to earn it or repay it. But that's grace, isn't it? It's something we must accept and try to pass on to others day by day. It is the highest calling we are called to.

"So thank you, one and all. Go now into the world, to your homes, your jobs, your schools, and to your bright futures, and show God's grace to everyone you meet. And the people said ..."

The auditorium erupted: "Amen!"

LATER IN THE CEREMONY, our graduating class lined up to receive our diplomas and MDiv stoles. I was two people behind Rowan in line. When Dr. Dunwoody called him across the stage to put the stole around his neck and give him his certificate, the chairman muffed it, as I was sure he would: "Rowan Roran Rayrich ..."

But I'd come prepared.

More loudly than I'd ever done in my life, I yelled from the side of the stage, *"Rowan Warren Wayrich! You go! WOO-HOOO!"*

CHAPTER 8

NIGHT CLASS

To know with certainty the road you travel,
you must close your eyes and walk in darkness.
—*John of the Cross, 1542–1591*

I note that Ms. Westcott, in the foregoing narrative, uses the word *geeky* with a certain amount of approbation, almost as if it were an earned degree ... a Bachelor of Geek; and I confess that her attitude makes me feel vindicated, for I'm often accused of geekiness myself.

For example, I have an old friend named Dudley Fitts, which is fairly geeky in itself, I suppose, but whenever I used to speak of him to others, I always felt compelled to explain in emphatic detail that he was not the same person as *the* Dudley Fitts, the poet, translator, and classical scholar. I never understood why people looked puzzled or even snickered at such moments. How was I to know they were unlikely to confuse my one-time college roommate with a long-deceased poet they'd never heard of in the first place?

You see, geeky.

In fact, it was Ms. Westcott—as a former classics major and the only other person I know who *has* read *the* Dudley Fitts —who recommended that I stop making the distinction.

I choose this particular example of my geekiness for a reason—because Dudley Fitts (my old friend, mind you, *not* the poet and classical scholar) teaches art at a Catholic high school in New Orleans, and years ago he had a promising student in his class named Tom Fouchee, who later became an art professor here at Cupperton. As the Little Prince used to say of his asteroid, it's a small world. Although I'll try not to mention either of the Dudley Fittses again, I *will* mention Tom Fouchee, for he is the *agent provocateur* behind much of what follows, and he's the absolute opposite of geeky.

LIKE SO MANY other chapters in my life, this one opens in my office on the third floor of Beetham Hall—this time, to the sound of a robust knock on the doorframe one afternoon at the beginning of January term and a deep mellifluous voice with a Creole accent saying, "*Bonjou*, Martin. Have a minute?"

"Tom! Of course. Come in, come in," I said. "What can I do for you?"

Thomas Fouchee fills a doorway to the brim rather than enters it. His expansive six-foot-three frame is something Rodin would have cast in bronze. He (Tom, that is, not Rodin) earned his MFA from LSU, teaches studio art and art history at Cupperton, and manages acquisitions for the Sheeres Art Museum on campus. His students adore him, and in the Department of Theophily's first semester, his class on "Images of the Divine in Art" had been filled to capacity.

In contrast to his size, his preferred medium of artistic expression is silver-point drawing. It's hard to imagine his thick, cigar-like fingers wielding the delicate jeweler's needle required of the technique, but his work is exquisite. As a Roman Catholic, he takes traditional iconographic details for his themes, but with a twist. He focuses on one small part of a given symbol and depicts it as if it were emerging from a vapor: a curved thorn branch curling out of a mist, or the eye and beak of a dove in a whirlwind. Several local churches display his pieces on their walls.

He entered, sat across from me, and said, "Could I ask a favor?"

"Of course."

"Here's the thing," he said. "The widow of an alum passed away and left Cupperton some money—almost a million dollars—and the will specified it was for 'religious art.'"

I whistled an impressed little whistle. "Lucky for the museum," I said.

"Maybe ... but ..."

"Don't tell me ... the seminary?"

"The chairman and his development committee are staking a claim. It seems the woman's late husband attended both the university and the School of Theology, and Dunwoody wants to commission some portraits and a long mural for the lobby of Erickson, showing the seminary's history."

"And in the final panel," I said, "I can just picture Dunwoody himself emerging like Modern Man in the March of Evolution."

Tom continued, "But I've got my eye on six or seven pieces for the museum—major works to fill in the collection—beautiful artworks—things the university would be proud of."

"I'm sure, but if you want me to pull strings with the seminary, I'm afraid that like the elder Pinocchio, I'm stringless."

"No, no," he said, "I was hoping for a letter of endorsement

... to President Costa and the Finance Committee. They make the decision. A recommendation from you as Theophily chair might swing it in my direction."

The notion that I had any influence over anyone at the university regarding million-dollar endowments was a shockingly new concept to me, much like one of those evolutionary apes first discovering that he could crack open nuts with a rock. "If you think it'll help, I'd be happy to try ... As Middleton said, 'I'll get you into heaven yet'!"

The gratifying upshot was that a month later, Tom was again in my office, as jubilant as a tambourine player in heaven. "It worked," he said. "I got the endowment. *Merci!* I can't thank you enough!"

"I had an inkling," I said. "So when's the unveiling?"

"The paintings will ship next month, so we'll have a big *fêt* —a party—over Alumni Weekend in April. I know you'll love them, Martin."

THIS STORY WOULD HAVE ENDED THERE, neat and clean, and we all could have shut this book, switched off the light, and gone to bed. But I'd forgotten one of the primary laws of physics: Every action has an equal and opposite reaction (which I've always suspected Sir Isaac Newton first formulated one morning after a night of heavy partying with his chums).

In my case, the equal and opposite reaction to my letter took the form of a visit from Dr. Dunwoody. The first week of April, he was at my office door, and from his cheery countenance I could tell he had something unpleasant on his mind.

While I might have anticipated his visit, I could never have foreseen his opening gambit: "I'm guessing your middle name begins with an *E* ..."

Hesitant, I said, "It's Edward. Why?"

"Hah!" He extracted a tattered paperback from the inner pocket of his jacket and lobbed it onto my desk, though the dramatic effect was marred somewhat by the book's sliding across the scattered papers and flopping onto the floor. I retrieved it—and recognized it immediately.

"Mina M. Rathbone, I presume ...," he said. I froze. Of all the people at Cupperton that I least wanted to know about her, Dunwoody was at the top of the list. "... Author of *An Assassin in the Stacks,*" he continued.

I groped for words. "Uh ... would you care to borrow *Blood in the Bookroom* or *The Skeleton of the Scholar*?"

"I've read them, thank you. I'm a fan of murder mysteries."

Struggling to keep my panic in check, I said, "So, I assume you're not here to have me sign your copy ... How'd you figure it out?"

"Allow me to present the evidence," he said, sounding like an inspector from Scotland Yard in a BBC series. "First, the Agèd Page Used Bookshop had about a half dozen remaindered copies of all three books, which suggested that the author might be local. Next, your young professor character quotes some fifteenth-century poet no one's ever heard of: 'For lack of money I could not speed'—"

"Anonymous, though often wrongly attributed to John Lydgate," I interjected.

"Whatever. No one in the world reads fifteenth-century poets but you—"

"Not true ... the archbishop—"

"But the clincher," he interrupted, "was when I realized that *Mina M. Rathbone* is an anagram for *Martin Bonham*, with an added *e*. So, I deduced the extra letter must be your middle initial." He paused as if expecting me to say, "Brilliant, Holmes." But I was speechless, in awe of his sleuthing skills, though it was clear that putting detective novels in Dunwoody's hands was not unlike giving a blowtorch to a toddler.

"So," I managed to squawk after a moment's silence, "... how'd you like them?"

"Not nearly as well-written as Ms. Lambert's—yes, I've figured out her pseudonym as well! Her books have far more charm and suspense. But all that aside, I raise this issue as a sort of admonition ... a bond of surety between us. Simply put, I'd hate for anyone to find out who Mina M. Rathbone is."

"Why should I care? You do realize, don't you, that I teach composition—?"

"But the pseudonym ...," he interrupted, "it suggests you'd rather not have your sordid past life known. My guess is that, with your academic work out of print, you are under some pressure to help elevate the English Department's academic standing, and lurid murder mysteries—written anonymously under a female pen name—might not fill the bill. Moreover, what would alumni donors think if they knew that the chair of the university's prestigious Department of Theophily," which he spoke in a mocking tone, "once wrote steamy potboilers? I only mention this in case I need a favor or two from you in future."

He had me dead to rights. Decades ago, not long after I came to Cupperton, Ms. Lambert and I discovered that we both loved classic whodunits, and, as a lark, we dared each other to write one. Under her anagrammatic pseudonym of E. Anabeth Miller, she has written seven installments in what she calls her Hiss and Hearse Series, about a pair of herpetologists who marry and solve crimes together—all of which continue to sell well. As for me, I was a penurious assistant professor at the time, much like my hero-detective in *An Assassin in the Stacks*, and I found that "for lack of money I could not speed," that is, I still had grad-school debts to pay. Our publisher preferred their racier detective romances to be written by women, hence my distaff nom de plume. My novel turned into a series of three, all modest in length, as well as in sales. Although they were, I confess, somewhat sophomoric (or as my old friend Dudley Fitts once characterized them, "Cheesy"), the advances did indeed help me speed. But I hadn't thought about Ms. Rathbone in years—or, in the words of Christopher Marlowe, "That was in another country, and besides, the wench is dead." May she rest in peace.

But Dunwoody was correct: that part of my past did not appear as a bullet point in my curriculum vitae, nor was it information that I cared to have bruited about campus. Loose lips sink chairmanships.

With Dunwoody still lurking troll-like in my office, I knew another shoe was hovering in the air. "So, what exactly do you want?" I asked.

"Funny you should ask. You see, I just discovered that you wrote a letter to the Finance Committee to persuade them to grant a certain endowment to the Art Museum. While it's too late to prevent that, I thought you might want to issue a public statement of regret for having written that letter since the funds were so shamefully used."

I furrowed my brow. "What are you talking about?"

"Ha! You don't know!" he said. "Yes, one of the paintings ... it's all black. Seriously ... a waste of resources and certainly *not* 'religious artwork.' I'm lobbying to have it sold and the money used for better purposes—a mural for the seminary, perhaps. So a nicely worded retraction from you to the Finance Committee, published in the campus paper, would be in order—timed to coincide with Alumni Weekend. Perhaps *Mina* could write it for you ..."

As soon as he left, I dashed across the quad to find Tom at the museum. He was busy preparing for the exhibit, which opened the following weekend—his *fêt*—but sensing my distress, he said, "You don't look well. What's up?" He led me into one of the side offices, where I told him all about my ill-spent youth, Mina, mystery novels, and Dunwoody's blackmail.

When I asked him about the offending painting, he shivered with excitement. "Yes, it's my favorite of the new pieces— a large Ad Reinhardt oil-on-canvas from 1956—a steal at a hundred and fifty thousand. It's called *Black on Black No. 14*. It's exquisite."

"*Black on Black*? That sounds like an old joke: 'A crow in a coalmine at midnight' kind of thing. Dunwoody says it's not religious art."

"Oh no. He's wrong. Frankly, I think *all* art is religious, but as far as Reinhardt, he was a major figure. I can't wait to unveil it. I think I'll be able to convince people if I can get them to listen. And anyway, the other pieces are more conventional: a small Medieval wood altarpiece of the crucifixion, a beautiful Gerrit van Honthorst sketch for *The Mocking of Christ*, and a Gwen John painting of a nun—all stunning. And listen," he added, "if Dunwoody's forcing you to write that letter, just do it. No need to give up your secret. I don't care about his threats —because there's no way I'm giving up the Reinhardt."

On the Wednesday morning before Alumni Weekend, Tom snared me on the steps of Beetham. I had the fateful letter in my hand and was about to deliver copies to the Finance Committee and the campus paper.

"That it?" he asked. I nodded. "Good. Tear it up. I don't think you'll need it. I'll explain later." Then he moved in closer and said in a hushed voice—"Listen—whatever you're doing tomorrow night at ten, cancel it. Be at the museum, rear loading dock. No excuses. Ten o'clock. A special invitation-only preview of the opening ... but *don't ... tell ... a soul.* Expect to see others there ... people you know. Just come," and he dashed off in the direction of the museum.

THE NEXT NIGHT, at a quarter to ten, I was walking across North Quad, when two shadowy figures appeared on the pathway that merged into mine. One of them said, "Marteen?"

"Graciela? Nate?"

Putting a finger to her lips, Graciela said, "Shh! It's all very hush-hush, yes? You must be going to the same place we are."

I saw something glint. "Is that an engagement ring?" I whispered.

She winked at me, and Nate beamed. "We're planning for October," she said.

Before long, we were joined by Alice Mears, Naazim el-Atar, Ms. Lambert, and three or four others. At the Sheeres Museum, we walked around to the back, where everything was dark. Tom was at the door of the loading-dock, smiling and putting his finger to his lips. "Shh." A local police officer was at his side. Stan Ahrens, the museum's security guard, escorted us to the main exhibit room, which, except for Stan's flashlight, was unlit. As my eyes adjusted, I spotted Katie and Tyrell in the dim vault of the hall, along with several other professors and a small group of students who I surmised were from the Art Department. A large rectangular frame hung on the back wall, draped with a white sheet. A laptop stood on a table in front of it, wired to a small projector.

As I look around, I recognized more people: Soo-jin Park from Biology, Josh Fields from Astronomy, and Rabbi Rachel Zeller, who, as an adjunct, has taught Jewish history at the university as well as "Psalmic Prayer and Poetry" for the Department of Theophily. It was quite a crowd. A buffet table was spread with hors d'oeuvres and assorted beverages—all murkily lit and festively mysterious.

Tom soon entered and said, "We all here? *Bonswa*. Thank you for coming. This should be fun. We're still waiting for our special guests—I'm hoping they haven't thought better of coming. But please look around, quietly, if you don't mind. Help yourselves to food." It was hard in that enlivened, puzzling atmosphere to suppress the occasional giggle as we chatted and scrutinized the various artworks on the darkened walls. Even the familiar pieces now looked unfamiliar, color-less, and lifeless.

A short time later, Tom reentered. Raising his hands, he said, "Okay. Time for complete silence. If you would, back yourselves against the walls—as far in the shadows as possible."

We did as we were told and held our breath. The moments ticked by.

Then—a shattering of glass from one of the side hallways. A thump, then a shuffling ... indistinct voices and whispered commands: "No, no, here ... this way." More shuffling.

Several dark figures entered the far end of the exhibit hall and scuffled in. When they reached the center of the room, someone, probably Stan, flicked on the overhead lights. We nearly ducked from the sudden glare, and one of the newcomers—a young woman—let out a stifled scream.

Tom stepped forward. "Welcome, welcome, all! *Bonswa!* We've been waiting for you. We're so glad you could make it!"

In all, there were four intruders, two male, two female, all seminarians, I believe—too stunned to move with all of us standing around and staring at them, though Stan and the police officer moved in behind to prevent escape just the same.

Tom said, "Officer Collins, would you mind calling your colleague at the police department to have our other special guest escorted to our soirée?" The officer nodded and left the room.

Tom then explained that the newcomers were, in his words, "distinguished members of the Fraternal Order of the Eleven-Nineteens," and that he'd received a tip that they were planning some mischief at the museum. I glanced over at the ever-resourceful Katie, who threw me a knowing wink and smiled. Tom continued, "I was hoping they'd go through with their plan because I wanted them to be here for the official unveiling. We even facilitated their attendance by disarming the alarms and unlocking the rear windows, though it appears they broke one of the windows anyway, not realizing it was unlocked. Very unprofessional." The intruders looked guilty, like Jean Valjean if he'd been caught with a truckload of the bishop's silver.

One of the women volunteered, "We weren't going to steal anything, ... we ... we were just going to hide one of the paint-ings ... for the weekend ... as a protest ..."

"The black one," said Tom, "yes?" Their silence said it all. "Listen, there's no harm done ... as long as you cooperate. Class should start shortly. And please, help yourself to refreshments —one and all."

We then milled around awkwardly, talking among ourselves, but somehow avoiding eye contact with the four intruders.

About a quarter of an hour later, Tom said, "Ah, I think I hear our last guest now."

Dunwoody, red in the face and gesticulating angrily, was escorted into the gallery by another local police officer. "What the devil's going on?" said Dunwoody. "What's all this?"

"A night class," Tom said cheerily. "I'm afraid we caught some of your students breaking and entering—"

"They're not my students," Dunwoody blustered, but as soon as he saw the four, he said, "Oh ... them."

Tom continued, "But I'll decide later whether to press charges or not. Windows have been broken, trespass has been committed, art-napping has been plotted, but for now, their fate hinges on your cooperation—so listen ... and learn ... *everyone.*"

Gritting his teeth, Dunwoody suppressed his rage.

Tom signaled to Stan to dim the lights once more. "All right. Let's begin. I'll open with a question, a conversation starter, which is this: Are we allowed, ethically, morally, to depict God's face in a painting? And more to the point, is it even possible?" I knew for a fact that these were his opening questions for his "Images of the Divine in Art" class.

Dr. el-Atar spoke up. "According to both the Qur'an and *hadith*, that is, the sayings of Mohammad, it is forbidden to depict Allah or Mohammad—as well as humans and animals. That's why much of Islamic religious art is geometric patterns and stylized leaves and flowers."

"In the Torah," said Rabbi Zeller, "the second command-ment prohibits graven images—idols—so Jewish religious art tends to focus on historical events, the Maccabees and such. In Exodus, God tells Moses that no one sees the face of God and lives. So no ... God should not be portrayed, nor is it even possible."

"And in Eastern Orthodoxy," said Dr. Mears, "icons never depict God the Father."

Tom said, "The same was true for Western Christianity for about a thousand years. Oh, the hand of God might appear occasionally, reaching awkwardly out of a cloud"—click, and the projected image of such a hand appeared on the sheet that was draped over the frame—"but things changed. By the Renaissance, painters in the West grew more comfortable depicting God the Father." He clicked through a series of paintings, ending with Michelangelo's famous Sistine Chapel fresco of God creating Adam. "The argument was that these weren't idols but symbolic representations—icons—visual aids that pointed beyond themselves. Most Christian artists, East and West, were more comfortable painting the face of Jesus and have done so from very early on." He clicked through images by Rembrandt, da Vinci, Velázquez, and others.

"But this poses a problem—what's called the James Bond Effect. The theory is that the actor you *first* saw portray James Bond—and there've been seven of them—is the one you'll prefer and the one you tend to visualize in your mind, even if unconsciously, when you read Ian Fleming's novels—just like it's hard *not* to visualize Daniel Radcliffe as Harry Potter. Faces tend to stick.

"Since the Renaissance, artists have fairly consistently depicted God as the classic 'old man with a white beard'"—he clicked through a dozen images as he spoke—"though you'll notice that the beard is more often gray than white, sometimes looking more like a retired Civil War general in a robe than the creator of heaven and earth. So, for many of us, that's the image that sticks in our mind's eye, even though we know it's absurd. But our penchant for that kind of facial recognition is deeply embedded in the human psyche ... Dr. Mears, what can you tell us about that?"

A bit startled to be called upon, the chair of our Psychology Department thought for a moment, then said, "Well, ... the ability to distinguish faces is located in the brain's temporal lobe and is considered one of the most important factors in human development. We can usually tell in an instant whether we've seen a face before, among many thousands. Faces are so deeply rooted in our brains that we even tend to see them where none exist—in wood grain, for instance, or rock formations or the front grille of my Honda Accord. Dogs can pick one scent out of thousands; cats hear things few other animals can; but one of our greatest human skills—our superpower, if you want to call it that—is our ability to distinguish among faces and read facial expressions. A baby's first significant social interactions are imitating the adult faces around her. Roger Moore, by the way, is the real James Bond!"

"Come on, Alice," I piped up suddenly, "you can't be serious, Sean Connery—"

"You're both wrong," said Tom. "*This* is the real James Bond." He clicked to a slide of Daniel Craig. Everyone laughed. "Which brings us to a second problem: does the name Warner Sallman ring a bell?"

No one responded, but with one click, we knew who Warner Sallman was. The image on the sheet was the familiar portrait of Jesus that must hang in every church in the country ... the one showing a softly glowing Jesus with wavy brown hair, a trimmed beard, an aquiline nose and longish face, posing three-quarters to his left and looking very European.

"Yes, Sallman painted this famous portrait, though it's based on centuries of similar portrayals, and it's the image of Jesus that persists in many people's minds. More than a billion copies—that's *billion* with a *b*—exist. That's a lot. For instance, a billion grains of sand weighs twenty-two thousand pounds. I grew up in a black Catholic church in New Orleans, and I think we had at least three copies of that picture. Sallman was a Chicago ad man in the 1940s and '50s, and he painted other famous pictures, like this one of Jesus holding a lamb"—click —"and this one of Jesus knocking at the heart's door"—click. "And Jesus looks pretty much the same throughout."

We studied the images. Tom said, "Now, for an experiment." He clicked to an image of the American flag, except unexpectedly shown in its complementary colors: green, black, and yellow. "You've all seen this optical illusion. It's a familiar middle-school science project. But let's try it. If you would, stare at the middle of the flag for thirty seconds"—he paused as we did so, and after a few moments, he added—"now, close your eyes. Do you see it? You should see the color negative—an all-American red, white, and blue flag, the complementary colors to green, black, and yellow. Given more time, I know Dr. Mears could explain to us why this happens. Now"—click— "who can tell me what this image is?"

One of the students said, "The Shroud of Turin."

"It is," said Tom, "... and it isn't. It's the supposed face of Jesus from the Shroud, but many people don't know that this familiar image is a digitally enhanced photo negative of the original. The actual Shroud looks like this." Ghostly, rust colored smudges appeared on the screen. "Those who believe the Shroud is authentic claim that by some chemical process the photo negative of Jesus's face and body was seared into the cloth. I don't argue one way or the other—nor does the Catholic church, by the way—but let's assume, for the sake of argument, that it's authentic. If so, can we then say that *this* is what Jesus looked like?"

"Both images are distorted," said Dr. Mears.

Katie spoke up, "The forehead seems too short and the eyes too high, and the nose looks too long. It looks more like a Byzantine icon."

"So even if it's authentic," said Tom, "the details are still in question. Which brings us to our last problem: 'The Treachery of Images.' Does that mean anything to anyone?"

Never being one to shy away from an opportunity to show off, I interjected, "It's a painting by René Magritte: *La trahison des images*, in French. It depicts a tobacco pipe, beneath which the artist has added the words *Ceci n'est pas un pipe*—'This is not a pipe.'"

Tom said, "Which means ...?"

"That the painting itself is not the pipe; it's just a representation, which is why it's called 'The *Treachery* of Images.' Even a photograph is only an image, never the thing itself."

"So, to paraphrase Magritte," said Tom, "*Ceci n'est pas Jésus* —this is not Jesus, even if it *is* Jesus ... Nor is *this* Jesus"; he clicked through a series of famous paintings by da Vinci, El Greco, Rembrandt, Blake, and others, "nor this"—click—"nor this"—click.

"But let's go back to our negative images, how our closed eyes—physiologically—take an image and flip it around ..."

He then slid the sheet off the painting and signaled to Stan to switch on the overhead lights. And there it was. The controversial black painting against a stark white wall.

"What's *this* an image of?" asked Tom.

Dunwoody spoke for the first time: "It's black. It's just black."

"Right," said Tom. "This is by twentieth-century artist Ad Reinhardt, who died in 1967. But look closely. Is it really just black?"

There was a long silence as we studied it. Then Katie said, "There's a slightly darker area, kind of a thick cross shape, in the middle. Just a hair darker."

"Which is why," said Tom, "it's called *Black on Black*. Does everyone see it? Now, let's try the American flag trick. Stare at that shape—let's go for a full minute this time." We did as we were told, and after a minute, Tom said, "Okay, now close your eyes. What do you see?"

A couple of people let out small gasps, and Tyrell said, "A bright white square against a black background, and there's a little brighter cross in the middle."

"Huh!" said Tom. "Light emerging from dark. Dr. Rojas, you're our resident expert on what's called the *via negativa*—'the negative way'—tell us about that, if you would."

"Of course," said Graciela. I suspect Tom had warned her ahead of time that he'd be calling on her. "It's the spiritual path that some mystics followed. Put simply, it's contemplating God by erasing from our minds everything that is *not* God. Santo Juan de la Cruz wrote about it in his *Dark Night of the Soul*—and Marteen could tell you about a medieval English book, *The Cloud of Unknowing*, which shares the same ideas. Theologians call it the 'apophatic' approach. People often think the 'dark night' means a sort of depression, feeling distant from God—but it's not that. It's a kind of spiritual honesty, a putting aside of all false images so that we're left with nothing but the One who is infinitely beyond our perceptions and preconceptions. And that can feel like a vast dark place. One of Santo Juan's most famous quotes is: 'To know with certainty the road you travel, you must close your eyes and walk in darkness.' The mystics thought we learn to know God best through God's unknowableness and *see* God best in God's unseeableness. It's a paradox."

"Thank you, Dr. Rojas," said Tom. "The modern mystic Thomas Merton once wrote, 'The only thing faith and hope do not give us is the clear vision of the God Whom we possess. We are united to God in darkness, because we have to hope.' Then Merton quoted Saint Paul in Romans: 'For we are saved by hope. But hope that is seen is not hope.' Reinhardt, who was a friend of Merton's, wrote that he wanted each of his paintings —get this—to be a 'free, unmanipulated and unmanipulatable, useless, unmarketable, irreducible, unphotographable, unreproducible, inexplicable icon'—in other words, absolutely *everything* that Sallman's Jesus is *not*, point by point. Did you catch that last word? *Icon*. He thought of this painting as an icon—and I don't believe he was speaking metaphorically. Now, if you'll indulge me ... one last image. This way." He walked across the exhibit hall to a door on the far side. We followed. "The stairway lights are on but take care. All the way up. I'll follow, and we'll meet on the roof."

The freshness of the chilly night air filled our lungs and reinvigorated us as our night class emerged onto the roof of the museum, well above the lights of campus. We looked around for artwork but saw none.

Quietly, Tom said, "Okay, we all here? Good. We are now, as Merton said, 'united to God in darkness.' Okay, everyone ... now look up." There were what seemed like thousands upon thousands of stars. "What's *that* an image of?"

Josh Fields laughed, "Okay, I'm just a semi-pagan astronomer, but I know what you're getting at. Martin has heard me say that I feel God's presence when I look at the stars. And I mean it. But now I think even they are too finite. The Divine is still beyond somehow."

Katie said, "Yeah! And remember Anselm of Canterbury? He said God is 'that beyond which a greater cannot be conceived'"

Josh added, "It's like the night sky itself is an icon, that all creation—the whole universe—is a spectacular icon painted by God, and even then, God is still that beyond which a greater cannot be conceived."

"Perfect," said Tom. Then turning to me: "It's a Theophily lesson, isn't it, Martin? Perhaps we love God by not presuming to know more than we actually do, and by just opening ourselves to the mystery we can't begin to comprehend, and to hope in things not seen. We can love God in the darkness."

IT WAS one in the morning when our night class ended. Many of us lingered there on the roof as Tom's art students brought up trays of wine glasses. Before Dunwoody and his seminarians could slip back down the stairs, however, Tom headed them off at the door. He called me over, along with the two police officers and Stan Ahrens. Addressing the students, Tom said, "What made you think you could get away with this art-napping idea?"

With her eyes downcast, one of the women said, "Well, Dr. Dunwoody said he wished someone would *do* something about that painting. So we just sort of ... *did* it."

"I said no such thing!" said Dunwoody. "At least, I mean ... I never meant ..."

"We assumed you were hinting," said one of the men. "We were just trying to help."

"Like Henry II," I added, "asking his knights, 'Will no one rid me of this turbulent priest?' after which they assassinated Thomas à Becket. How history repeats itself!"

"Dr. Dunwoody, what should I do?" said Tom. "Officer Collins here says it's up to me if I want to press charges. Should I have him arrest these students, who, by the way, seem to be implicating *you*? It could mean their expulsion and a reprimand for the seminary—"

Dunwoody was no fool. He'd read enough mystery novels to piece out where this was headed, so he looked at me with a hard glare and said, "Okay, Bonham. Here's the deal: if I forego my 'pledge of surety,' do you think you could convince

Professor Fouchee to forget about this whole incident? ... I will never mention a certain mystery writer's name again, and I will withdraw my objection to the painting. You'll have no protests from the seminary. I promise."

I glanced back over at Tom. He gave me a quick nod, and I said, "Incident? What incident? You see, it's forgotten already. From this point forward, we will mutually pledge to immerse our secrets in the river Lethe, and they will become, in the words of Dudley Fitts, like 'a dark foreflowing song of silence.'"

Perking up at the name, Tom said to me, "Dudley Fitts? My high school art teacher ... your old friend?"

"No, no," I said, "the poet and classical scholar."

CHAPTER 9
A WALK IN THE WOODS

Your enjoyment of the world is never right till every morning
you awake in Heaven; see yourself in your Father's Palace; and
look upon the skies, the earth, and the air as Celestial Joys:
having such a revered esteem of all, as if you were among the
Angels.
—*Thomas Traherne, 1636–1674*

Dear Disciplinary Committee:

I, Martin E. Bonham, would like to thank Chairwoman Lambert and the other members of the Cupperton Faculty Disciplinary Committee for this opportunity to respond to the allegations made against me by the chairman of the Seminary and School of Theology and to enter into the official transcript my own version of events. While Dr. Dunwoody's narrative and mine are similar in their broad outlines, his smacks of melodrama, while mine, as you will see, partakes of the picaresque—with a pair of comic sidekicks in our case ... and no hero. And yet, be it stated unequivocally here at the outset that (1) I never callously abandoned Dr.

Dunwoody in his hour of need, nor (2) did I ever make light of his misfortunes by "chortling," as he claims.

I herewith present my case.

———

As you know, the university's Employee Picnic and Field Day takes place every year on the first Saturday of May and provides professors, staff, and their family members a bit of "heart-easing mirth" before the end of term. This year the event was held at Mahkwa State Park, noted for its lush flora, wooded hills, and glistening lake.

I was driven to the gathering by Ms. Westcott and her friend Tyrell Robson. As we cleared the last copse of trees on our approach to the parking area, I could see several of my academic confrères clustered around a picnic table near the marge of Bear Lake, and even from a distance I perceived they were engaged in vigorous conversation. The two most engaged, judging from their animated gestures, were Dr. Soo-jin "Sue" Park (Biology) and Professor Tom Fouchee (Art), though also present were Dr. Graciela Rojas (Romance Languages) and her fiancé, Nathan Herkenroeder (IT), Professor Carl Evans (Theater), and two or three others, including Dr. Dunwoody. Since their fervid discussion provides an essential context for understanding the day's later misadventures, I feel compelled to transcribe it here as accurately as memory permits.

As Ms. Westcott, Tyrell, and I approached, Dr. Park hailed me: "Martin, over here ... we need you to weigh in." When I joined them, she explained, "It's like this: since Tom's night class last week, something's been bugging me. I've begun to think that an overemphasis on the *via negativa* ultimately leads to a negation of the natural world. As a biologist, I find that unacceptable. God created Nature, so why would we push it aside?" She was referencing a rather unusual class that Professor Fouchee had conducted at the Sheeres Museum a week earlier in connection with the current art exhibition—a class that most of those present had attended, and one that had displeased Dr. Dunwoody in particular.

Before I could answer, Tom interjected, "And I've been trying to explain to Sue that, yes, I understand what she's saying, but the Catholic mystics were trying to get down to spiritual basics and avoid any hint of idolatry. They didn't want any *created* thing to distract from their openness to God, or worse, to be *mistaken* for God—"

Sue shot back, "And I've tried explaining to Tom that the whole notion of 'the dark night' can become just as much of an idol as anything else, right? And there's something vaguely gnostic about it ... like a secret kind of knowledge. It elevates the spiritual world at the expense of the material, don't you think, Martin?" She was growing heated. "What was it Augustine said about the higher and lower things ...?"

As our resident Latinist, Ms. Westcott provided the quotation, "'While the higher things are better than the lower things, the sum of all creation is better than the higher things alone.'"

"Precisely," said Sue. "Doesn't the *via negativa* sort of stress the higher things alone?"

So, as you can see, I was being put on the proverbial spot.

Dr. Rojas, ever the peacemaker, interjected, "Even at their most spiritual, the mystics still talked about Nature, yes? Santa Teresa used *la mariposa*—the butterfly—as a symbol of new life in God. She used gardening as a metaphor for cultivating the spiritual life, with the Holy Spirit nourishing the soul just as water nourishes the roots of trees. And even Santo Juan de la

Cruz was walking in a garden when he had his vision of the *dark night.*"

"And the cloud of unknowing is a *cloud*, after all," Ms. Westcott added—which made me realize that the day was indeed growing overcast. "Here's what I think," Ms. Westcott continued, "'walking in the dark' is only possible because light exists, because there's a *via positiva* as well. Remember Meister Eckhart ... his famous quotation about 'every creature is a word of God.' He says if you study Nature, you may be excused from even listening to sermons —because everything in the natural world teaches us about God. I think that's about as good a definition of the *via positiva* as you can get. Psalm 19 says, 'The heavens declare the glory of God ...'"

Carl Evans spoke up, "And in *As You Like It*, Shakespeare says there are 'tongues in trees, books in the running brooks, sermons in stone, and good in everything.'" (I admit to wishing that I'd thought to quote that bit first.)

"Nope," said Sue, "not buying it. I still think Tom's negating Nature, and the rest of you are only valuing it insofar as it provides stale metaphors for spiritual things. That's *my* definition of idolatry! I'm talking about something else altogether. What if God just wants us to enjoy creation—and care for it—as a *bonum per se*, a good in itself? Maybe the things of the natural world *aren't* a bunch of hidden spiritual lessons. Maybe they're our fellow creatures. Like it or not, we were *created*; we're part of Nature. Francis of Assisi called the sun and moon his brother and sister—"

Tom shot back, "Yeah, but your resistance to any spiritual content in Nature smacks of iconoclasm to me." He too was getting heated.

Sue responded, "No, no, you misunderstand. Look at it this way: maybe one of the reasons God made the world was to give us *joy*. You think? Somewhere in the Jewish Kabbalah it says,

'When you stand before the Judgment Seat, you'll be asked to explain why you did *not* indulge in all the allowable pleasures.' Nature is, if nothing else, an allowable pleasure.

"Look," Sue continued, "while we've been sitting here, gabbling like hens, I spotted a dabchick over there popping in and out of the cattails ... it's a pied-billed grebe. And instead of letting this discussion go on and on, I should have pointed out the belted kingfisher ... right there ... sitting on that silver birch ... you see him? He's blue and has kind of a tousled crest. He's watching for fish. If we wait a second, he'll dive ... wait ..."

We did, and a few moments later the bird dived. It was stunning, reminding me of Gerard Manley Hopkins's poem "As Kingfishers Catch Fire."

"Hear that rat-a-tat-tat?" Sue said. "That's a pileated woodpecker. And I love this park because it's like a museum of ferns. Walk the trails, and you'll see. There are ordinary lady ferns everywhere with their fiddlehead fronds, but you'll also find maidenhair ferns—look for the black stems and the small, bushy palm-branch-shaped fronds. And you'll see walking ferns ... which are called that because they send out a long, pointed leaf, and wherever the tip touches the ground, a new fern grows. It walks! I even saw a horsetail fern here once—which is rare this far south. They're one of the oldest plants on earth. But you see, I don't think there's any spiritual meaning to it all. Those things just *are*, and they're beautiful; they fill me with awe. All I know is that I feel a deep love for God just for making all this variety and wonder and joy, and for allowing us to share it."

We sat there, absorbed in the scene until Tom broke the silence: "Okay, Martin—who's right?"

Everyone laughed.

Fortunately, I had no need to render judgment because my thoughts had run in an entirely different direction. "Like Archbishop Townsend last fall," I said, "I turn to the poets, and I'm thinking—"

"Hey! Listen up, everyone—choose partners!" We jumped. Coach Brock Schrader of the Phys. Ed. Department, roaring like a drill sergeant (which he'd once been), swept down upon us like a wolf on the fold. He was mustering teams for the field activities, and the first event, he announced, was the three-legged race. Ms. Westcott and her friend Tyrell gleefully volunteered, as did Dr. Rojas and her fiancé. I thought it a gracious gesture on Tom Fouchee's part to ask Sue Park to be his partner, despite the differences in their statures and religious views. She was delighted.

For my part, I felt as though a lead weight had dropped from my throat to my stomach. Years of involuntary summer camp as a youth had soured me on such hurly-burly, so, with the adrenal response of a highly strung squirrel, I skittered off toward a nearby sign that read, "To the Hiking Trails." Suddenly, fern hunting sounded like a wonderful idea.

Curious to report, no sooner had I crested the first hill than whom should I see not thirty paces ahead of me but the chairman of the Seminary and School of Theology? He too was clearly not a fan of three-legged races.

At first, walking in the woods beside Dr. Dunwoody was akin to walking alone—except for the inscrutable, doleful aura that seemed to emanate from his vicinity. My attempts at conversation were met with curt monosyllables, though after about five minutes, I hit upon a topic that elicited a certain garrulousness from him. "So what'd you think of the discussion?" I asked.

"All nonsense!" he said in a sharpish tone. "About as exciting as a chess match on the radio."

Although I knew that Dr. Dunwoody could be like the wasp —that is, apt to find offense where none is intended—I probed: "You're not still sore about the other night, are you? ... Tom's class and all ..."

"Phah! No, that whole thing was a stupid misunderstanding. And as far as Nature," he said, "Origen settled the matter eighteen centuries ago. Nature provides for our spiritual and physical needs. That's it. Period. What a boring bunch of eggheads," he added.

"Hold on," I said, "I'm impressed with Dr. Park ... she knows her stuff—"

"Yeah, well, too much, I think. I heard some story about her ... apparently, she was in the middle of a lecture and heard a bird tweeting outside. So she set her notes aside, opened the window, and spent the rest of the hour quoting every poem she could think of about birds and making a complete idiot of herself. The students thought she was a goofball."

Under the circumstances, I deemed it prudent not to disclose the fact that the professor in question was actually me. I'd quoted Milton to the students—"To hear the lark begin his flight / And singing startle the dull night ..." and Shelley— "Hail to thee, blithe Spirit! / Bird thou never wert ...," some John Clare and two or three others. As far as I knew, the students were blissfully enchanted.

For the next half hour, as our discussion continued, I avoided any further mention of birds, but I also found myself in the curious position of defending not just my academic colleagues but all of Nature as well. In his turn, while quoting some theologian or other, the chairman would preemptively apologize on my behalf, "It's all right, Bonham. I don't expect you to understand ..."

At one point, he said, "So, what *were* you going to say about *poets* before Schrader interrupted?"

I *was* going to share something Thomas Traherne wrote, that "the world is a mirror of infinite beauty, ... the place of Angels and the Gate of Heaven," but knowing the bitter reception such thoughts would be met with in the present situation, I demurred. I just said, "Uh ... just something about Nature being a mirror ..."

———

AT A CERTAIN STAGE in our odyssey, we heard the rumble of thunder, like a sinister minor chord in the distance. We grew quiet and plodded heavily on with some apprehension. I grew strangely conscious of each footstep, watching the leaves and dirt and tree roots pass underfoot. The sky soon darkened even further, and then the clouds began to roil oddly, like a time-lapse video in a National Geographic special. I suggested that we turn back, but Dr. Dunwoody said, "The park's up this way."

"No, actually, I believe it's back that way."

"Hmph," he said.

I stopped.

He kept walking.

I stood there, not knowing what to do. Reluctantly, I traipsed after him. Then, as the first fat dollops of rain greeted my face, I called out, "Wait up." He didn't. I kept traipsing.

Ten minutes later, the sky delivered what the Book of Job aptly calls the "small rain and the great rain," and the sinister minor chords were no longer distant. At one point we jumped when a flash of lightning struck not far off and we heard a tremendous boom a moment later, which was followed by what sounded like a not-too-distant tree crashing to the ground. Fortunately, that was the only bolt of lightning to strike nearby.

There comes a point, when one is caught in a heavy down-pour, when one's clothing becomes so saturated that it feels as though one were wearing cold lead pajamas, and then there also comes a point at which one no longer cares. It didn't take long for me to reach the first point. The second followed within minutes. Still, thinking that seeking assistance might be advisable, I extracted my phone from my shirt pocket to find that water bubbles had seeped beneath the screen and rendered it mute. I shouted ahead to Dr. Dunwoody, "Does your phone work?"

He yelled back, "What phone?"

When I caught up to him, he said, "All right, I think we need to go this way," and he pointed down a ravine. No path was evident. His intention, apparently, was to bushwhack.

"But that's not the way back to the campground," I shouted over the swooshing of rain.

"It's a shortcut. Trust me," he shouted back. "The trail just keeps doubling back on itself, so I know the campground's just over the hill on the other side of the ravine."

Knowing, as Robert Frost once wrote, "how way leads on to way," I argued that we should stay on the tried-and-true path, for it would eventually lead somewhere helpful. That's the nature of paths ... to lead somewhere. And if anyone was looking for us, they'd most likely follow the trails.

"Phaw," he responded. "We've been going in circles. Listen, the park is just over that hill. I hear them calling for us."

I heard nothing but the rain slashing through the trees.

Since I'm a firm believer in allowing people to learn from their mistakes, and since I was also concerned for his safety, I resolved to accompany him on his road less traveled, which was, in fact, no road at all. Boldly, we waded knee-deep into the lush, wet ferns and descended into the ravine.

"Oh, look," I called out, "black stems, palm-shaped leaves —these must be Sue's maidenhair ferns ..."

I had expected no response and wasn't disappointed.

The footing grew progressively soggier as we neared the low point, and my shoes made a sucking sound with each heavy footfall in the quaggy mud. A moment later Dr. Dunwoody made an indistinct noise that, had it been distinct, I'm sure would have amounted to profanity. One of his shoes had been suctioned off by the muck. It took him several moments to fish it out, though his stockinged foot was now every bit as mucky as the shoe he placed over it.

Before long, as we slogged up the brushy side of the opposite slope, I noticed that the briars were beginning to catch at my pant legs, and soon they were catching at my sleeves as well. "Just keep going," instructed the chairman. "We're almost there." His indistinct noises returned.

That strategy worked for the next ten feet or so, but soon the briars grew so thick that I could hardly move. Thickets have the uncanny knack of closing in around you, much like the vegetable world's equivalent of a swarm of bees. "This must be what being hog-tied feels like," I said.

Dr. Dunwoody, now silent, was in the same predicament.

"Let's go back to the trail," I said.

"No, we've gone this far ... we just need to push ahead."

"Also known as the Vietnam Syndrome," I muttered to myself. I was beginning to reach my limit.

So, we delicately plucked one thorn branch after another from our clothing, like undoing dozens of rusty zippers, so we could take another stride forward, only to be mired once again and repeat the process.

In time, about halfway up the hill, we emerged from the thicket with our arms and faces and fingers bloodied and our clothing torn. Ancient Chinese torturers used to administer what they called "death by a thousand cuts"—but since Dr. Dunwoody and I did not die, I calculate that the number of our cuts must have registered somewhere in the mid eight hundreds.

"Ha! See, we made it," said Dr. Dunwoody. As we trudged up the hill, he added, "So tell me, Bonham, what was the meaning of *that* in your little Theophily world? It didn't give us much *joy*, did it?"

"The meaning," I grumbled, "is that we're at the top, and the park is *nowhere* to be seen."

Indeed, like the mountaineering bear in the children's song, all we could see was the other side. Our only option was to ascend the next hill, which was steeper than the first, but once we stumbled to its summit, my fears were again confirmed. Another hilltop. No park.

Bear in mind that I followed in Dr. Dunwoody's wake at all times, and in no manner of speaking could I be said to have led him into danger as he claims. I merely served as a reluctant acolyte to the dangers he created for himself.

⸻

Now, as to the accusation that I "chortled" when Dr. Dunwoody was beset by wild beasts—which he characterized to your committee as "rabid wolverines"—allow me a factual reportage.

Several minutes after we had crested the fourth or fifth hill, the rain let up somewhat, and we did at least discover a narrow path that appeared to lead to a two-track dirt access road a short way off. A positive sign. As we plodded along, soaked, scratched, and shivering, we heard a peculiar scraping sound on a nearby tree trunk. Two young raccoons (which, for those of you who like to know such things, are called kits) were shinnying down, and once they had reached terra firma, they waddled plumply across the path about ten feet in front of us. "Uh-oh," I said, and fretful like the porpentine, I stopped dead in my tracks.

"What?" snorted Dr. Dunwoody. "You afraid? Keep walking. They're just babies. They're gone now."

"Yes, I know, but the mother may be in the neighborhood," I replied, "and she may be prepared to defend her progeny tooth and nail ... 'the female of the species being more deadly than the male'—"

"What?" He harrumphed and kept walking.

"It's Kipling," I said as the frightened little beasts made a rustling sound somewhere in the undergrowth, "though I believe he was talking about she-bears, not raccoons—"

"No, you idiot, I mean—we're not hurting them, so why would the mother be upset—?"

At that instant, coincidentally, the very topic of our conversation emerged from the bushes, and despite Dr. Dunwoody's opinion to the contrary, she was quite visibly upset. With a look of crazed hatred in her eyes, she squared off right in front of us, not unlike Spartacus before the Roman legions, and curled her lips back to display her formidable dental work. The noise she made was midway between a high hiss and a snarling growl—the raccoon equivalent, I suppose, of *banzai*. It was her way of saying that treading the purlieus between her and her kits was verboten.

I must have jumped three feet in the air while Dr. Dunwoody dashed back down the hill in what the Roman legions would have referred to as an *anabasis*, a tactical retreat. As for the agitated beast, having won the day, she turned and skulked off into the underbrush after her brood.

Backtracking, I found Dr. Dunwoody, shoeless once again —both shoes this time—seated on the ground, panting, muddy, and miserable. The only thing that could be even remotely construed as "chortling" was when I quoted, less than tactfully, I admit, the famous stage direction from act three of Shakespeare's *Winter's Tale*: "'Exit, pursued by a bear'!" While I may have chuckled once, and once only, as I said it, I certainly did not chortle—I know the difference—but I quickly realized that Dr. Dunwoody was in pain and that levity is lost on the afflicted.

Clutching his ankle, he said, "Help me up—I think I'm hurt."

With effort, I brought him to an upright position, not without a bit of stumbling, losing our balance, and cursing on both sides, but as soon as we tried to walk, with him leaning heavily on my shoulder, it was clear that something was amiss. We hobbled to the shoulder of the access road. Grimly I realized we hadn't escaped the three-legged race after all.

"It's no good," he said. "You'll have to get help." I plopped him down at the base of a tree.

Once again, I was faced with a dilemma. Should I leave Dr. Dunwoody to seek help, or should I remain with him? What if the lightning returned? How badly was he injured? I checked my phone again. Still waterlogged.

He growled, "So where's your *via positiva* now, Bonham. You happy?"

Bitterly I retorted, "Well, *Origen* certainly hasn't been much help!"

"Just shut up and get help ... and make sure you come back!"

Needing no further prompting, I started jogging down the access road.

"No! The other way, Bonham!"

"It's *this* way," I said firmly.

And that, in a nutshell, defines our relationship. You see, Nature *is* a mirror.

When faced with this quandary, I knew what I had to do: head in the proper direction and not look back. It was clear that the chairman had learned nothing from his previous mistakes, or, in the immortal words of Dudley Fitts (an old friend of mine, *not* the poet and classical scholar), "Rats in mazes learn. People don't learn."

WITHIN A MINUTE OR TWO, I could no longer hear Dr. Dunwoody shouting at me to head in the other direction ("... you idiot! ..."), and after ten more minutes, I arrived at a gravel road that I knew, from a convenient directional signpost, led back to the campground. Soon I arrived at the picnic area, where Coach Schrader, with his back to me, had his phone to his ear. He turned, saw me, and barked into the phone, "Hold it! Here's one of 'em now. Just showed up ... no ... not the little bald one —the other one."

At that moment Ms. Westcott, Mr. Robson, and Dr. Park ran to embrace me. They too were soaked and much the worse for wear. I felt awful knowing they'd been so distressed.

"Where's the other guy?" Coach Schrader asked.

"Back up the road. Not far. He's hurt."

Tyrell ran to get his car.

Ms. Westcott said, "We had three teams out looking for you. Where were you? We must have circled the trails three times. We were about to call the state patrol!"

"Well, we sort of strayed off the path ..."

"You what? Why would you do that?"

"It's a long story," I said.

"Why didn't you call?"

"My phone's soaked."

"The old flip phone, right? I've told you ..."

When Tyrell pulled up in his car, we all piled in and raced down the muddy ruts to the place where I'd last seen Dr. Dunwoody. No sooner had we arrived, climbed out, and scanned the area than Coach Schrader asked the obvious question: "Where is he?" Dr. Dunwoody was gone—vanished like the snows of yesteryear.

We hadn't stood there for more than a minute, perplexed and preparing to beat the bushes for the missing chairman, when Ms. Westcott's phone buzzed. It was a text message from Tom Fouchee, who had led one of the other search parties: "Dr Dun OK. Headed to hosp."

We later learned that he'd been rescued not long after I'd left him. Apparently, hiking from the opposite direction and alerted to his location by his yelling at me to "go the other way," were representatives of the Sasquatch Club, whose purpose, as you know, is to trek into the woods periodically in hopes of befriending Big Foot. Thoughtfully, they carry with them a cooler of beer, should Big Foot be thirsty, so, luckily for Dr. Dunwoody, these students were able not only to give him aid and succor but to apply ice to his afflicted ankle and share their towels and rain gear. More helpful yet, they called someone who then called Tom Fouchee to say that they had carried Dr. Dunwoody to a nearby access road, bundled him into one of their cars, and were transporting him to the emergency room in Ware, where he was later found to have suffered a sprained ankle as well as superficial cuts.

Lest anyone conclude that I was unconcerned about the chairman's fate, I went to his house the next day with a get-well card, a new pair of socks, and a copy of my book of fifteenth-century religious poets, which I inscribed with a quotation from Shakespeare: "One touch of nature makes the whole world kin." I thought it particularly appropriate. An efficient seminarian met me at the door, accepted the package, and told me that the chairman was not receiving visitors.

Only the day before yesterday was I informed that he'd lodged a formal complaint against me with the Faculty Disciplinary Committee.

In conclusion, I share this thought: I'm sure you remember the great Victorian critic John Ruskin's disparagement of what he termed "the pathetic fallacy," that is, the unfortunate sentimental tendency in literature to attribute human intention and emotion to objects, especially in Nature, such as when Coleridge writes that the last leaf on the tree "dances as often as dance it can" or when Charles Kingsley describes the sea as the "cruel, crawling foam."

I take a different view. I believe that the pathetic fallacy is not so much a literary indiscretion as it is God's intentional sense of divine whimsy. Allow me an example.

When Ms. Westcott, Mr. Robson, Dr. Park, Coach Schrader, and I returned to the parking area, preparing to return to campus, something quite astonishing happened—and I wished Dr. Dunwoody had been present to share it. As we stood there, the clouds seemed to part "as a scroll when it is rolled together," leaving the evening sun to shimmer blindingly in the west, and the air above us—the whole expanse of the sky—filled with a tingling freshness, as if some celestial refrigerator door had just opened. Nature had altered its mood, and, as Dr. Park had suggested, it filled us with joy ... for there, behind us, to the east, was the most vividly brilliant double rainbow I've ever seen, arching from somewhere beyond Bear Lake to somewhere beyond the woods in which I'd just been bemired, as if embracing the whole world and every last, lost soul in it—granting a much-needed blessing on "the planet on which so many millions of us fight, and sin, and agonize, and die." Although wet and shivering, I felt in my bones what Wordsworth meant when he wrote, "My heart leaps up when I behold / A rainbow in the sky." It is no pathetic fallacy to say that somewhere in the deep, electrifying colors of that rainbow, the loving, unpredictable, wild God of the universe was smiling.

And thus, as Chaucer was wont to say, endeth my tale ...

I WOULD LIKE to extend my heartfelt thanks to Chairwoman Lambert and the entire Disciplinary Committee for allowing me this opportunity to clear the air, so to speak, and to provide an accurate chronicle of the events that took place at the Employee Picnic and Field Day, and I would like to thank all those who participated in the search-and-rescue operation. I am deeply appreciative.

I've also made a substantial monetary contribution to the Sasquatch Club's coffers in Dr. Dunwoody's name.

I hope I have convinced you that I am innocent of the charges laid against me, and in the words of Petronius Arbiter, "May all your guardian angels punish me if I lie."

Sincerely,

Martin E. Bonham, PhD
Professor of English
Chair, Department of Theophily

CHAPTER 10
THE DISCIPLINARY COMMITTEE

We suffer because we have no humility
and we do not love our brother.
From love of our brother comes the love of God.
—*Silouan the Athonite, 1866–1938*

In the dim stillness of the conference room on the library's ground floor, I sat ... a full hour ahead of the scheduled meeting. I fidgeted and brooded ... and appreciated as never before just how Thomas Moore's last rose of summer must have felt, "blooming alone, all her lovely companions faded and gone."

The college was at the beginning of its June Interim, that peculiar annual fortnight between the spring and summer terms during which all normal activities cease. The students scatter like chaff before the wind, commencement is but a recent memory, and most of the staff and faculty whisk their families away to places far more interesting than sleepy Midwestern towns. If you encounter anyone on campus, the odds are they're either lost or trimming the hedges. This year, Graciela had spirited Nate off to Arizona to meet her mother; the Evanses were touring Broadway with the girls; and according to reliable sources, Dolly De Angeli had absconded to Las Vegas, gripping in one hand the arm of a dapper, unidentified older gentleman, and in the other, a stout sack of quarters. She's reputed to be something of a slot-machine savant.

The indispensable Katie remained, though she too was planning to depart once the results of the Faculty Disciplinary Committee's report had been delivered. She and Tyrell were bound for parts unknown to all but themselves. And of course, Ms. Lambert and President Costa were still on campus, for it was they who had convened this conclave. The president had even missed the first day of a scheduled spiritual retreat to attend, though Ms. Lambert, I knew for a fact, relishes staying on campus during Interim for the creative scope it offers her fiction writing.

But my thoughts turned mostly to Katie and our conversation earlier that morning. The previous evening, she'd texted "7 am CTea be there," and in case I neglected to check my phone, as sometimes occurs, I found Post-it notes bearing similar messages stuck to my office door, my faculty mailbox, and the picket gate in front of my house.

Having been so lavishly summoned, I made certain to arrive on time at the designated location the next morning, where I found Katie pacing before the entrance like an overwrought panther. No sooner had I opened my mouth in salutation than she said, "Shh ... there's news. Just shut up and listen," and she spun around and strode resolutely into the CupperTea. She was clearly in one of her stringent moods.

The café was vacant and deafeningly quiet as we stepped to the counter, and even the barista just nodded as we ordered our drinks—as though he too was loath to desecrate the still-ness of Interim.

"Here's the deal," Katie said in a hushed tone. "The committee ... the report ... it's about more than just the flap at the faculty picnic. They've been interviewing people all over campus ... for months apparently ... about you and Dunwoody and your stupid, stupid feud. This whole thing's about to blow up. Ms. Adams told me she sneaked a peek at the report over at Admin ... and Costa's not happy, the provost's not happy, the dean's not happy, and some *major* changes are coming."

"Like what?" Our drinks arrived. We took our customary seats by the window. My chai jiggled in my hand.

"I don't know. She couldn't say, but it doesn't look good." A long silence ensued. Finally, she added, "You know it's up to you, right? Everything could fall apart if you don't ... well ..."

"What?"

"If you don't *humble* yourself a little!"

"Throw myself on the mercy of the court—"

"Exactly."

"Confess my sins before the council of the elders—"

"Yes."

"Say *mea culpa* three times and beat my breast—"

"M.B., *stop it!* You're not taking this seriously." She locked me in a hard, convicting stare, as though the sheer weight of it would cause me to crack. It did. I looked away.

When I looked back, she was still staring at me. I said, "Don't you have a phone to check or something?" Her stare turned to a glare. I added, "And what should I apologize for? I am as innocent as a lamb and numbered among the pure of heart—well, the *relatively* pure of heart."

"Easy for you to be glib, boomer, but look, if the Theophily Department folds, I'm out of a job—one I happen to love, by the way—while you get to retire with a pension in a few years and pop off to some doddery old English professors' rest home where you can quote Dickens at each other all day. You don't get it, do you? We've worked too hard—"

I was waiting for her to take a breath so I could say, "Katie, I'm sorry; I do take this seriously," when her phone buzzed. She glanced at the text. "It's Tyrell," she said. She took a deep breath and tried to compose herself. "I better answer."

She bowed her head, and, as she stabbed her phone's keypad furiously with her thumbs like a kalimba player playing jazz, I studied her as one might study the brush-strokes of a Van Gogh. How different she was from the Katie who sat in English Mystics 401 two years earlier and told me she didn't love God. While her hair was still dark and dramatic, she'd swapped her heavy glasses for contact lenses over the winter. She looked like a different person. Elegant and glowing. But it was more than that, something indefinable. Although she was still a goth whirlwind in black leggings, she now seemed more confident. Centered. Formidable.

And her tattoos! She was an illustrated history of Theophily's first year. There was the *All shall be well* on her right deltoid and the Graciela-inspired *Beloved* on her left. As a souvenir of Reverend Walker's visit (and in solidarity with the teenagers at the Caring Zone), she'd added the image of a broken chain to the back of her neck; and, as she reported, a picture of a "good angel" graced her right shoulder blade. A scripty *Be Still* ... had materialized on the inside of her left forearm after, I think, Tom Fouchee's night class, and probably others about which it's best not to inquire. Katie, as the television sportscasters say, had skin in the game. I also spotted a new piercing—a sort of rough miniature spike, like a tiny version of the ones used in the crucifixion, that ran through the upper lobe of her right ear in two places.

She set her phone down. "Tyrell's picking me up as soon as the meeting's over."

"Your new piercing—"

"The industrial—"

"What?"

"It's called an industrial," she said.

"I like it—quite visceral. Were you perhaps thinking of Isaiah ... where he says the Messiah was 'pierced for our transgressions and bruised for our iniquities—'?"

"What? No. What are you talking about?" She tilted her head and squinted at me as if I'd spoken in Tagalog. "No. I just always wanted one. And don't change the subject. You know what you need to do, right?"

"Yes ... apologize ... to everyone ... plead if I must. I'll say I'm sorry for any enmity between the seminary and our department ... between Dunwoody and me. I will do my best, Katie. Don't worry, I'll be an adult."

"As if," she said. "I just hope it's enough."

AND SO, as I sat alone in the gloom of the darkened conference room, awaiting the others' arrival, this question occurred to me: How long had it been since I'd asked Katie about the status of her ongoing spiritual crisis, the one that launched the Department of Theophily two years earlier? Six months? More? Where had the time gone? "The old hour glass spins its thread of sand," as John Clare wrote. Had I been so absorbed in my own petty dramas that I'd forgotten about her?

Suddenly, my affection for Katie felt heartbreaking somehow, deeper than before, and I saw, as though I'd just awakened from a trance, that she'd enriched my life far more than I could ever repay. The reality struck me like a cosh: Katie Westcott was not only the future of the Department of Theophily, she was its heart and soul, its very core. And she always had been. Her honesty. Her earnestness. Her ironic little sparks of joy.

With a click, the overhead lights came on. "Oh, you're here!" Ms. Lambert spoke from the doorway. For those of you who don't know her, Ms. Lambert is a compact, highly energetic woman with grizzled hair, either tied back in a jaunty ponytail or in the traditional librarian's bun. Her hazel eyes, peering over the top of her demi-lune reading glasses, are quick and perceptive, unlikely to miss the smallest detail, much like the heroine in her Hiss and Hearse detective novels. She's the kind of woman who, while not at all unattractive, becomes even more attractive as one gets to know her. She is the most polymathic person I've ever met, a cornucopia of wide-ranging trivia, to the extent that Katie, who used to work in the library, once referred to her as "the human internet." Ms. Lambert is my oldest and truest friend on campus

"This shouldn't take long," she said. "The president's on her way, and Dr. Dunwoody'll be here shortly."

"Shortly ...," I mumbled, "he can do no other."

She smiled, then raised an eyebrow. "You look anxious."

"Me? Never. Why?"

"Yeah, like Kafka in a mugshot."

She sat in the chair opposite and placed two sheets of paper on the table. I could see that the heading on the top sheet read FDC—for *Faculty Disciplinary Committee*. One sheet for me and one for Dunwoody, which I took as a positive sign. One page. How bad could it be?

"I confess this meeting has me frazzled," I said, "but I was actually thinking about Katie ... how redoubtable she's become ... and how much the department means to her ... to both of us."

"You're lucky to have her, I know, but *relax*, okay? As far as this meeting goes—"

At that moment, President Costa, who probably never relaxes even in her sleep, walked into the room as briskly as if she were planning to walk through the far wall. Her face was rigidly expressionless. Without saying a word, she swiveled suddenly and sat in the chair next to Ms. Lambert, looking indeed like someone in need of a spiritual retreat. She laid a thickish folder on the table, marked *APC*, which could only stand for *Academic Program Committee*, and that's when it dawned on me that this meeting was not just about Dunwoody and me and our "stupid, stupid feud," as Katie put it, but about programs, classes, departments—our future. This was what Ms. Adams meant when she told Katie that major changes were afoot.

A minute later, Dunwoody entered. He hesitated momentarily as he pondered whether to appropriate the chair next to mine or the one farther over. Ms. Lambert, glancing over her demi-lunes, also noticed his hesitation and rolled her eyes slightly as he chose the one farther away.

"All right, we're all here," she began.

"If I may," I spoke up, "before we begin, I'd just like to say I sincerely apologize—"

"Dr. Bonham," President Costa interrupted, "we'll have time for discussion later, but for now, we have an agenda to get through, and I have a plane to catch. Thank you both for being here. So, Ms. Lambert, please start with the Disciplinary Committee's report ..."

Ms. Lambert, handing one of her sheets to Dunwoody and the other to me, said, "I'll try to make this as quick and painless as possible"—a phrase, I thought, that must surely be embroidered on the throw pillows of executioners and dentists everywhere. "On this page you'll see the findings of the committee's inquiries as well as its recommendations."

Dunwoody and I scanned the single-spaced pages in front of us, but before I could comment, he spoke up: "This seems to be about me only; is the one you gave Dr. Bonham about him?"

"No, they're the same."

And indeed, the page bullet-pointed every stunt and shenanigan that Dunwoody had pulled in the past two years— the Forum on Faith, the banquet, the archbishop's visit—plus a couple I hadn't even known about, such as mobilizing seminarians to boycott Theophily classes. His eyes bulged slightly as he fumed, "So, why doesn't this show any of the things Bonham has done to *me!*"

Calmly, Ms. Lambert replied, "For instance?"

"Well, he tricked me into talking to all those grade school children."

President Costa piped up, "No, actually, I was the one who suggested that to my daughter, Amanda. You clearly—intentionally—put Dr. Bonham in an uncomfortable situation at the Forum on Faith ... by planting students in the audience ... so I wanted to see how you'd handle an uncomfortable situation yourself. And by all reports, Dr. Bonham saved the day."

Dunwoody sputtered, "Hardly, but ... well ... what about ..."

He paused. He thought for a moment. Then he thought harder. It occurred to me that he'd drawn a blank because everything I'd done to him had been but a defensive maneuver to blunt whatever he'd done to me first, though I scanned the page once more to make sure that attempted water-balloonings weren't mentioned.

"... what about the faculty picnic?" Dunwoody finally said.

"The committee read both your account and Dr. Bonham's," said Ms. Lambert, "and we didn't find fault on either side. It was an unfortunate misunderstanding."

"So, Bonham's this perfect little angel, eh? There've been *no* complaints about him and his department at all?"

President Costa stepped in. "Yes, we did receive one complaint ... from a certain Caring Zone church in Baldwin. They said that Dr. Bonham and some others, led by Reverend Walker, had disrupted one of their Sunday-morning services last fall. I had to talk them out of pressing charges against the university. When I called Reverend Walker for an explanation, he told me that someone who looked a lot like you had urged him to attend that service. What can you tell us about that?"

Dunwoody sat there for several seconds, seeming to shrink visibly. Then, he decided to play his last ace. "Well, you *do* know that he wrote dirty novels under a pseudonym?"

"Of course," said Ms. Lambert, in a slow, measured tone, as if addressing a toddler. "First, they're not dirty, and second, the administration's well aware ... and has known about them for years. No one has any objection."

President Costa added, "He does teach composition, you know. I've read them myself and rather like them."

This all came as news to me. At that moment, I must have looked as smug as only someone who is trying not to look smug can look. I nearly whooped aloud. Dunwoody seemed defeated, as though, in Abraham Cowley's phrase, his "soul to a strange somewhere fled."

"You'll see at the bottom," said Ms. Lambert, "that the only action the Disciplinary Committee recommends at this time is an official warning for you, Dr. Dunwoody, as well as an annual review by the faculty dean of any complaints about either of you. Any rudeness or disrespect from this point on will be grounds for serious disciplinary action or even dismissal."

"And tenure won't protect you," President Costa added. "Understood?"

I nodded, but Dunwoody said, "But his whole attitude, his presumption, as if he knows anything about religion—his whole department, in fact ... You're impinging on the seminary's territory by letting anyone and everyone lecture about faith. It's all so uninformed and pretentious! And after this meeting, I can guarantee you Bonham's going to be insufferable."

"Pretentious?" Ms. Lambert said, somewhat harshly. "You think the Department of Theophily is pretentious? Dr. Dunwoody, you have a professor in the seminary who, because he has two doctoral degrees, *insists* on being addressed as 'Dr. Dr. Barnes.' I know for a fact that another professor in your department has padded his resumé with fake publications, and another claims membership in an academic society of which he appears to be the *only* member. I'm not sure *you* are in a position to talk about *pretentious*! The Department of Theophily is not your personal piñata. It has to stop."

Stunned by her tone as much as her words, Dunwoody looked as if he'd been sandbagged. He sat there, staring at Ms. Lambert with wide, sad eyes. A long silence, and suddenly I became aware of the fluorescent lights buzzing softly above our heads.

"Now, for the Program Committee's report ...," began President Costa, mercifully changing the subject. She handed her folder to Dunwoody. "This report concerns the seminary solely, but since the final recommendations involve the Department of Theophily in part, I'd like you, as chair, to be present, Dr. Bonham."

Again, I nodded.

"The chief recommendations," said President Costa, "are, first, the student group known as the Eleven-Nineteens is to be disbanded at once. Simply being a member will be grounds for immediate dismissal. No appeal, no exceptions. Second, all seminarians will be required to include at least two Theophily classes among their electives, to broaden their educational experience. Again, no exceptions. Third, and most importantly, a restructuring of the seminary's hiring procedures and practices goes into effect immediately. The seminary can expect meticulous oversight from the academic dean and the administration—"

Dunwoody objected, "What in the world's wrong with our hiring practices?"

"Simply put, you hire only men. Aside from Ms. Adams, you've hired only two women in the past ten years—as adjuncts—and you've hired no minority candidates."

"What about Dr. Kapule?"

"Yes, he *is* half Hawaiian, but you have no blacks, no Hispanics, no one with disabilities, and no Asians or Pacific Islanders—apart from Dr. Kapule. You'll see at the end of our recommendations that we ask you to adopt the Department of Theophily as an informal model for faculty configuration. Even though Dr. Bonham drew his staff from the existing faculty, as well as some local clergy, still, it turns out that his is one of the most diverse departments in the entire Midwest Collegiate Association. We're proposing it as a model for every department.

"I should also point out," continued the president, "that the Department of Theophily has proven to be tremendously popular with students and in its first year has created a great deal of positive press for the university. *U.S. News and World Report* now cites Cupperton as one of its top ten 'up-and-coming' small universities and calls the new department 'innovative.' Dr. Bonham and Katie Westcott have created a remarkable sense of renewal and inclusivity on campus. Look at how many disciplines they've brought together. Science professors are connecting with humanities professors, and department heads are talking to one another. Any number of professors are waiting in line to create their own Theophily courses. Even *Dr. Dr.* Barnes asked me recently if he might approach Dr. Bonham with a course offering ...”

I made a mental note of this because Barnes, earnest soul that he is, is considered one of the most soporific lecturers on campus. Katie once told me that Barnes had confided to someone that he'd dreamed he was giving a lecture one time and when he awoke, he was.

The president continued, “So, if you expect the seminary to survive, Dr. Dunwoody, you're going to have to change with the times. It's not a threat; it's a reality.”

Ms. Lambert added, “Nationwide, only twenty-five percent of all tenured seminary faculty are women, which is terribly low—but Cupperton has zero!”

President Costa continued, “Look, diversity is strength. Your enrollment has been lagging; fewer academics want to teach here; prospective seminarians have told us that they can't come here because of the faculty makeup; alumni have started to divert funding elsewhere ...”

Turning crimson, Dunwoody said, “Look, this is nothing but affirmative action—quota filling—because the fact is, qualified women are hard to find—”

“No,” interjected the president, “this is fact-based hiring. We've kept files on the women and minority applicants you've rejected in the past ten years: one is now assistant dean at Duke Divinity, others are full professors at such places as Wheaton, Notre Dame, Princeton, and Fuller, and three of them have received AAR book awards. It grieves me to think that they could have been among *our* faculty.”

Dunwoody seemed to be caught off guard, but after thinking for a moment, he said, “Yes, yes, that's all well and good, but ... but need I remind you that *all* of Jesus's disciples were men?"

I cringed and felt a sudden urge to duck. In the face of two such commanding women, this line of attack seemed ill-considered, if not ill-fated. "The Charge of the Light Brigade" came to mind. And I was right. Ms. Lambert, having reached her breaking point, said rather forcefully, "And need I remind you, Dr. Dunwoody, that *you're* not Jesus?"

"Well, that's not fair—"

"And need I also remind you that the disciples were Middle Eastern Jews *without* theology degrees? How many Middle Eastern Jews do you have on your faculty?" Again, Dunwoody, stunned, glared at her. She continued, "And the gospel of Luke says that not only did the women travel with the disciples— Mary, Joanna, and the others—but they also supported the disciples financially 'out of their own means.' Are you one of those men who believe women shouldn't even talk in church and should keep their heads covered and ...?" She ran out of breath.

"Well, no, I didn't mean that—"

"Then what *do* you mean?" There was an awkward silence. Ms. Lambert added, "And need I remind you that women were the first to see the resurrected Christ—"

President Costa, like a school crossing guard, held up her hand to indicate that Ms. Lambert should stop. Calmly, the president said, "Bottom line—the administration will review all new applicants and are encouraging you to consider quali-fied women and minority candidates when they apply—for your own survival. It's not hard. We already exercise this over-sight for the undergraduate school, and it's time that the semi-nary be brought under the same guidelines."

Seeing Dunwoody slump in his chair like a scolded puppy aroused an unexpected empathy in me. Perhaps the chastisement had been too severe, too personal, and in all honesty, I knew I was as guilty as he was. Inwardly, I'd harbored an intense animus toward him, and yet here I was, having escaped all accountability for my own attitudes. Hadn't Jesus said, "Anyone who is angry with a brother or sister will be subject to judgment"?

When Dunwoody raised his head, strangely, he looked not at President Costa but at Ms. Lambert once again, apparently still stung by her outburst.

President Costa concluded, "So, one final recommendation—to encourage you and Dr. Bonham to put all this behind you, I'm requesting—no, mandating—that the seminary and the Department of Theophily work together to cosponsor an international, interfaith festival this fall. The Events Committee has wanted to do this for years, and this seems to be the perfect opportunity ... a chance for different religious and ethnic communities in the Tri-Comms area to come together to share their foods, music, and culture, and your two departments will be the ideal sponsors. Reaching out to other faith groups is one way of loving God. Don't you think? I will ask Ms. Adams and Ms. Westcott to act as committee cochairs, and Ms. Lambert will help, but you two *will* work with them to make sure this happens. Understood?"

"In spades," I said.

Dunwoody nodded slowly and, after a pause, grunted, "Are we done?"

President Costa, in a pleading tone, said, "I'll say one more thing. One of my favorite saints, Silouan the Athonite, said, 'Our brother is our life' and 'From love of our brother comes the love of God.' I don't believe it can be stated any more simply than that. If you love God even remotely as much as you claim, then I need you to remember it ... And yes, we're done."

With that, Dunwoody stood up and tromped heavily out the door.

KATIE WAS STANDING across the quad as I exited the library. She sprinted over to me, her heavy backpack swinging side to side as she ran.

"Wow!" she said, "I just saw Dr. Dunwoody go by, and he didn't look happy. What's the scoop?"

I narrated, to the best of my ability, the events I'd just witnessed, and in response, Katie hugged me as though I'd saved her life, squealed in my ear—"*Eee!*"—then jumped up and down. "They see us as a model! That's dope!" she exclaimed. "And an interfaith festival! Wow! I can't wait to tell Tyrell. Can the Bethel choir perform? I'd love that." She turned in the direction of a car parked at the north end of the quad and gave a thumbs-up. Tyrell honked in return. "You did it!" she said to me. "You knew exactly what to say. You're a genius!" I decided not to tell her that I'd hardly said a word. "Thank you," she said, "I'll be able to enjoy my trip now. What a relief!" She gave me another hug. "Wow! Okay then. That's it. Tyrell and I are heading out. Camping. See ya."

As she was about to dash off, I said, "Katie, hold on."

"Yeah?"

"I've been meaning to ask—what's happened to your ... you know ... your feeling that you don't love God? Has that changed at all?"

"Oh *that*!" she said. "It's a long story, but mostly, yeah, I still have lots and lots of doubts and depressions, but I don't let them bug me as much anymore ... how should I put it?" She set her backpack on the ground and thought for a moment. She held up an index finger in Tyrell's direction to indicate that she'd be another minute. "Okay, here's the thing. God made me like I am—organized, analytical, geeky—that's me. Right? But, you see, I use all that when I do the work God's given me to do day by day, and part of that is just caring for the people I know ... and for anyone God puts in my path. And day by day, I trust that the next step I take is exactly the one that God wants me to take. If I screw up, then God has something for me to learn. For me, that's what loving God is. It's trust. I was expecting it to be a huge, deep feeling of some kind, like the mystics—a big emotional thing, a beautiful madness, like you said, but it's not. It's mostly just doing the work, caring for people every day—which is pretty much what Jesus did—and as much as I can, I trust the next step. And somehow, I find joy in that. Make sense?"

"That's dope," I said. She smiled.

Hoisting her backpack over her shoulder once again, she turned and started to march off toward Tyrell, but before she'd taken more than a few steps, she stopped and plucked a package from her pack. She tossed it to me. "Almost forget. Ms. Lambert stopped by last night and told me to give you this, but only *after* the meeting today. Have a good Interim! Bye."

From its heft, I could tell the package contained a book or two, which I assumed to be some of Ms. Lambert's new academic work—the books she writes when she's not writing mysteries. As I strolled home, I tore the brown wrapper from the package and found that they were not books that she'd penned at all: instead, they were volumes five and six of the complete works of Thomas Traherne. I was confused. Why give me those? They were precisely the volumes that had fallen victim to my thwarted water-ballooning of Dunwoody last winter. Then it dawned on me. This was her way of telling me that Carl had told her the whole story but that she had opted not to mention it in the report. It was a sly sort of wink. I grinned. I was grateful, though I wondered if he'd told her about the pants. Then again, yes, how could he *not* have?

―――――

THAT NIGHT, just as I was placing my toothbrush back into its customary drinking cup on the sink, I heard an aggressive pounding on my front door, the kind SWAT teams make on crime shows when they're about to take down a suspect. I nearly jumped out of my slippers. Wrapping my robe around my shoulders, I padded downstairs and peeped through the peephole. My heart sank. It was Dunwoody, pacing beneath the lurid glow of the porch light, mumbling, and waving his hands around as though he were reprimanding a dimwitted seminarian.

Just as I was toying with the idea of pretending not to be at home, he banged on the door again and yelled, "Bonham! I know you're in there; the lights are on."

"What do you want?"

"Just to talk. Nothing else. I'm not angry. It's important."

I opened the door and jerked my head to one side to indicate that he should come in. I left the door ajar in case a quick getaway was required.

He shuffled into the living room and settled himself, uninvited, on my favorite reading chair by the fireplace. "Okay, look, I've had something on my mind all day ...," he said, "I knew I wasn't going to sleep tonight if I didn't get it off my chest ... Could I have a glass of water?"

"What? That's what you've had on your mind all day?"

He gave me a dark look. "I'm thirsty, Bonham!" I traipsed to the kitchen and returned.

He drank the water slowly, caught his breath, then dropped his chin to his chest. In an uncharacteristically soft tone, he said, "Look, let's put all that other stuff behind us. I'm sorry. For everything. I want to start fresh ... no tricks, I promise ... Can we be friends?"

"No!" I said reflexively. "... Maybe ... I don't know ... why?"

"Because I need your help ... I didn't know who else to ask. I need advice. Something occurred to me at the meeting today, which I didn't even quite realize until then ... you seem to know her better than anyone on campus ... it's just ... what can you tell me ... about Ms. Lambert?"

CHAPTER II
MS. LAMBERT'S STORY

The place of prayer is a precious habitation;
for I now saw that the prayers of the saints
were precious incense; ... I saw this habitation to be safe,
—to be inwardly quiet when there were
great stirrings and commotions in the world.
—*John Woolman, 1720–1772*

Since I (Ms. Lambert) was one of the two people involved in what has come to be known as "the incident," Martin asked me to write this next installment of his informal history of the Department of Theophily. Despite reservations, I accepted the challenge due largely to Katie Westcott's promise that two copies of Martin's finished manuscript would be donated to the library's archives. The story of Theophily, I'm convinced, needs to be preserved, and, as you'll see, I briefly became one of its central characters.

Also, since I can never talk about "the incident" without Martin saying it, I will save him the trouble by saying it myself right here at the start: "It came down to the wire." Indeed.

I. WEDNESDAY

North Quad was eerily quiet except for the hum of cicadas, the buzz of the earnest bees among the hydrangeas by the library entrance, and the drone of a distant lawnmower, which proved that at least one other person was still on campus. It was the kind of steamy, languid day on which you'd least expect something out of the ordinary to happen. Only two days had passed since the Disciplinary Review, and I was still a bit shaken.

My plan was to tidy up in the reference room until midday and then to write at home all afternoon (my publisher having asked for my next Hiss and Hearse novel by September). So, after purposefully locking myself in the library that morning, turning the air conditioning to High, and hanging a sign on the front entrance that read, "LIBRARY CLOSED—SEE YOU AT SUMMER TERM," I began the process of organizing paperwork, answering emails, returning unclaimed holds to the shelves, and doing all those other tasks that can be quite meditative when done alone. I relish the focused solitude of June Interim.

Then, above the strains of the Debussy I'd piped through the library's intercom from my phone, I became aware of a faint thumping ... and a far-off voice ... someone was shouting. I switched off the Debussy. Thump, thump, thump. More shouting. As I approached the glass doors of the entrance, I could see a dark silhouette looming outside, and while visions of fictional villains danced in my head, I soon saw that it was only Dr. Dunwoody. "There you are! Ms. Lambert! Hello! May I come in?" he called as he waved through the glass.

After Monday's tense meeting, I thought it best to speak with him in public, so I stepped out into the humid sun-drenched air.

"Hello," he said, nodding his head slightly. He seemed nervous. "I was wondering if, you know ... if we might talk." When the door snapped shut behind me, he said, "Oh, no! You haven't locked yourself out, have you?"

"I've got a key."

"Always prepared, eh? Right, well, I'll start by apologizing. I'm sorry for my irritability ... you know ... at the meeting. I can be temperamental. It was immature of me. You were right about the things you said, and I'm very, very sorry."

"It was a difficult meeting," I said. "I know it was hard. I said some harsh things, but all things considered, I think it went well. Thank you for your concern."

"Yes, yes, I think it went well too. Change is good. So ... you know, I was wondering if I might make it up to you by buying you an iced tea or something at the CupperTea ..."

What is going on? I thought. This desperately contrite side of the chairman was something I'd never seen in my thirty years at Cupperton, and he was clearly failing to live up to his reputation as someone who, as Martin says, suffers from a chronic Napoleon complex.

"Oh," he said, "and I brought you this." He handed me a small box of chocolates. "As a peace offering, you might say." I took it with a slight shudder because, unlike my close friends, he was apparently unaware that I'm allergic to chocolate—I love it, but it gives me hives and stomach cramps.

"How kind. Thank you. Uh ... sure, iced tea would be great."

As we walked across North Quad, past the hydrangeas, the painted boulder, and Phipps Auditorium, we continued chatting, but rather than asking me the usual get-to-know-you questions—like Where are you from? and What's your favorite movie?—his first question was about my academic credentials. He was astonished that I had a doctorate.

"Then why," he asked, "does everyone call you *Ms.* Lambert?"

"Oh, that's Martin's doing," I said. "Years ago, I told him I thought academic titles were pretentious, that I wanted to appear open and accessible to the students ... a resource, a friend even, and not an authority figure. So Martin said, 'Then I shall henceforth refer to you as *Dear Ms. Lambert in the library*,' and the epithet stuck—minus the *Dear*. I've grown to like it."

"But you lose a lot of respect, don't you?"

"That's the point. I get more respect as the affable campus librarian than as the lettered Doctor of Library Science and Communications from the University of Washington. People who know me know about my various degrees. I double-majored in English and history as an undergrad; I got an MA in American history and, because I had nearly enough credits, I got another MA in research methodology. I did my doctoral thesis—which was later published—on peace movements in the twentieth century—I belong to the Religious Society of Friends ... the Quakers."

By that time, we'd reached the CupperTea, where he opened the door for me with a gallantly artless sort of flourish. Inside, we ordered drinks and seated ourselves at what I knew to be Martin and Katie's regular booth by the window. The vacant café and the overwhelming silence seemed to exaggerate our own lack of things to talk about. I studied the many initials carved in the wooden tabletop.

Finally, he asked, "So, are you and Bonham ... close?"

The question took me off guard. "Well, yes, he was the first real friend I made at Cupperton more than three decades ago," I said. "I remember this slim young man—he had brown hair back then and a silly mustache—approaching the reference desk in a sort of panic one day and saying, 'Tell me everything you know about *The Wedding of Sir Gawain and Dame Ragnelle*.'

He was writing an article or something about medieval Arthurian poems. I responded, 'All I know is I wasn't invited.' We laughed, and our friendship began."

"So, it's not like you dated or anything?"

I wondered where this was going. "Not really. Early on, I thought maybe something would develop, but neither of us are the dating-and-marrying type," and then I added with a bit of emphasis, "*at all*! But yes, we're close … platonic friends, you might say … so platonic, in fact, we even talk about Plato. Martin's a *Symposium* type—a romantic. I lean more toward the *Apology* … you know, courtroom scenes and executions."

"Like in your novels!" he said.

"Yes, I've sort of taken Socrates's remark 'let not injustice run faster than death' as something of a theme for my books."

"You know, I've read *all* your E. Anabeth Miller mysteries— I love them! Bonham's are lifeless by comparison; he's like some blunt-fingered Neanderthal pounding on a rock. Yours are nuanced and complex, so full of color and excitement —"

"I should get my publisher to approach you for a blurb—"

"And if I'm not mistaken, your anagram indicates that your middle initial is *I*. Correct?"

"Spot on," I said. "Helena Irene Lambert, though my friends call me Lena for short—so, please call me Lena. You see, before I was born, my mother was in a production of *Midsummer Night's Dream*." He looked puzzled, so I added, "She played the part of Helena."

"Oh, of course … and do call me Neil."

"So, why do you ask about Martin?"

"Oh, nothing. You just mention him a lot. I wondered if you and he were ever … an item."

"Hardly," I answered.

"Well, you see, from what he told me I wasn't sure."

"Wait … you talked with Martin—about *me*?"

"No, no, no, just in passing. You see ... after the meeting I'm trying to improve my image, get to know people better. More changes for the better." He laughed uncomfortably.

We chatted some more, mostly about mutual acquaintances and plans for the summer, and our awkwardness eased up a bit. I would even say we grew more relaxed. Then, as we were leaving the CupperTea, he asked if he might see me again. Thinking it best to meet him on my own terms, I suggested that we have lunch at my house on Friday. "We can eat on the front porch. I've just had the decking redone and added some new furniture."

"I'd love that," he said. "I'll be there."

II. Friday

Feeling apprehensive and cautious, I pottered around the porch, double-checking the place settings and whatnot. The new wicker table and chairs seemed perfectly suited to my house, a late Victorian, painted white with blue-gray trim and filigree, on what is called "faculty row," just north of campus.

When I looked up, I saw someone strolling casually down the sidewalk—wearing neatly creased white pants, a double-breasted navy blazer, and most oddly of all, a shimmery gold silk ascot. It was Dr. Dunwoody—Neil—and he looked as if he'd just stepped off a yacht, lacking only a white boating cap with crossed anchors.

"Right on time," I called.

As he approached, he held out a bouquet of freshly picked daisies, and again, I realized that he was unaware of my allergy to several kinds of wildflowers, daisies among them. "How lovely. Thank you," I said. "Why don't you bring them inside, and we can put them in a vase."

As he followed me through the front hallway, Belle, my

bullmastiff, approached him for a welcoming sniff. She loves strangers and is as gentle a dog as ever licked a hand. When Martin visits, she spends most of her time with her head in his lap, drooling all over his corduroy pants. Martin adores her. But Neil, apparently unaccustomed to one-hundred-and-fifty-pound dogs with heads like boulders, said in an unnaturally high voice, only a few notes lower than a falsetto, "Hello, doggie. Good dog. Nice doggie," and even more strangely, when I led him to the kitchen, he began to walk with an odd rolling of his hips, as though he were doing a Bette Davis impersonation. It was odd.

I had him put the flowers in a vase while I spooned the marinated chickpea salad onto plates and poured the iced tea. As we walked back through the living room with our plates and glasses in hand, he resumed his "nice doggie" swaying routine.

"Belle, kitchen!" I said as Neil and I exited onto the porch.

"You afraid of dogs?" I asked.

"No, no, of course not. But someone mentioned to me that Belle dislikes men, that the secret to getting along with her is to, you know, sort of convince her you're not a male."

"Hmm. That wasn't *Martin* by any chance, was it?"

"Uh, yes, I believe it was."

A pattern was emerging. Martin was up to no good. Not wanting to arouse more animosity between the two of them than necessary, I played along. "Oh, yes, I see. Well, Belle is quite past that stage. She's very gentle now—she even likes doctors of theology!"

Seating ourselves at the wicker table, we proceeded to eat ... and chat. "So, tell me about your writing," he said. "What are you working on?"

I told him, in far more detail than necessary, about my current project—the eighth Hiss and Hearse novel, to be called

The Black Snakes of Brisbane, which grew out of my trip to Australia two summers ago. I always visit the cities in which my heroine and her husband solve their snake-related mysteries. I also mentioned the academic study I'd been working on about conscientious objectors during World War Two. I get carried away when talking about my books. At the end of my lengthy monologue, I asked, "And how about you?"

He delivered an equally lengthy monologue about the Bible translation committee he serves on and about being the preliminary translator for the book of Proverbs. It sounded interesting. The new translation is to be called the New International Contemporary English Bible, or the NICE Bible for short. The publisher, he explained, plans to market it by showing photographs of vibrant young people reading the book in warm, intimate settings—in front of a fire, on a beach, camping, sitting in bed as the morning sun streams through the curtains—with the sales pitch printed beneath: "Have a NICE day."

Just as I was pondering whether that was the best approach for a new Bible translation, he said, "You know something? Katie Westcott's question about loving God ... well, I've thought about that ... often ... and I think I most love God when I'm working on this translation. It's the strangest feeling, as if I'm connecting with something vast and important. I love that feeling ... but don't tell Bonham ... because, you know, it's a Theophily thing!" We laughed.

Somehow, that broke the ice. As the afternoon grew more breezy and pleasant, so did the conversation. Almost without realizing it, we began sharing stories about our families and our schooling, about our failures and successes, our hopes and disappointments. He told me that he was from Piqua, Ohio, and was the next-to-last of eleven children. "My parents," he said somewhat ironically, "would have had more children if only they'd gotten along better!"

His farmer father, he confessed, was never abusive, but still, he could be cold and unresponsive, while his mother was prone to protracted silences and even more protracted grudges. He was shamed, sometimes harshly, for all sorts of minor misdeeds throughout his childhood. Lacking approval from his parents, he transferred that desperate need to God and always felt he could never quite live up to expectations. It made me think of that French adage: *"Tout comprendre, c'est tout pardonner"*—"to understand all is to forgive all." And after so many years of knowing Dr. Dunwoody only by reputation, I was just beginning to understand ... and to forgive.

Also, after decades of living alone, I found it acutely thrilling to be enjoying myself in the company of an intelligent man who was taking such an obvious interest in me, so, after lunch, when he asked, "May I see you again?" I answered, without hesitation, "Of course."

THAT EVENING, I heatedly punched the keypad on my phone.

"Martin, it's Lena," I said when he answered. "You've *got* ... to ... *stop!*"

"What?"

"You told Neil that Belle dislikes men."

"Oh, that. Well, I may have garnished the brick a bit—"

"And you must have told him that I like men in ascots, right?—because I recently told you that I thought ascots look like a sea creature crawling out of the man's shirt. Oh, and let me guess, you also told him I love chocolate and daisies, right?"

There was a long silence, then, "Lena, I know. I'm sorry. I thought it might help if you were trying to put him off—"

"Don't interfere!"

"The truth is," he stammered, "I don't know what I'd do if you were to ... well ... You see, he came to my house late Monday night, the day of the meeting, in utter despair and wanted my advice. He's convinced he's in love with you ... You aren't going to marry him, are you?"

"You know something? You don't know the first thing about him—"

"So, you *are* considering it!"

"Listen! There's a lot you don't know."

"Like what?"

"Okay, for one thing, *why* he gets so intense about the seminary."

"Because he's a bore?"

"No. Because he was once married." More silence on the other end of the phone. "Yeah, that's right. And get this, his wife died in a car accident after they'd been married only two years. Not only that, but she died as she was driving back from the doctor's office, where she'd gone to find out if she was pregnant." Martin was still speechless. "Her name was Laura, and her nickname for him was Kees—short for Cornelius. They'd decided that if they had a girl, they'd name her Katherine because they loved the name Katie. So, why do you think he was so upset when Ms. Westcott went over to the Theophily side? He felt completely paternal toward her—and he felt as if you'd stolen her! When Laura died, he threw himself into his studies to cope, got his second and third doctorates, was hired at Cupperton, and now he's chairman. He does it all for her ... for Laura. It's like he still wants her to be proud of him. But I don't think he ever properly grieved, and he said it wasn't until the Disciplinary Review that something kind of broke inside him. He said he couldn't deal with his denial any longer, of not talking about it. He couldn't deal with himself anymore. Frankly, he said I reminded him of his wife—that the reason he loved her was her utter honesty and willingness to stand up to him. She was tough. That's apparently why he finds me attractive."

"So you *are* going to marry him?"

"Martin, *stop*! No, I'm not. But I find your jealousy rather odd because it's not as though *you* ever took an interest!" I knew the instant I said it, it was hurtful. "I'm sorry. It's just ... you *know* I'd never adjust to marriage. I don't *want* romance. I like my life as it is."

"I know we're just friends, but I thought that you and I ... as *friends*, you know ... were kind of exclusive ... you know, a *thing*."

"We've known each other for more than thirty years, and you've never so much as hinted that you and I were 'a thing.' In fact, I sort of wondered if you were gay." Again, I regretted it.

"I'm not," he said. "I'm surprised you'd think that ... and so what if I were?"

"Look, Martin, I love you dearly, and I'm sorry. Our friendship means the world to me—but you know as well as I do that even if you *were* interested, I'm just *not* the marrying type. And you aren't either. I suspect you're descended from a long line of celibate bachelors! Look, I like Cornelius. He's kind and smart, he's good to talk to, and he can even be funny ..." I could hear Martin grunt "... and I love the attention. At our age we need all the friends we can get. But no, I'm not marrying anyone."

"But does he know that?"

"No. Not yet. We're having another date, if you want to call it that, on Sunday. He's taking me on a picnic. I'll break it to him then."

"The old 'just friends' routine?"

"I suppose. I assumed that at a certain age, I wouldn't have to deal with that anymore."

"Lena, for what it's worth, any man would be blessed to be married to you. You know that, right?"

I laughed a loud embarrassed laugh and said, "As I said, just stop! I can't imagine anyone being attracted to me."

"No—*you* stop. You *are* attractive—don't forget that. And as my old friend Dudley Fitts used to say, 'The sexiest part of a woman's body is her mind.'"

III. Sunday

The day was bright, cloudless, and breezy, and the air was cooler than it had been for the past week—about as perfect a June day for a picnic as one could wish for. After returning from Friends Meeting at noon, I changed into what I thought was appropriate picnic attire—loose white linen slacks, a yellow, long-sleeved pullover blouse, and what I thought was a thoroughly natty white Panama hat, with a red bandana hatband and matching red clutch handbag. I was in that odd position of having to tell Neil we were "just friends" but still wanting him to find me absolutely alluring.

When he knocked a few minutes later, I opened the door. He was basketless. I thought, uh-oh, was I supposed to provide the food? As he patted Belle sweetly on the head, he said, "Okay, I have a surprise. This way." He led me down faculty row, back toward campus, past the CupperTea, and across North and South Quads until I realized we were headed not toward the arboretum but toward Erickson Hall, the seminary building.

"Aren't we going on a picnic?" I asked.

"Just wait."

He punched a code into the keypad by the front door of

Erickson. It buzzed, and we walked inside. There, he punched more numbers on another keypad to disarm the alarm system, after which he took my hand and led me to the main stairs. "This way," he said. When we reached the third floor—I was winded—he turned to the right and walked toward his office. Inside, atop his cluttered desk, sat a large picnic basket with a checked tablecloth neatly folded on top. A doily heart, like a grade-school Valentine, hung from the handle.

"For someone special," he said and smiled, as he put his hand in his pocket.

Panicked, I thought, oh no, does he have a ring? Is he going to propose? No sooner did that thought cross my mind than he withdrew his hand and grasped the basket's handle. "Let's go," he said. But it was enough to convince me that now was the time for honesty—before this special, red doily-heart picnic went too far.

"Neil, we need to talk."

"Of course." He directed me to the chair next to his desk. He sat on his desk chair and rolled it close to mine. I gazed out the window. A white butterfly flitted past as the hazy summer trees swayed lazily in the empty quad outside. The awkward moment weighed on me.

"Okay," I began, "you see, I don't know exactly what your intentions are"—as I said it, I knew it sounded lame—"and maybe I'm misreading this whole situation, but I need to explain some things. You've been very kind, very sweet, but to put it plainly, I'm not looking for an intimate relationship right now, for personal reasons as well as professional ones. First, I just can't handle a romance at this point in my life, and second, *no one* knows this yet, but I'll be leaving Cupperton in January. I've been offered a job ... abroad ..." He looked stunned. "... at the Bodleian Library in Oxford ... England. It's something I've wanted for years."

There was a brief silence during which Neil continued to stare at me. I glanced over his shoulder once more, at the luminous trees swaying silently beyond the window.

I continued, "You see, at the University of Washington I studied with Dr. Marlys Davis, who later got a position as the U.S. History reference librarian at the Bodleian. She's retiring and suggested that I apply for her position. I did and I got it. You're the first person I've told—after President Costa, that is. This means a lot to me, and while I want us to remain friends, I just can't have attachments complicating things right now. You're a wonderful person, so smart and caring, and I know we'll keep in touch. But ... that's what I needed to tell you."

He continued to stare at me for what seemed like a long time. His eyes didn't look sad so much as empathic. Finally, he said, "Oxford! Oh, I can't tell you how happy that makes me. How wonderful! Absolutely perfect! As I've gotten to know you, I've become convinced that you're wasted here at Cupperton, and I'm so glad for this opportunity. I suspect Bonham will be crushed ... but I have a confession as well. I'm relieved —disappointed of course, but relieved. I've wondered whether I was up for a serious relationship myself. I'm not as young as I was ... and, of course, I have my work. I need friends more than romance."

He stood, leaned over me, put a hand on each side of my face, and gave me a soft sort of kiss on the forehead. "Friends then!" he said. Then, grasping the handle of the basket once more, he said in an upbeat tone, "Now that that's settled, let's not waste a perfectly good picnic, eh? And I still want to show you my surprise." His cheeriness made the tension vanish.

He led me down the hallway to a door that opened onto the rear service stairs, where we began to climb once again—two more flights up until we seemed to be standing in a small closet-like space with a single, heavy fire door on one side.

When he opened it, I was blinded by the penetrating sunlight. We were on the roof of Erickson, standing above the fifth-floor offices—six stories in the air. My eyes adjusted, and I took in the spectacular view.

"You like it? Other than the observatory, it's the highest point on campus, with the best view. Look, you can see the old brick water tower in Palmyra"—he pointed—"way over there."

"This is amazing! I had no idea!"

"It's a well-kept secret. And look here." There in the middle of tar-paper-and-gravel roofing material was a rug on which stood a small, roofed structure, like a gazebo. Beneath it stood two chairs and a table, and in the middle was a vase full of daylilies. My absolute favorites—partly because I'm not allergic to them. Martin must have told him ...

"The seminarians created this as a place to bring dates to —and, as they sometimes claim, to study. They call it Mount Gilead. You like it?"

We walked the perimeter, taking in the view from every direction. South Quad lay immediately below us, and Murphy Chapel and North Quad beyond that. To the west, beyond the treetops and the observatory dome, you could distantly see Palmyra's neat rows of houses, and, to the northeast, part of the river park in Ware. Jet trails streaked the sky far in the northwest where the city airport was, seventy miles away. To the east, you could see the trees of the arboretum, the lily garden, a bit of the labyrinth, and the bend in the river where it feeds into the reservoir beyond. To the south was nothing but trees as far as the eye could see. It was stunning.

Seating himself at the shaded table, he pulled a bottle of wine from the basket—Chateau Ste. Michelle Indian Wells Merlot. My favorite! Again, Martin must have told him. I was suddenly tempted to withdraw my "just friends" talk.

He rummaged roughly through the basket, grumbled, then

rummaged again. "Uh-oh. I seem to have forgotten the corkscrew. I have a pocketknife in my office with a corkscrew on it. I'll run down and get it. Be right back." He walked to the door. There was a pause. He stood motionless for a moment or two.

Eventually I asked, "Neil? You okay?"

"Um, it's locked."

"You have a key ..."

"No ... there's no keyhole anyway. You've got your phone, right?"

"Oh, no, it's in my handbag ... in your office. So, are we ... stuck?"

In a mild panic, we tried twisting the doorknob, jerking it, pushing it, even kicking the door. We tried prying our fingers into the crack around the doorjamb. No use. The seconds dragged by.

"Anything in your basket that would help?" I asked.

"Only sandwiches and fruit. I don't even have any silverware."

"Maybe someone's down there—in the quad ... or over in the arboretum," I said.

We walked to the northeast corner of the retaining wall, with South Quad to our left and the arboretum to our right, and took a deep breath. "Help! Is anybody there? Help! Anybody! Up here!"

In our hearts we knew it was no good. We were stranded six stories above campus ... during June Interim ... and on a Sunday no less. We saw four or five cars pass in the distance beyond North Quad, zipping past the CupperTea and the Music Annex, but though we waved like castaways on a desert island, we knew they were too far away.

We walked the perimeter again, scanning in all directions. Trees, deserted campus buildings, distant hills. The tennis courts behind the athletic building were empty. After yelling a few more times, we gave up. Despondent, we sat at the table.

"Someone's bound to walk by sooner or later," he said.

"How long's that going to take? It's a ghost town down there."

He shrugged.

"We should pray," I said.

He nodded. "You're right." Then, folding his hands and bowing his head, he began intoning in a high voice, as if talking to Belle, "Dear Lord, earnestly do we beseech thee—"

"Neil, no, let's pray silently. I do better that way. You know … double the prayer power."

"Oh, right, right. Sure." And he bowed his head again as I stood.

After a few seconds, he popped his head up and grumbled, "What *are* you doing?"

"I'm praying. What do you think?"

"You look like you're walking around," he said somewhat severely and added, "and your eyes are open!"

"So?" I snapped. "That's how I pray. The psalmist says, 'I will lift up mine eyes unto the hills from whence cometh my help.' I don't know about you, but I'm looking for help."

He squinted at me in disapproval. "I suppose," he said.

"Look, if I'm going to ask God to get us off this roof," I said, "then I'm going to keep my eyes open. So, you just pray your way and I'll pray mine. And we won't stop till we get an answer. Okay?"

"Fine," he said a bit huffily as he bowed his head once more.

Silently, I prayed something like this: "Okay, God, hold us in your Light. This is actually pretty funny. I know we aren't going to die up here; our bleached bones won't be discovered years from now, like in my *Black Mambas of Barundi*. I'm confident I'll sleep in my own little bed tonight, but I'm curious to see just how you're going to get us out of this. It's all so awkward ... and inconvenient. Please help."

Again, I circled the perimeter, scanning the tops of the trees, taking in all the far-flung, empty, seemingly uncaring world below. I watched the jet trails in the distance and saw a turkey buzzard circling overhead. Not a good sign. I scrutinized the base of the retaining wall in case I'd missed something that might help—a crowbar would have been nice. Nothing.

I leaned my elbows on the wall and cast a forlorn gaze over South Quad. Still, no one was down there. Resting my chin on my hands, I realized I must look like a gargoyle—Erickson Hall's own female gargoyle in a Panama sun hat. That thought sparked another—reminding me of my third novel, *The Pythons of Paris*. In one scene my heroine climbs the stairs of the north tower of Notre Dame to admire the cathedral's array of stone sculptures—"one-horned hellcats, malevolent pachyderms, human-devouring dogs, needle-billed goblin birds, and rain-water-spewing fiends." But of all the gargoyles, she decides that her favorite is Stryga, the most famous of all, the Spitting Gargoyle, who, as I wrote, "broods eternally over the city, with his chin resting on his hands, two blunt horns sprouting from his head, and his tongue sticking out ... like a snub-nosed stone Nietzsche blowing raspberries at the world." Martin once told me how much he admired that line. Then, as my heroine descends the tower, she notices an odd little door to one side— a door that later becomes the key to solving the story's mystery.

The door! I needed to study the service door once again. I walked to it. A metal plate covered the crack where the bolt goes into the frame, so inserting something thin, like a credit card or a butter knife to ease back the bolt, would not be an option—all of which was pointless, since I didn't have a credit card or butter knife. Three heavy hinges fastened the door to the frame. Even if I'd had a screwdriver, the screws were corroded and seemed unlikely to twist.

Just as I was praying, "God, please don't tell me you're suggesting we climb down the outside of Erickson like Quasimodo," I noticed something. A small hole in the center of the doorknob. Of course. How simple. I remembered something that my heroine had done in another novel. When confronted with a locked door at the Roman zoo, she inserted a stiff wire into a similar hole, and voilà. I'd researched lock picking at the time. Manufacturers, in fact, provide those holes for emergencies like this.

"Right! Now, God," I prayed, "what about a wire?" Again, I scanned the rooftop for something small and stiff enough to insert into the tiny hole. No wire. "Okay, God, I'm waiting."

Then, I felt a palpitation in my chest. A heart flutter? Anxiety? The answer dawned on me. Seldom have I had a prayer answered so immediately ... and viscerally.

I glanced back to make sure that Neil was still praying. I threw my hat down and quickly pulled my long-sleeved blouse over my head, then unsnapped my bra in back, and after peeking once more to make sure that Neil still had his eyes closed, I slid off my bra. Naked from the waist up for those few seconds, I felt vulnerable—but also mischievous. I felt this impulse to do a little dance to celebrate the absurdity of the moment—a half-naked female gargoyle of a certain age prancing on a rooftop while the chair of the seminary prays just a few feet away. I quickly pulled my blouse back over my head.

I turned one of the bra cups inside out and plucked at the lining. The threads were stiff, but I managed to make a small hole through which I could pull out the flat, curved wire. I inserted it into the hole. I jiggled it, moving it in and out, and kept quietly twisting the knob. Jiggle, turn, jiggle, turn, jiggle, turn, until I finally heard the soft click I was waiting for. I pulled the door open, inserted my shoe as a door stop, and unlocked the mechanism from inside, just in case.

Having no convenient place to hide the now partly shredded bra, I impulsively tossed it over the side into the trees. Since then, I've often imagined small birds nesting in its contours or perhaps some startled seminarian, gazing out a classroom window, wondering how it got there. In the weeks that followed, I scanned the trees on Erickson's south side, thinking I'd catch a glimpse of white, but it seemed to have vanished.

Neil was still praying. To get his attention, I loudly said, "Thank you, God. Amen!" He looked up, saw the open door, and his jaw dropped. I said, "God answered my prayer."

"But ... how? How did you do it?" But before I could answer, he added, "And how do you know it wasn't *my* prayer God answered?"

That was the old Dr. Dunwoody I knew, but I deferred to him. "You know, you're right. God answered *our* prayers. But look, Neil, let's get out of here. Grab the basket ... because I've got an idea. Maybe the best idea yet. I'll tell you on the way."

"But how did you do it?" he repeated.

As we descended the five flights of stairs and emerged onto the fresh, welcoming lawn of South Quad, I explained the whole thing, after which he said, "Of course ... just like your heroine in *The Vipers of the Vatican* when she breaks into the serpentarium at the Roman zoo to find the brass key hidden in the nest of African bush vipers."

"Wow! You really *have* read my books!"

A QUARTER OF AN HOUR LATER, we were standing at Martin's door, picnic basket in hand. We knocked. "Martin! You there? Hey, Martin!"

Martin cracked the door and peeked at us dubiously.

"Let us in! ... We bear good tidings ... and we've brought food!" I said.

"What's going on?" He opened the door.

"First," I said, handing him the basket, "I'm here to announce that from this point on, you and Neil are going to be friends, best buds, amigos—otherwise, *neither* of you will be a friend of mine. Ever! Got it? I'm serious. Damon and Pythias! Tolkien and Lewis! Calvin and Hobbes!"

The two men looked at each other skeptically ... but nodded.

"Second, you do realize, don't you, that you have only three and half months to organize the interfaith festival? When Summer Term starts next week, I'll contact Katie and Ms. Adams, and we'll get the ball rolling—together we'll make this the best international confab this side of the United Nations—and I suggest we call it an All-Faiths Festival instead. Sounds more inclusive. Third, Neil and I have a story—one that will memorialize the moment when the Department of Theophily and the seminary buried the hatchet for good, wiped the slate clean, proffered the olive branch, kissed and made up. Okay? Say amen!"

Again, nod, nod.

"Say it!" I repeated sternly.

"Amen."

"Amen."

"And in the course of our story, Neil and I discovered a Theophily concept of our own this afternoon!"

Then, taking turns, laughing as we did so, Neil and I told the whole tale of our rooftop adventure—"the incident"—and by the end, even Martin was chuckling. "And here's the Theophily part," I concluded, "like the psalmist says: 'I love the Lord because he has heard my voice and my supplications.' Our prayers were heard, Martin! God listens!"

He thought for a moment, looked at Neil and me, and smiled. "Indeed. But it came down to the wire!"

CHAPTER 12

THE ALL-FAITHS FESTIVAL

Both read the Bible day & night,
But thou readst black where I read white.
—*William Blake (1757–1827)*

"Woe unto you, you *hypocrites*! ... You appear beautiful outward but are full of *dead men's bones* and uncleanness ..." Those words thundered across the brick courtyard in front of the Student Stores as I (Martin) strolled onto campus the morning of the All-Faiths Festival. "You shall be cast into the furnace of fire where there'll be weeping and *gnashing* of *teeth!*"

Like me, Brother Jonas had risen with the birds, though in his case the apparent mission was to heap admonitions of doom upon the heads of the exhibitors who were arriving early to set up their tables, tents, and booths, and to haul their carts of food and beverages to North Quad. Today Brother Jonas seemed more tightly wound than usual. No doubt, he'd seen the posters heralding the festival, which he must have felt granted him an even more wide-ranging license to fulminate —more wide-ranging than the petty castigation that was already his primary mode of communication.

He stood atop his customary bench overlooking the CUSS. "You *think* you're Christians," he bellowed at us passersby, two of whom, by the way, were turbaned Sikhs who were lugging folding tables, "but you're whited sepulchers, appearing righteous unto men, but within, you are full of *hypocrisy* and *iniquity!*"

Normally, Brother Jonas is a neatly self-regulating system; that is, the louder he rants, the less anyone pays attention. Although I'd often seen him preaching in the CUSS, my only face-to-face encounter with him had been two years earlier when Katie and I approached him during our Theophily research as he was being shouted down by frat boys. This morning, though, I felt disinclined to ignore him. Feeling responsible for the festival's success, and, as if guided by some unseen hand, I pivoted in his direction. While it is uncharacteristic of me to accost street preachers publicly, my own castigation muscles being somewhat atrophied, still, some efficient bud-nipping seemed called for.

More than that, I was also operating, as if enchanted, under the influence of a powerful dream I'd had that morning. Although I teach medieval dream poetry in my lit classes —*Pearl, The Parlement of Foules, Piers Plowman*—I seldom remember my own dreams, which seem to vanish "as a cloud with the morrowtide, and as dew passing forth early." This one was no exception, though I remembered that it involved the day's festivities somehow. It left a deep, if vague, impression, mysterious and sublime, and for the past hour or so I seemed to dwell, as if in tropical sunshine, within its warm incandescence. I felt enlivened, and I was not about to let the Brother Jonases of the world cast a pall over my joy.

I strode across the bricks and positioned myself, matador-like, directly before him. I peered up into his face. He seemed to be in his early forties, and at such close range, I found myself astonished by his neatly pressed slacks, spotless shirt, and carefully combed and slicked-back black hair. It seemed counterintuitive somehow. Street preachers are not necessarily street people. Although he tried to ignore me, I could tell he was discomfited, for he turned slightly to the side as he shouted, "*Woe* unto you, you blind guides who strain at a gnat and swallow a camel!" He was clearly not used to having anyone encroach so deeply into his personal space.

"Excuse me!" I said. "Excuse me!"

He turned to the other side, still preaching, though his cadence faltered. "Woe unto ... unto you—"

"Excuse me!" I repeated.

"What?" he snapped. "What do you want? Can't you see I'm *talking*?"

"I was wondering ... how do you *know* everyone's a hypocrite? Have you actually *talked* to everyone?"

He pondered, then said, "*All* have sinned, and Isaiah says, 'Everyone is a hypocrite'—"

"But you're not Isaiah—"

"'And every mouth speaketh folly'—"

"Except yours, right? Seriously, how do you know you're not doing more harm than good? I mean, most people just look at you and say, 'If that's Christianity, I don't want any part of it!' Can't you see you alienate people?"

"The preaching of the cross is foolishness to them that perish!" he intoned. "The Lord has gifted me with the ministry of rebuke—he that hath ears to hear, let him hear."

"But *who* hears? Do you have followers? How many converts have you made this week? This month? *Who's listening?*"

He seemed to blanch for a moment. He pondered again, no doubt flipping through the selective little Bible concordance in his neatly combed head. "I am the voice of one crying in the wilderness—"

"And you're not John the Baptist either!" I said impatiently. "You're too well dressed! You know, Jesus said we could discern false prophets by their *lack* of fruit. You got fruit? You ever ask yourself what good you're actually doing? It's almost as though you're trying to convince *yourself* about faith and God, not anyone else. And just because you bray like Balaam's ass doesn't mean you speak for God."

Since that seemed as good an exit line as any, I turned and stomped up the pathway between the Student Union and Murphy Chapel toward North Quad. It took Brother Jonas all of ten seconds to resume his pious stream-of-consciousness, shouting in my direction, "Jesus said his disciples would be *hated* of all men for his name's sake, that he that endureth till the end shall be saved …"

In addition to being a self-regulating system, Brother Jonas is also a self-justifying one … and little did I know he was but a foreshadowing of things to come.

As I emerged into North Quad, I was still shaking inwardly, so much so, in fact, that I was relieved to see a familiar face, even though that face belonged to Cornelius Dunwoody.

"Bonham!" he called out cheerily. "Perfect weather, eh?" He was right. The fall colors were at their peak. The extravagant reds and golds of the towering oaks and maples that dotted the quad were breathtaking, and the ivy on the walls of academic buildings was crisping into scarlet. It was one of those chilly, sun-brimmed, crystalline autumn days, which seem, in Keats's words, to "swell the gourd, and plump the hazel shells / With a sweet kernel." Or as my father used to say, "Football weather."

"Absolutely!" I responded.

I could tell Dunwoody had been superintending the exhibitors who were setting up their booths and tents, giving them whatever unhelpfully constructive criticism he felt they needed. "Say, Dunwoody, did you see Brother Jonas in the CUSS? You think we should do something?"

"Don't pay him any attention. That's what he wants. As Proverbs says, 'Answering a fool according to his folly only makes him feel wise in his own eyes.' *You're* not thinking of confronting him, are you?"

I paused and changed the subject. "So, reviewing the troops, I see ... how's it going?"

I wish I could say that Dunwoody and I had become bosom pals during our three months of festival planning. Despite Ms. Lambert's spirited efforts, I could not bring myself to call him Neil, nor could he bring himself to call me Martin, so we tacitly agreed to maintain our relationship on a surname-only basis (especially after he saw my reaction when he once called me Marty). Still, as we worked cheek by jowl with the committee's trio of *femmes formidables*—Katie, Ms. Lambert, and Ms. Adams —Dunwoody and I became mutually tolerant allies. A sort of *pax professorum* prevailed.

The planning process itself proved far more involved than I'd expected ... wheels within wheels, as it were, to the extent that our committee soon found itself adopting Karl Marx's pithy "from each according to his ability" as something of a watchword. Katie and I, for instance, being already known to the Tri-Comms religious community due to our Theophily contacts, reached out to a couple dozen establishments, inviting them to participate by providing food, publicity for their group, and, if possible, musical performances. Twenty-one churches and other organizations had agreed to participate. Ms. Adams, we discovered, had an absolute genius for all things administrative. She filed the necessary paperwork with the university and the town; rented two hundred folding chairs, a small performance stage with a sound system, and four porta-potties. She purchased the necessary liability insurance and arranged for parking, maintenance, and cleanup. Our publicity was safely in the hands of Ms. Lambert, who prepared ads for the local papers, radio stations, and social media, and, with Katie's help, designed and printed the posters that hung in store windows and on church bulletin boards throughout the Tri-Comms area.

And Dunwoody? He made himself useful by checking in every few days to see how we were progressing. He fancied himself our supervisor, which gave him the illusion of being indispensable while remaining harmless. To his credit, he was an enthusiastic cheerleader for the entire project, and he was indeed the first committee member on the scene that morning as I arrived.

I'D LARGELY FORGOTTEN the donnybrook with Brother Jonas by the time people began strolling onto North Quad for the festivities. Shortly after eleven, the three formidable women, along with Dunwoody and me, surveyed the red-brick pathways that crisscrossed the quad as they began to bustle noisily with students, retirees, young couples with baby strollers, assorted local burghers, and a few rambunctious teenagers-at-large.

So many professors and local clergy were either in attendance or staffing the booths that the event felt like Old Home Week. Excitement was in the air ... as was the aroma of the exhibitors' exotic street foods. At the Korean Baptists' tent, for instance, Sue Park stood by a large silver chafing dish filled with *dak-kkochi*, barbequed chicken on a stick, and the church's pastor spooned out bowls of *kimchi*, repeating with each dollop, "Very spicy ... very spicy." Across from them was the Islamic Center's booth, where Naazim el-Atar stood at a steaming griddle, frying *samosas*, small vegetable-filled pastry pockets. Tall copper urns furnished Turkish coffee and tea.

The Sikhs from the nearby gurdwara offered *achari paneer tikka*, a kind of spicy fried cheese on a stick, and farther down the row, Rabbi Rachel Zeller and four members of her synagogue sold *hamantasch*—fruit-filled pastries. President Costa and Alice Mears, at the St. Athanasios Greek Orthodox tent, sold *souvlaki* (more meat on a stick), and the tiny storefront church of Iglesia de María de la Paz, Graciela's church, was selling "walking tacos"—though Graciela and Nate were out of town that weekend, making preparations for their wedding, which was to take place at Murphy Chapel in a mere two weeks.

I fully expected the Methodists to offer three-bean salad at their table, but to my surprise they provided seven varieties of ice cream with sprinkles and hot fudge. Free—or for what they appropriately called a "free-will" offering.

The festival, it seemed, was poised on the brink of success. Things were humming along so neatly that I could almost imagine, in some tiny way, how the Creator must have felt at sundown on the sixth day of creation and saw that it was good.

AT NOON, Carl Evans, our master of ceremonies, stepped onto the raised platform in the shadow of the oaks, tapped the microphone, and in his Emcee-from-*Cabaret* voice said, "*Willkommen, bien-*

venus, *bienvenidos, ahlan wa sahlan,* welcome—welcome, *everyone* to Cupperton's First Annual All-Faiths Festival!" which was greeted with polite applause. As people from all around the quad began making their way to the semicircle of folding chairs, Carl introduced the first performers of the afternoon. Six Punjabi men from the gurdwara stepped up onto the stage to give a demonstration of bhangra dancing, accompanied by a recording of boisterous Indian music—a delightfully upbeat start to the festival. The crowd loved it and showed their approval by clapping along.

As Katie, Ms. Lambert, Ms. Adams, Dunwoody, and I stood on the lawn on the west side of the quad, enjoying the colorful turbaned dancers and the pulsating music reverberating off the walls of the academic buildings, a stout, white-haired woman sauntered past. She was being led by two small dogs on leashes—fluffy, white dustmop-like canines of vague parentage. Katie, always charmed by animals, asked if she might pet them. "Of course," said the woman.

"Welcome to the festival," I said. "Where are you from?"

"The city. I'm meeting some church folks here."

Kneeling on the grass as the dogs frolicked and vied for her attention, Katie scratched their ears and asked the woman, "What are their names?"

"Smith and Wesson," she answered. "I have a Doberman at home named Glock, but I can't trust him in crowds."

Ms. Lambert, Ms. Adams, Dunwoody, and I exchanged glances.

"How adorable," exclaimed Katie. "How'd you come up with those names?"

The woman gave her a funny look. Awkwardly, I interjected, "Well, we're so glad you're here. Be sure to check out the food booths. The Bethel AME Gospel Choir is up next. Plenty of chairs ... grab a seat!"

"I'll do that," said the woman. Then, turning and glancing back toward Beetham Hall, she said suddenly, "Oh, there he is! That's my pastor." She waved and shouted, "Pastor Jack—over here!" I turned. The man waved back.

Although the moniker didn't register with me, the face was unmistakable. It was that of the buzzcut, adolescent-badgering preacher we'd seen at the Caring Zone in Baldwin the year before when we visited with Reverend Walker. Wide-eyed, Katie stared at the man as though she'd seen Grendel's Dam emerging from her cave.

"Sister Jean," he said as he approached us, "you beat us here. How's it going?" He studied me for a moment, smiled, and said, "Well, well, we meet again! I should have guessed. How providential! God always has a plan"—he extended his hand—"Jack Eisley ... "

Leaning on my parents' exhaustive etiquette training, which stressed being gracious in all circumstances, especially the most awkward, I shook his hand, and with as much composure as I could muster, I said, "I'm Martin Bonham. This is Katie Westcott ... and Neil Dunwoody, Lena Lambert, and Pam Adams. Welcome to the All-Faiths Festival. We hope you enjoy it!"

Somewhat darkly he said, "Oh, I'm sure we will. So where's your large friend, the one who was with you last year? Couldn't make it today, huh? ... Oh, and by the way"—he pointed over my shoulder—"would you mind calling off your attack dog ... the woman back there? She seems to be giving one of my flock a hard time."

I glanced again toward Beetham. A wiry red-haired figure, which I knew immediately to be Dolly De Angeli, was talking animatedly to someone, though judging by her gestures, *upbraiding* would be more accurate. Her hands flailed as if she were explaining how a wind turbine works. I excused myself and dashed in her direction.

As I drew near, I could see that Dolly was trying to convince a heavyset young man, who was wearing camouflaged fatigues and had some sort of skeletal-looking rifle strapped across his back, that he was not welcome on campus. "And what would your poor mother think—dressing up like a soldier and walking around with a gun? We got kids here! And look at the gut on ya!" She poked a bony finger in his chest. He backed up slowly, not sure how to respond to this strawberry-haired virago. "I bet you don't even have a girlfriend!"

"Hey, Dolly—Dolly!" I said as I reached her. "It's okay—it's okay."

"Hiya, hon," she said to me. "Say, tell this wise guy he can't bring a gun here."

"Listen," I said to her, "let's head back to the quad. Everybody's welcome here today, right? He's not going to hurt anybody."

"How you know that?" she said but reluctantly backed away, still glaring Medusa-like at the man.

Taking her hand gently, I said, "Come on, Dolly." Turning to the young man, I added, "You're welcome here, son. I know you're not here to make trouble." It occurred to me that never in my life had I ever called anyone "son" before. As we walked back up the quad, I said to Dolly, "It's an open-carry state. We may not like it, but there it is. The university's only policy is that people can't take guns into the buildings."

By the time we reached the others, Pastor Jack and the dog-fancier had disappeared, though Dunwoody pointed and said, "We've got *more* company," and by the way he said it, I knew it wasn't good. A group of about twenty determined-looking individuals were approaching from the direction of the museum, some carrying American flags, some signs. As they approached, I could read such slogans as "Repent or Perish," "Take Our Nation Back," "No Sharia Law," "Woke Is a Joke," and one that I couldn't help but take personally, "Professors Are the Enemy." One woman wore a "God, Guns, and Guts" T-shirt, which, for some unfathomable reason displayed a skull and crossbones, and several of the men were carrying firearms. They marched boldly across the quad, past the painted rock, past the exhibition booths, and toward the stage, casting hard glances in every direction.

They joined Pastor Jack, who was standing next to the stage.

The Sikhs had not quite finished their dance when one of the pastor's supporters managed to unplug whatever device was providing the music. The dancers stopped and seemed to hang in midair momentarily like marionettes. Pastor Jack, with a wide, indulgent smile, strode up onto the stage and waved his hand back and forth at them, as though sweeping crumbs from a table. He approached the microphone. Several of the gun-toters closed ranks behind him, and men with flags stood on each side. "Is this on?" his voice boomed out over the quad ... causing some feedback at first. "That better? Can you all hear me? Good! God's peace, everyone! We've come here today to share a much-needed word from the Lord!"

I was trembling. Ms. Adams turned to me and said, "Martin, I just realized ... I didn't even think of hiring security!"

Pastor Jack's voice thundered from the speakers, "We've come to your All-Faiths Festival with one mission today—to testify to the fact that there's only *one* faith—the true gospel of Jesus Christ. Who's gonna give me an amen?"

Dunwoody asked, "Who are these people?"

"You don't *know*?" I was astonished. "... The Caring Zone, Baldwin—where you sent Reverend Walker last year! You mean you've never been there?"

He was quiet for a moment. "No. I just ... I had no idea."

Pastor Jack preached on. "I suspect many of you are Christians, or at least *think* you are, but you need to ask yourselves if you've really been filled with the Holy Spirit and had a genuine personal experience with the one true Lord and Savior, Jesus Christ, the Son of God. But I can also see from just looking at many of you that you don't know the Lord, so I'm here tell you that no matter what kind of cult you belong to or what your skin color is or what god you pray to, your job right now is to repent and let Jesus into your heart. Today!"

Suddenly, a crackling of what sounded like gunfire echoed among the brick facades of North Quad. I jumped. My heart seemed to stop. Spinning around, I realized it was only teenagers setting off a string of firecrackers somewhere near the library, but it was enough to make Pastor Jack's followers grip their guns tighter and scan the area with dark scowls.

"Katie," I said quietly, "call the police."

"Right, M.B." She took out her phone and walked a few paces off.

"Thank you," Paster Jack shouted in the direction of the teenagers, who were now scurrying away, "for that rousing Fourth of July welcome! God bless America, everyone! Amen! Now, as I was saying, I know I wasn't invited to be here today" —he paused, looked at his followers behind him, and added in an ironic tone, "My invitation must have gotten lost in the mail!" The followers chuckled. "But you see, I realized, I got a First Amendment right to speak, just like all of you, and I brought my friends here so they could exercise their *Second* Amendment right to protect my *First* Amendment right. Ha! That's the way it works, right? So, it's like this, folks, even if anyone tries to interfere, one way or another, *y'all* gonna meet Jesus today! Ha-ha!" He had an ominous way of drawing out the word *y'all*. His adherents nodded and chuckled again.

With a Bible in one hand, I thought, and a gun in the other, Pastor Jack and his flock were threatening us with both. I recalled Reverend Walker talking about those who base their faith in their animosity toward anyone different from them. The challenge, he said, is in responding to them without becoming like them.

Katie returned and whispered, "The police say they can't do anything unless they actually threaten violence. They said they know Pastor Jack and he's not a problem, but they'll try to send someone over."

"This seems threatening to me," I said. I sidled over to Ms. Lambert and Dunwoody. "Lena, you've studied peace and resistance movements. Any ideas?"

She pondered for a moment, scanning the quad and watching the local folks starting to scatter—thinking with their feet, as my father used to say. Then her gaze rested on Pastor Jack. I could see her eyes narrow. "It may not work," she said, "but something from Saint Pete comes to mind. Okay, huddle up, everyone." And she pulled us into a tight circle and began to outline a plan. *The* plan.

Pastor Jack rumbled on: "When I saw your posters, I thought right away of the very first commandment. Remember that one? It says, 'Thou shalt have no other gods before me.' Sound familiar? So even *God* says there's no such thing as 'all faiths'; there's just *one* faith. You know, even our money says, 'One Nation Under God,' not 'One Nation Under *Lots* of Gods.' This nation will only become one when we've converted everybody to the God who sent Jesus Christ to die on the cross for you and me. So ... later, we're gonna have an altar call—we're not leaving till we've saved some lost souls. I'm serious. No matter what kind of pagan religion you're mixed up in, Jesus wants to save you. Can I get an amen?" His followers obliged.

By this point, many of the locals had fled, though a few

seemed too intimidated to budge. A couple of teenagers lingered to see what would happen next.

"Okay," said Ms. Lambert after she finished detailing the plan to us. "You got it?"

"Yes," I said as we broke our huddle.

"Got it!" said Dunwoody, and he shuffled off.

"Brilliant," said Katie, who then jogged over to Tyrell and whispered in his ear. He, in turn, went from choir member to choir member, whispering to each. Ms. Adams jogged down the line of booths and tables and shared the plan with the exhibitors, while Dunwoody conferred with some faculty members who then conferred with some students.

Within a minute, the five of us regrouped and joined hands —Katie on my right and Ms. Lambert on my left with Dunwoody and Ms. Adams beyond her. Tyrell and the entire Bethel AME Zion Gospel Choir strung out to the right of Katie, and soon, professors, students, seminarians, exhibitors, and a couple of dozen others had joined, hand-in-hand, as we started to encircle the stage.

Pastor Eisley kept on going. "Yeah, just gather 'round, everybody, that's right. So, how does God want his people to deal with foreigners and their religions? I'll tell you. Deuteronomy says, 'When thou art come into the land which the Lord thy God giveth thee'—and you know God's talking about America too—'thou shalt not learn to do after the abominations of those other nations,' and 'Ye shall hew down the graven images of their gods and destroy the names of them out of that place.' Jeremiah says those idols are 'like scarecrows in a cucumber field.' ..."

Ms. Lambert's plan was simple. It contained just three brief directives: "Join hands. Keep silent. Pray with love."

For myself, I was too distracted to pray anything but the single word *help*, but I was at least able to tune out Pastor

Eisley's harangue as he launched into some sermon about Nadab and Abihu being consumed by fire for an unworthy sacrifice. I glanced around the circle.

Even many who hadn't heard the plan—like Carl and Sara Evans and Dr. el-Atar—understood what was going on and joined in. I spotted Dolly De Angeli holding the hand of microbiology professor Bill Fredericks ... and there was Dr. Kapule and Dr. Dr. Barnes and Sue Park and Tom Fouchee and Rabbi Rachel Zeller ... and even President Costa and Alice Mears, both of whom had rushed over from the St. Athanasios booth. Soon, the line of hand-holders had grown so large that it managed to link up behind the stage, completing the circle—a ring of silent prayer. Most oddly of all, Brother Jonas was there too, on the far side of the ring. Curious.

I squeezed Ms. Lambert's hand on my left and Katie's on the right, and they squeezed mine back. We prayed. Knowing how Ms. Lambert insists on praying with her eyes open, I lifted my own gaze up into the radiant, blue autumn sky above me, which seemed to go on forever. It was so clear, so peaceful. I felt I didn't need to pray for help at that point, for all the help one could ask for was already present in that glorious sky. It was itself a prayer. The voice filling the quad became only a distant buzz.

AND THEN I REMEMBERED.

My dream.

It flooded back so clearly that it was like dreaming it again.

First, I recalled floating upward. As if flying. Up and up. When I looked down, I was fifty, maybe a hundred feet above North Quad. A festival—our festival—was in progress. From my dream perspective, I could see the square-roofed tents, the rectangle of the performers' stage, the specks of the folding chairs. From above, I saw the stately oaks dotting the quad, and in the middle was the pinpoint of the painted boulder, the university's memorial landmark, seeming like the hub of a wheel ... a wheel that began to turn slowly. I remembered feeling suddenly disoriented and a bit nauseated.

As I floated higher in the dream, I could see the crowds of people below, with all their faiths and ethnicities, certainties and struggles, and as I rose, they began to cluster together oddly, like water droplets in a cloud ... a cloud that shifted from place to place, first in one direction and then in another, sad and aimless somehow, and the sound they made was like the murmur of a distant, crowded stadium in which thousands of voices, rather than cheering, were praying aloud, pleading and sorrowful, or was it joyful and praising? I couldn't tell. So far removed was I that the sound of their voices was nothing more than a sort of tidal surge—softer, louder, softer, louder. A cold wind enveloped me, and as blue air turned to black, I realized that I wasn't floating over the quad at all, but I was watching, from thousands of miles away, a cold, swirling, blue-and-white, radiant planet spinning in the dark.

That was the end.

As I stood there, still gazing up into the endless blue sky, I recounted the dream to myself again and again to make sure I'd remember it, until it occurred to me that everything was quiet. No distant buzz. No hostile voice boomed over the loudspeakers. I blinked and glanced at Katie, then at Lena. I wasn't even sure how much time had passed, but Pastor Jack and his flock were shuffling off, disgruntled apparently, and heading back to their cars in the lots behind the Student Stores and the museum. Even Smith and Wesson were waddling whitely off into the distance.

We unclasped hands. "Hold it. What happened?" I asked Katie.

"Did you fall asleep? My dad falls asleep when he prays."

"Maybe. No," I said, "not exactly ... but my mind was elsewhere. What's going on?"

"Well, Pastor Jack was stymied. Nobody responded to his altar call. In fact, nobody responded to anything. We just stood there silently. How could you not hear him saying all that stuff about 'faithless and perverse' and 'hardness of heart'?"

"Well, I was trying for a higher perspective, I suppose."

Katie just shook her head. She then turned to Tyrell and said. "Okay, Ty, I think now's the time. Let's go! Quick."

Tyrell pointed to the right and the left, singling out his choir members and indicating that they should head toward the stage, and since Katie herself had become a member of the Bethel Choir, she followed. After they'd filed onto the platform, Tyrell raised his hands for the downbeat, and they rocketed into a song that, judging from its much-repeated refrain, was called "Every Praise to Our God"—with Kyeesha Reed performing one of the solos.

Lena, Dunwoody, and I were still standing shoulder to shoulder. I turned to Lena and asked, "So ... Saint Peter?"

She gave me a blank look.

"You know, you said something from Saint Peter gave you the idea."

"Oh, right. No, not Saint Peter ... Saint Pete—one of my other heroes—Saint Pete Seeger, the folksinger. Do you remember what he inscribed on his banjo?" I shrugged. "He wrote, 'This machine surrounds hate and forces it to surrender.' That seemed as good a plan as any."

We were silent for a time. As the choir began its second number, Dunwoody leaned toward me. "You know, Bonham, this reminds me of that verse where Jesus talks about hypocrisy and whited sepulchers. You could use this in one of your Theophily classes sometime, eh? It's just all too easy to *think* we love God when it's really our own presumption and pride—our religiosity—that we're in love with ... and not just this Pastor Jack, but all of us."

"It's funny ... I was discussing whited sepulchers with someone just this morning," I said. "It's as though faith is a razor-sharp sword, and we need to be careful which end we hand to others. How about we teach that class together?"

WITHIN HALF AN HOUR, the festivities had returned to their previous level of bustle and busyness—and again, I saw that it was good. People had formed lines at the food booths, and the Bethel Choir was wrapping up its performance with their signature encore, "You Are Welcome in This Place." Katie beamed from the choir's second row.

Dunwoody had drifted away and was chatting with some students by the boulder, and Ms. Adams, now sporting a small white-lace bonnet, was greeting people at her church's booth. (I would never have guessed that she was a Mennonite.)

Dolly De Angeli, I noted with interest, was in a cozy tête-à-tête with microbiology professor Dr. Bill Fredericks, who was back at his post, serving warm doughnuts and hot coffee at the Word of Life Pentecostal booth.

I asked Lena, "Do you know ... is Bill Fredericks married?"

"Widowed, I think. Why?"

"Just wondering."

And, finally, one lone police officer strolled up the pathway toward me, holding *souvlaki* in his hand. "So, did you call the police?" he asked. "What's up? Everything all right?"

I nodded. "Yes, everything's all right."

Minutes later, as four young women from Sue Park's Church we're singing hymns in Korean, I felt a tap on my shoulder. I turned—and was stunned. It was Brother Jonas. I'd only seen him close up at ground level once before, and he was shorter than I remembered, less imposing without a bench beneath him. In one hand he held his Bible and in the other, a triple-scoop ice cream cone, which was dripping pink and blue streaks down his forearm and staining the rolled cuff of his neatly pressed white shirt, though he seemed gleefully oblivious.

"Hey, again," he said in a normal tone—normal for most people, though oddly subdued for him. "The Methodists are giving away free ice cream ... I got Superman. I'll get you some if you want. And just so you know, don't let Jack Eisley bug you. What a stupid stunt! It was rude. They should have known it would turn people off! And guns! Unbelievable! I've known him for years, and he doesn't know the first thing about evangelism ... and he doesn't know the Bible as well as he likes to pretend. Just thought you'd want to know. And say, I've been asking around about you, and from what I hear, you're all right. You all did good today with that prayer-circle thing. Glad I could be here!" He paused and looked at me with a wide-eyed, sincere expression. "Say, you know, we ought to get coffee sometime. See ya." And he walked away.

By three o'clock, I was finally alone. Seated on a folding chair, relaxing and relishing some *souvlaki* of my own, I reflected on the bizarre and tumultuous events of the day. A profound weariness had overtaken me. Rarely have I experienced such a wide range of exhausting emotions in such a short time.

A group of orange-robed Hindus from the temple in Ware, accompanying themselves on a pump harmonium, began chanting a kirtan from the stage, and its melodic repetitions had a soothing, almost hypnotic, effect. I was about to drop my chin to my chest and shut my eyes when a familiar figure emerged on the pathway beside Beetham. It was the Reverend Joseph Clark, my old Episcopalian buddy from the Forum on Faith. He wore his usual black tunic and clerical collar and looked voluminous as always—what G. K. Chesterton might have looked like dressed as a penguin.

He walked briskly in my direction, his face beaming. This time, the button on his tunic read "CERTIFIED EMOTIONAL SUPPORT PRIEST." Reluctantly, I stood. Grasping my hand energetically, he gushed, "Doc Bonham, my good man, great to see you! So sorry to be late—it's an hour's drive from the city—but what a glorious event! 'How good and pleasant when God's people live together in unity!' Right?" With his other hand, he thumped my shoulder vigorously several times. "Right? Right? Am I right?"

I grinned and said wearily, "You're right."

With a glowing, paternal smile, he scanned the food tents, the young families, the retirees, the rambunctious teenagers, the Hindu chanters—taking it all in, he nodded his approval and, with eyes twinkling, said, "Hope I haven't missed anything!"

CHAPTER 13

INTO THE LABYRINTH

Whoever possesses the present moment possesses God.
Whoever possesses the present moment possesses everything.
The present moment is enough.
Don't let anything trouble you.
—*Teresa of Ávila, 1515–1582 (attr.)*

"So, Bonham," Dunwoody abruptly breaks the silence as we sit with Lena on a bench in the arboretum on that chilly late afternoon in October, "tell me, just how do *you* answer Katie's questions?"

THE THREE OF us had taken a break—sought refuge, really—from Graciela and Nate's wedding reception—not that the event was in any way unsatisfactory or one champagne bubble less than wholly effervescent, but amid all the flashing lights of the disco ball and the young people laughing and dancing to the DJ's *thump-da-thump-thump*, we had begun to feel our age.

After exchanging a few quick glances, Lena, Dunwoody, and I ducked covertly through the sliding glass doors of the Banquet Hall's rear balcony, feeling not unlike teenagers cutting class.

A minute later, we were strolling aimlessly down the sloped path behind the hall toward the arboretum, where we made our way along the winding pathways and eventually settled ourselves on the stone bench next to the brick-paved labyrinth. Even from that vantage point, through the damp trees and thin mist, we could make out the indistinct, joyous chatter from the hall above, as if from a radio in a distant room of an empty house, playing neither music nor words, but a sort of happy, cadenced hum.

The late afternoon's lowering sky suited my mood—"The gloaming spreads her waning shade," as Byron wrote, and with that thought, the breeze seemed to grow a tad chillier. I shivered.

Although delighted by Lena's appointment to the Bodleian, I grieved nonetheless, so much so that Alice Mears had suggested several weeks earlier that I might be experiencing Elizabeth Kübler-Ross's Five Stages of Grief. Since June, I'd passed through Denial ("Lena, you're joking!"), Anger ("Why didn't you *tell* me you were applying? And why did you tell Dunwoody first?"), and Bargaining ("Perhaps President Costa might consent to a raise to keep you here ..."). By the day of the All-Faiths Festival, I'd hit Depression ("Who's going to laugh at my obscure literary allusions?").

Lena had chided, "Martin, I'm *not* dying! We'll stay in touch. It'll be okay!"

I didn't reach the fifth and final stage—Acceptance—until the day of Graciela and Nate's wedding, or, to be precise, until Lena, Dunwoody, and I were sitting on that bench in the arboretum. When I said to Lena, "You'll have to title your next book *The Adders of Oxford*," she responded, "Trust me, I'll dedicate it to you and Neil." At that moment, I achieved Acceptance. I would miss her, yes, but I still had time—a couple of months, in fact—for an extended waving of the handkerchief. And I knew, as she said, it would be okay.

———

THE WEDDING itself had been dazzling. Graciela was beautiful beyond belief. The ceremony in Murphy Chapel, conducted in both English and Spanish, was a modest affair with only about fifty people in attendance, mostly younger, and since Graciela's father had died several years earlier, she'd asked me to walk her down the aisle. It was an unexpected and wholly undeserved honor for which I was solemnly grateful. To the strains of "La Paloma," played tenderly on piano by Tyrell, I slow-walked Graciela, her hand in the crook of my arm, to the altar, where I gently placed that hand in Nate's. I then returned to the pew, where I sat next to Graciela's mother, who, as an older version of Graciela, seemed also to be knit from the same combination of deep smiles, serenity, and soulfulness.

Never have I seen a more resplendent bride ... a sort of heart-stopping shimmer radiated from her as she stood in the half-light of the chapel's candles, her eyes flashing and her black hair sparkling beneath the white lace of the veil.

The only hiccup in the ceremony was when the dangling sleeve of the priest's chasuble briefly caught fire during the candle exchange, causing gasps throughout the chapel and eliciting a brisk emergency response from the ever-efficient Katie, who was one of Graciela's bridesmaids, with the help of a young acolyte stationed in the wings. After the priest had been successfully put out, everything hummed along smoothly, if a bit smokily, and Graciela's smile as she and Nate stepped quickly back up the aisle at the end of the service was more than enough to make any lingering apprehension vanish.

Afterward, as Lena and I paced slowly across South Quad toward the reception at the Banquet Hall, Lena linked her arm in mine and quoted, "'The fairest creature that ever he saw, without measure.'"

"... is from what?" I asked.

"*The Wedding of Sir Gawain and Dame Ragnelle.* Do you remember when you first came into the library decades ago and asked me what I knew about that poem?"

"Of course. And you told me that you hadn't been invited."

"Well, today we were." She squeezed my arm.

———

"So, BONHAM," Dunwoody says as we sit by the labyrinth that chilly late afternoon, "tell me, just how do *you* answer Katie's questions?"

Although I've pondered that often, I've never been asked to verbalize a response before, so I take a few moments to muster my thoughts.

"Oh, I've learned so much from everyone," I begin. "When Katie first posed those questions to me—it's been, what, more than two years now?—I began asking myself, What does *love* mean? If the key to loving God is loving others, what does love even look like? How do I ordinarily show people that I truly, deeply love them? The answer dawned on me slowly, though it was surprisingly simple. How do I love others? I pay attention to them. Close attention. I try to be present—fully present—to focus on them, be aware of their concerns, ask questions.

"But unlike my friends, God is *always* present, always right here. So, as often as I can, I remind myself of that Presence, to pay attention to it, to open myself to it, and when I do, I start talking. Just naturally. Usually, it's a sort of narration in my head, as if to say, 'Here I am,' 'This is what I'm thinking,' 'These are the important things for me right now,' 'What do you think?' 'What's important to you?' It becomes a dialogue. It's prayer.

"Even when I'm silent, when I'm not narrating in my head, it's still prayer because I'm aware that I'm never alone. God said to the psalmist, 'Be still and know that I am God.' Even when my life is filled with activity and chaos, I can usually find that still place inside. Perhaps I love God more in those silences because that is when I give my fullest attention. It's contemplation. Resting in Presence. I find great hope in that line from the fourteenth-century mystic and poet Richard Rolle ... he says, 'Me and my loving—Love makes them both one.'

"As far as Katie's second question, '*When* do you most love God?' it has only one possible answer: the present moment. It's all we have. Whether I'm paying attention or talking or being still, right now is my only chance. As Teresa of Ávila said, 'Whoever possesses the present moment possesses God.'

"I also love my friends by telling them how grateful I am for their kindnesses and attention and love, and for who they are. With God, I'm grateful for ... well, for everything. That's part of my inner narration. I wake each morning and think, 'Thank you for this air, this sky, this food, this breath, this life.' Thomas Traherne says we should think of all those things as 'Celestial Joys' as if we 'were among the angels.' And, of course, I trust my friends. I know they want only the best for me—and who could I possibly trust more than God?

"Does all that amount to loving God with all my heart, mind, soul, and strength? I don't know, but it's the best I can do. And anyway, I wonder whether that verse isn't more of a promise than a commandment, a foreshadowing of things to come, when, with no distractions at all, we're fully present with that Presence."

Dunwoody nods slowly but remains silent. Lena lightly places her hand on my arm. We sit there quietly for several minutes, being present, as the muffled thrumming of the reception behind us mixes with the rustle of the cold wind in the trees. The temperature continues to drop in the deepening twilight. And somehow my gratitude deepens as well.

I shiver and say, "You know, here ... the labyrinth ... this is my favorite place on campus."

Lena, ever the wellspring of trivia, says, "It's a full-size reproduction of the one on the floor of Chartres Cathedral ... thirteenth century ... you knew that, right?"

"No, I didn't." Then I ask, "Dunwoody, have you ever walked the labyrinth?"

"Never occurred to me. I thought it was a game."

"Well," says Lena, "it *is* a game in a way, but it's also a meditation. It's not a maze though. A labyrinth has just one path ... it's convoluted ... four short, straight passages, and thirty-one curving ones, but you can't get lost. And there's a destination. A center. You walk it slowly, following the lighter-colored paving stones, winding in the direction they lead you —eleven layers of pathway. Altogether, the path is nine hundred feet long, almost a sixth of a mile—folding back-and-forth upon itself, loop after loop. I read somewhere that that's about three hundred and sixty steps for the average person, as many steps as there are degrees in a circle, about as many steps as there are days in the year. If you live to be ninety, that's one footstep for every three months of your life. Four steps for every year, one passing season with each step."

We sit there, silent, pondering her words. I've never seen Dunwoody so attentive.

She continues, "Labyrinths have been used for meditation

for centuries. As you walk, you try to imagine God walking beside you ... and in front of you, beside you, behind you. You think about the twists and turns your life has taken, about what has happened through the years and all that will happen in the years to come ... you think about inevitability and time passing. Each U-turn in the path is like a major turning in your own life. And you pray.

"The entrance to the labyrinth faces east." She points. "And the final straight path to the center does too. That's because east is the direction of the rising sun and, traditionally, the direction of Jerusalem. But it also faces the most beautiful part of our arboretum, the lily garden. I'm sure the gardener planned it this way, making sure that lilies of one kind or another would be in bloom much of the year. I love the lilies. First are the white Easter lilies, then the Asiatics and Turk's caps, the speckled hybrids and trumpets. Then in midsummer, there are the yellow daylilies and the white Madonnas, and finally, in the fall, the bright orange tiger lilies, which I love most of all. The Easter lily is the symbol for Jesus, of course, but in a way, they all are—the trumpets, the Madonnas, and the tiger lilies ... 'Christ the tiger,' as Eliot said. They represent beauty and variety and constancy—and an unfailing hope that never grows weary, because Jesus—and our goal of becoming more like him—is the path itself. 'I am the way,' he said. And do you remember who he said that to? To Thomas, the doubter, but also the one who said he would follow Jesus anywhere.

"At the center, over there, you can see a small circle in the bricks with six scallop shapes around the edge. That represents heaven ... life's journey complete. Jesus is there too—the companion of your journey and the journey's end as well. Scholars disagree about the significance of the scallops. But to me, it's simple. It's a flower with six petals, a lily. To be in the middle is to be where the pure nectar is, the very heart of God."

There are no lilies blooming now, just a few bare stalks, but I can remember how they looked in all their brilliance, month after month, waving in the sunlight, and I can dimly make out the scalloped paving stones in the center. We sit there, each thinking our own thoughts, hardly breathing, not wanting to spoil the moment.

Finally I ask, "So, what are we waiting for?"

"It's too dark," Dunwoody grumbles. "I can't see." But then his tone softens. He says to Lena, "Maybe if you help ..."

Rising from the bench, she says, "We'll help each other ... hand to shoulder. Martin, you first." Dunwoody and I stand. Lena places Dunwoody's hand, from behind, on her shoulder and then places her hand on mine.

Slowly, in the twilight, we enter the labyrinth and begin our long, careful shambling along the lighter colored bricks, watching them slip beneath our feet, step by step. First, a short, straight path, then, to the left, a curving quarter circle. A U-turn to the right and another quarter circle. We say nothing. I try to imagine that fourth presence here, and I pray silently, if a tad self-consciously, but earnestly all the same—"Here I am; I am present; I am grateful"—as the days and the seasons slip under our feet, another and another and another.

And this is precisely where our story ends—and Graciela's and Nate's, and Katie's and Tyrell's, and Kyeesha's and Carl's and Dolly's and all the others', and yours too, reader—with Lena Lambert, Cornelius Dunwoody, and me, Martin Bonham, along with an unseen Fourth, still in the middle of our respective journeys, knowing how far we've come, uncertain of how far we've yet to go. The love of that Fourth impels us forward, season by season, step by step, toward the Center where I suspect all of us—and the Fourth—will embrace ... and be embraced.

The journey to the Center may be more arduous than any of us can imagine or more joyous than any of us can hope for. Perhaps both.

The journey to the Center may take either more steps than we expect or fewer.

But either way, there will be exactly the right number of steps to get there.

Notes on the Text
(BY DR. MARTIN BONHAM)

In his role as publisher at Strawberry Hill, Horace Walpole (1717–1797) once requested that his friend, the poet Thomas Gray (1716–1771), provide annotations for an edition of his poems, to which Gray responded, "If a thing cannot be understood without notes, it had better not be understood at all." Gray eventually relented and provided the notes.

I too was averse to annotating the references in the foregoing narrative, but Katie Westcott, who has always felt that I lean too heavily on literary allusions, insisted that such annotations might be helpful to the reader. I said, "Don't people *read*? Shouldn't they already *know* these books and authors? Don't they *trust* me?"

She said, "Some will, sure, but others will think you're throwing in quotes just to sound smart."

"So, you're accusing me of inserting 'the scantlings of learning to dignify my book,' as Austin Dobson once wrote?"

"See, you're doing it again! How do readers know you're not just making this stuff up?"

I resented the implication. "I *never* make stuff up," I replied.

"Then prove it," she said.

So, having argued myself into a corner, I, like Thomas Gray, hereby grudgingly provide the sources for the quotations and allusions in this book (at least all those not sufficiently explained in the text). *Note*: If you suffer from insomnia, I recommend you turn to this section and begin reading slowly and with great attention.

CHAPTER 1: THE DEPARTMENT OF THEOPHILY

Epigraph: In the valley of this restless mind: This is the opening quatrain of an anonymous fifteenth-century Middle English poem, "Qui Amore Langueo" ("Because I Languish for Love"). The poem's Latin title is a quotation from the Vulgate's rendering of the Song of Songs, or Canticles, 2:5. It can be found in *The Oxford Book of English Mystical Verse* (1921) and other anthologies.

buttonholed by that raven: Edgar Allan Poe (1809–1849), "The Raven" (1845). (You didn't really need me to point that out, I suspect.)

Florio's translation of Montaigne: John Florio (1553–1625) was the first to translate the *Essais* of Michel de Montaigne (1533–1592) into English; the last volume of his translation was published in 1603. Montaigne coined the term *essay*, which in French means "an attempt"—which, in Montaigne's case, meant the attempt to grasp all the aspects of whatever subject he was writing about. Some scholars theorize that Florio may have written some of Shakespeare's plays, which is complete nonsense. Don't get me started.

Religious Poets of the Fifteenth Century: That is, poets whom no one's ever heard of, like John Audelay (died c. 1426); Henry Bradshaw (c. 1450–1513); John Walton, who did a verse translation of Boethius (first part of the fifteenth century); and a host of anonymous bards, like the one quoted in the epigraph to this chapter. I love those old poems.

wandering lonely as a cloud: If you're not familiar with "I Wandered Lonely as a Cloud" (better known as "Daffodils") by William Wordsworth (1770–1850), then your secondary school education failed you. You should get your money back. It was published in 1807 and is perhaps Wordsworth's most anthologized poem.

sloughs of despond ("swamps of despair"): An allusion, of course, to *Pilgrim's Progress* by John Bunyan (1628–1688). It is in such a swamp that the main character, Christian, finds himself sinking because of the weight of his sins. In the US, by the way, *slough* is pronounced as to rhyme with *clue*, while in the UK it rhymes with *cow*. This information might come in handy the next time you use the word in conversation.

the Great Commandment: Matthew 22:37–39 and Mark 12:29–31 paraphrased.

we love God because God first loved us: 1 John 4:19 paraphrased.

religious pantomime: From Friedrich Nietzsche (1844–1900), *Human, All Too Human: A Book for Free Spirits* (1879), Aphorism 396. Katie found this in the Penguin edition, which I once saw her extract from her backpack. At that time, she was friends with Rowan Wayrich, who'd been a German major at Oberlin and, I suspect, gave her that book.

beautiful madness: From John Ruskin (1819–1900), "Traffic," in the collection *The Crown of Wild Olive* (1866). This lecture was delivered at the town hall in Bradford, England, April 21, 1864, and what it has to say about commerce, aesthetics, and morality is as relevant today as it was then. Why Ruskin isn't read anymore I will never understand.

as an honeycomb: Proverbs 16:24 KJV.

The Fire of Love and *The Doctrine of the Heart*: The first is a major work by English mystic Richard Rolle (c. 1300–1349), who was known as "The Hermit of Hampole"; and the second is an anonymous Middle English translation of a Latin treatise; the Latin original dates from the early thirteenth century.

Sartre ... adrift in a rowboat: I heard this somewhere in my remote past. Life is not long enough to track down every last reference, though the quotation sounds as if it should be from *Being and Nothingness* (1943) by Jean-Paul Sartre (1905–1980). Otherwise, content yourself with Sartre's other famous quote about rowboats: "Only the person who isn't rowing has time to rock the boat." I frankly don't know where that one comes from either. Maybe Katie is right and I just make these things up.

starry welkin and the Bowl of Night: The first is Shakespeare, *Midsummer Night's Dream* (c. 1595), act 3, scene 2; the second is from the opening line of "The Rubaiyat of Omar Khayyam" (1859) as famously translated by Edward FitzGerald (1809–1883). Even if you haven't read the latter, you are certainly familiar with many of its oft-quoted lines: "A Jug of Wine, a Loaf of Bread, and Thou" and "The Moving Finger writes: and, having writ, / Moves on."

perverse and crooked generation ... the Lord thy God is a consuming fire ... who have forsaken the right way ... if thou are lukewarm: Respectively, Philippians 2:15, Deuteronomy 4:24, 2 Peter 2:15, Revelation 3:16, all KJV or as recollected by Brother Jonas.

Somewhere Kierkegaard tells the story: Søren Kierkegaard (1813–1855), *Works of Love* (1847).

It's the most wonderful time of the year: This ever-popular, perennial Christmas song was first recorded by Andy Williams in 1963 on his record *The Andy Williams Christmas Album*. The song was written by Edward Pola and George Wyle. Wyle, Ms. Lambert informs me, also wrote the famous theme for the

Gilligan's Island television show. That bit of trivia should come in handy next Christmas when you're driving to grandma's and hear "It's the Most Wonderful Time" on the radio. Life is never dull with interesting facts on hand.

cover all the spiritual territory that the seminary doesn't: Of his time as a student at Oxford, Thomas Traherne (1637–1674) wrote, "There I saw that Logic, Ethics, Physics, Metaphysics, Geometry, Astronomy, Poesy, Medicine, Grammar, Music, Rhetoric, all kinds of Arts, Trades, and Mechanisms that adorned the world pertained to felicity; ... I saw into the nature of the Sea, the Heavens, the Sun, the Moon and Stars, the Elements, Minerals, and Vegetables—all which appeared like the King's Daughter, all glorious within" (*Centuries of Meditations*, III, 36). Although Traherne wrote that book in the early 1670s, it was not published until 1908. He is, indeed, an inspiration for the Department of Theophily.

saboteurs chucking our sabots: The word *saboteur* comes from the French *sabot* ("shoe") and refers to factory workers in days long past who would protest their working conditions by throwing their wooden shoes into the giant gears of the factory's machinery—an act of *sabotage*.

We are only as strong as we are united: From J. K. Rowling (b. 1965), *Harry Potter and the Goblet of Fire* (2000), chapter 37.

Fortune favored the bold: From an old Latin proverb: *audentes Fortuna iuvat*. I confess I like to throw in Latin and French phrases in part to justify having paid for a college education.

Samson between his pillars: Judges 16:29–30.

deserved the compliment of rational opposition: From Jane Austen (1775–1817), *Sense and Sensibility* (1811), chapter 36.

Deep into that darkness peering: From Poe, "The Raven" (again).

CHAPTER 2: THE FORUM ON FAITH

Epigraph: Our good Lord answered to all the questions and doubts: From Julian of Norwich's *Revelations of Divine Love*, chapter XV. Julian (1343–c. 1416) was an English anchoress and mystic who received a series of mystical revelations on May 8, 1373, at the age of thirty, while she was stricken with a life-threatening illness.

stout Cortez: John Keats (1795–1821), "On First Looking into Chapman's Homer" (1816).

Greeks bearing gifts: Virgil (70–19 BCE), *Aeneid*, II, 49.

Wycliffe's translation: If you can make sense of Chaucer's Middle English, then I highly recommend Wycliffe's translations of portions of the Bible. There are some astonishing turns of phrase, many of which often found their way into the Tyndale and King James Bibles.

Basil of Caesarea: Basil of Caesarea (c. 329–379 CE), also known as Basil the Great, discusses the possibility of animals in heaven in *The Hexaemeron* ("The Six Days [of Creation]"). As Dunwoody said, he was on the negative side.

Tertullian: Tertullian (155–240 CE), *A Treatise on the Soul*. Also on the negative side.

man and beast Thou savest: Psalm 36:6 *Young's Literal Translation*. Wycliffe renders this, "Thou schalt saue men and beestis." Who can argue with "beasties" being saved?

God will unite all things: Ephesians 1:10 ESV.

tame animals in heaven: C. S. Lewis (1898–1963) in *The Problem of Pain* (1940), chapter 9. Lewis includes an interesting reflection on the immortality of animals. Although largely unconvinced by arguments in favor of animals in heaven, Lewis allows the distant possibility that some animals, tamed and deeply loved by humans, might be present. He does indeed conjecture that hell for people might well be heaven for mosquitos.

God is love: 1 John 4:8, the same in nearly every English translation.

all shall be well: This is by far the most famous quotation from Julian's *Revelations of Divine Love*; it occurs in chapter 27.

CHAPTER 3: THE BANQUET

Epigraph: If, my Lord, a kiss signifies peace: From *Conceptions of the Love of God* (1577) by Teresa of Ávila (1515–1582). This minor work is her commentary on Canticles. Teresa boldly used images of romantic love to discuss our relationship with God.

like David ... dancing before the Lord: 2 Samuel 6:14.

languorous ecstasy: From a poem by Paul Verlaine (1844–1896), "C'est l'extase langoureuse," in his 1872 collection *Romances sans paroles*. Does anyone aside from French majors read Verlaine anymore, or has he been entirely overshadowed by Rimbaud?

Time's wingèd chariot: Andrew Marvell (1621–1678), "To His Coy Mistress," published posthumously in 1681, though he probably wrote it when he was in his forties.

were the river but a cup less quick: The poet Moro referred to here is *not* Maurizio Moro, the sixteenth-century madrigal writer, but rather Craig Moro (b. 1953), a dear friend of the author. The poem quoted is from an untitled chapbook of student poetry and art, dated 1971.

The Flyting: I can proudly say that I gave this name to the campus literary magazine years ago. I was trying to encourage students in my writing class to write with more "edge," to stop being so tentative, so poetic, and, instead, to express what they felt. I told them about the medieval custom of "flyting," that is, the exchange of poetic insults. Our word *flouting* is a linguistic descendant. Before a duel, for instance (as in Rostand's *Cyrano de Bergerac*), the opponents would insult each other with increasingly vituperative and creative epithets. It is not unlike the African American custom of "the dozens," in which inventive insults are exchanged, often starting with "your mama ..." We thought the name was perfect, hinting at both poetic chutzpah as well as flights of poetic fancy.

Gandalf before the Battle of Helm's Deep: J. R. R. Tolkien (1892–1973), *The Lord of the Rings, The Two Towers* (1954), book III, chapter 7.

untamed barbaric yawp: Walt Whitman (1819–1892): "I too am not a bit tamed, I too am untranslatable, / I sound my barbaric yawp over the roofs of the world," from "Song of Myself" (1855), 52.

O for your kiss! For your love: As mentioned by Graciela, she is quoting Marcia Falk (b. 1946), *Song of Songs: A New Translation (Love Lyrics from the Bible)* (1993). I've given this volume to numerous young couples as a wedding gift. Inspiration indeed!

Oh si él me besara con ósculos: Canticles 1:2, Santa Biblia Reina-Valera.

little foxes: Song of Solomon 2:15, paraphrase.

One's whole life for a kiss: Graciela is paraphrasing the poem by Sufi Muslim poet and mystic Jalal ad-Din Rumi (1207–1273), "I would like to kiss you," which she most likely found in *The Essential Rumi*, translated by poet Coleman Barks (b. 1937).

Porque fuerte es como la muerte el amor: Canticles 8:6, Santa Biblia Reina-Valera.

Trust God, for you are exactly where you are meant to be: I haven't checked with Graciela, but I believe this quotation is from a prayer in Teresa's *Interior Castle* (1577).

CHAPTER 4: A MINISTRY OF PROFANITY

Epigraph: These ministers make religion a cold and flinty-hearted thing: This is from the famous address by Frederick Douglass (1818–1895) delivered on July 5, 1852, to the women of the Rochester Anti-Slavery Sewing Society.

is it well with her soul … peace like a river: Paraphrased from the hymn "It Is Well with My Soul" (1873) by Horatio G. Spafford (1828–1888); though quoting it casually, I have the deepest admiration for this hymn and its author. If you don't know the story behind this magnificent hymn, please look up Spafford online.

The Lord hath anointed: Isaiah 61:1 KJV.

To loose the bands of wickedness: Isaiah 58:6 KJV.

"Peace in the Valley": Written in 1937 by Thomas A. Dorsey (1899–1993), a true legend in gospel music.

"You Are Welcome in This Place": This gospel song, also known as "Lord, You Are Welcome," is by Kurt Lykes.

bright Phoebus: Eighteenth-century poet Thomas Yalden (1670–1736) coined this term in his poetic fable "The Owl and the Sun," in *The British Poets Vol. XLVI: The Poems of Isaac Watts and Thomas Yalden* (1822).

"Take My Hand, Precious Lord": Like "Peace in the Valley," this one (written in 1932) was also composed by Thomas A. Dorsey.

wherever two or three are gathered: Matthew 18:20 paraphrased.

"We Gather Together": Hymn written in 1597 by Andrianus Valerius (1575–1625) and translated into English in 1894 by Theodore Baker (1851–1934).

"Oh, for a Thousand Tongues to Sing": Written by Charles Wesley (1707–1788) in 1739.

Mr. Herod: The story of Herod and John the Baptist is found in Mark 6:14–29.

contrary gospel ... anathema esto: Galatians 1:9. Paul writes, "If anyone is preaching to you a gospel contrary to what you received, let him be condemned to hell!" (NET).

CHAPTER 5: A VISIT FROM THE ARCHBISHOP

Epigraph: At last we hapless men / Know all our haplessness: From "Veni Creator" by Alice Meynell (1847–1922) and published in *The Poems of Alice Meynell: Complete Edition* (1923). Bishop Townsend will have more to say about this poem later in this chapter.

A tale I know has gone about: The Dunstan verse is from a poem *The True Legend of St. Dunstan and the Devil* (1871) by Edward G. Flight and illustrated by George Cruikshank. The poet dismisses the pincers episode as a fabrication but endorses the idea that Dunstan put a horseshoe on the devil's cloven hoof, which is supposed to have led to the superstition that a horseshoe hung over one's door keeps the devil away. Osbern of Canterbury (late eleventh century) in his *Life of St. Dunstan*, reports that after Dunstan tweezed the devil's nose, the devil cried out: "Alas! What has this bald fellow done to the devil?"

Jeremy Taylor Prize: Named for Jeremy Taylor (1613–1667), an Anglican cleric whom Samuel Taylor Coleridge dubbed "the Shakespeare of Divines." His most enduring work is *The Rule and Exercises of Holy Living* (1650).

"O Love That Will Not Let Me Go": A hymn by Scottish minister and writer George Matheson (1842–1906). Written in 1882, it originally appeared under the title "O Love That Wilt Not Let Me Go" in *Life and Work* magazine in 1883 and then in the *Scottish Hymnal* the following year.

"I Sing of a Maid That Is Matchless": Aside from my own anthology, this can be found under the title "I Syng of a Mayden" in innumerable collections of Middle English poetry, such as *The Oxford Book of Medieval English Verse* (1970) by Celia Sisam (b. 1926).

Now am I seated as my soul delights: I tracked down the precise citation: Shakespeare, *Henry VI Part 3*, act 5, scene 7.

God's in his heaven and all's right with the world: Robert Browning (1812–1889), "Pippa Passes" (1841), close paraphrase.

She openeth her mouth with wisdom: Proverbs 31:26 KJV. At this time, Dunwoody was working on a translation of the book of Proverbs for a new version of the Bible.

A man's wisdom maketh his face to shine: Ecclesiastes 8:1.

Always forgive your enemies: The bishop is playing fast and loose with his sources here because no evidence exists that Oscar Wilde (1854–1900) ever wrote this. Columnist Walter Winchell (1897–1972), in 1954, seems to be the earliest purveyor of this quip, which he attributes to Wilde. If Wilde never said it, I suspect he would have remarked, "Oh, would that I had!"

"Felix Randal": English Jesuit priest Gerard Manley Hopkins (1844–1889) wrote this sonnet in 1880, though, like most of his poems, it was first published posthumously in 1918 in *The Poems of Gerard Manley Hopkins*.

"The Hound of Heaven": Written by Francis Thompson (1859–1907) and first published in 1893.

"Baby Elephant Walk": A comic tune composed by Henry Mancini (1924–1994) for the 1962 film *Hatari!*

"Für Elise": An elementary piano composition by Ludwig van Beethoven (1770–1827), now sadly relegated to being one of the world's most popular telephone ringtones. A disparaging legend is that Beethoven wrote this for one of his

piano students, a young girl named Elise. When she attempted to play it, she stumbled several times, in response to which, Beethoven rapped her knuckles with a stick. That was, apparently, a common pedagogical technique at the time. Nothing like the threat of violence to improve one's musicianship.

CHAPTER 6: SHOULDER ANGELS

Epigraph: The angel of righteousness is delicate and modest: From the anonymous second-century document *The Shepherd of Hermas*, 5th Revelation, Commandment 6. See note below.

The devillish Engine back recoiles: John Milton (1608–1674), *Paradise Lost* (1667), book 4.

An idea that is not dangerous: From a book-length dialogue, called *The Critic as Artist*, by Oscar Wilde (1854–1900), published in 1891. It outlines Wilde's own theory of aesthetics.

convergence of the twain: The title of a well-known poem by Thomas Hardy (1840–1928) about the sinking of *Titanic*. First written in 1912, the poem appeared in his *Selected Poems* (1916) and chillingly refers to the ship and the iceberg as "coincident / … twin halves of one august event."

Thus doth Fortune turn her wheel: This is the gist of what Geoffrey Chaucer (1343–1400) wrote in line 509 of "The Monk's Tale" from *The Canterbury Tales*. The actual quote is "Thus kan Fortune hir wheel governe and gye."

the complete works of Thomas Traherne: Restoration cleric Thomas Traherne (1637–1674) was a prolific writer and poet, one of the great English mystics whom I highlight in my 402 class along with William Blake, Walt Whitman, and others. The set to which I refer, which has now added a seventh volume, is the work of scholar Jan Ross, who is something of a prodigy in the field of literary research. Most of Traherne's works were not even published until the twentieth century—

and some of them were published in Ross's set for the first time —all carefully transcribed from Traherne's handwritten manuscripts. Thank you, Ms. Ross!

an orchestra unto himself: A paraphrase from the fourth section of Chesterton's "Variations on an Air," in which the author does a pastiche of Whitman: "I take no notice of any accompaniment; / I myself am a complete orchestra." Look for it in *The Collected Poems of G. K. Chesterton*.

"Let Me Entertain You": From the 1959 musical *Gypsy*, with music by Jule Styne (1905–1994) and lyrics by the late Stephen Sondheim (1930–2021).

"Albert and the Lion": This classic bit of comic dance-hall verse was written by poet and performer Marriott Edgar (1880–1951) but was made famous as a stage monologue by Stanley Holloway (1890–1982). You can find it on YouTube. Holloway is best remembered for having created the role of Alfred P. Doolittle in *My Fair Lady*, both on the stage and later in the film adaptation starring Audrey Hepburn and Rex Harrison.

Heat not a furnace for your foe: Shakespeare, *Henry VIII*, act 2, scene 4. This is Norfolk's advice to Buckingham.

Count Ugolino: Dante, *Inferno*, Book XXXIII. The story is complicated. Suffice it to say that Count Ugolino, in payback for the misdeeds done to him in life by a certain archbishop named Ruggieri, is condemned to gnawing on the archbishop's skull for all eternity.

Doctor Faustus: This play by Christopher Marlowe (1564–1593) was probably first performed around 1592. The line quoted is from act 5, scene 2.

The Castle of Perseverance: An anonymous English morality play, the earliest complete play in English to have come down to us. Internal evidence suggests that the play was written before 1425. The manuscript is archived in the Folger Shakespeare Library, Washington, D.C. The quotation, modernized, is from the prologue (called "The Banns").

The Shepherd of Hermas: This anonymous Christian work, written in Greek, from the first part of the second century, reads like a primitive and somewhat baffling novella, in which a former slave recounts a series of visions he has received. A good and bad angel appear in one of those visions. Some early church fathers accepted the work as canonical.

That which I should do, I don't: I believe Katie is referring to Romans 7:19–20.

We have erred and strayed from thy ways: From the Order for Daily Morning Prayer, the first section of the Book of Common Prayer.

rubbish heap of history: This was the epithet used by Italian poet Francesco Petrarch (1304–1374) to describe Rome when he visited that city.

Dunwoody ex machina: Carl's quip references the phrase *Deus ex machina* ("god out of the machine"), which describes the device in ancient Greek theater of having a god miraculously descend from the sky (lowered in a chair by ropes and pulleys from above, hence the "machine") to resolve seemingly irresolvable plot issues.

"De Profundis": The long, bitter letter, written in 1897 by Oscar Wilde (1854–1900) to his former lover, Lord Alfred Douglas. The edition I found for Carl is not old, but it is rare, fewer than five hundred copies were printed—in a facsimile edition of Wilde's original handwritten manuscript, published by the British Museum in 2000.

Ethics: This seminal work by the Dutch rationalist philosopher Baruch Spinoza (1632–1677) was published the year he died. He is credited, among other things, with demolishing all remnants of medieval scholasticism.

CHAPTER 7: MS. WESTCOTT'S STORY

Katie asked me to annotate her chapter. So (as she so crisply phrases it), "here goes":

Epigraph: God, kindle Thou in my heart within: The epigraph I chose for Katie's contribution is from Alexander Carmichael's magisterial collection of Scottish Gaelic blessings, prayers, and incantations, the two-volume *Carmina Gadelica*, published in 1900. There is so much richness in his translations that it is nearly impossible to overrate them.

Umberto Eco's Foucault's Pendulum: Published in Italian in 1988 and translated into English by William Weaver in 1989. The more widely known book by Umberto Eco (1932–2016), also highly recommended, is *The Name of the Rose* (English, 1983).

The Da Vinci Code and *Indiana Jones and the Last Crusade*: Directed, respectively, by Ron Howard (2006) and Steven Spielberg (1989).

It is probable that improbable things will happen: Aristotle, *Rhetoric 24:9*. And yes, I'm proud of Katie for throwing in this reference. Like the medieval monks, she knows her classical Greek every bit as well as her biblical Greek.

The Romance of the Rose: A thirteenth-century French courtly poem, *Le Roman de la Rose* (1230/1270), begun by Guillaume de Lorris (c. 1200–c. 1240) and completed by Jean de Meun (c. 1240–c. 1305). This was one of the most popular works of secular verse in Medieval France.

C. S. Lewis: The Allegory of Love: A Study in Medieval Tradition by C. S. Lewis (1898–1963) was published by the Oxford University Press in 1936.

Unto half my kingdom: An allusion to Herod's words to Salome (Mark 6:23).

Rowan's valedictory address: Although nothing was

borrowed directly, parts of Rowan's address seem to have been inspired by the book *What's So Amazing about Grace?* (1997) by Philip Yancey (b. 1949). Yancey's book is itself amazing.

Kierkegaard talks about ... Abraham: Søren Kierkegaard (1813–1855), *Fear and Trembling* (1843). I do not know what edition Rowan Wayrich read, but I recommend the recent translation by Kierkegaard scholar Bruce H. Kirmmse (b. 1943). One Danish scholar has said that Kierkegaard's prose is so complex that he's actually easier to read in English translation.

And the people said ... : 1 Chronicles 16:36.

CHAPTER 8: NIGHT CLASS

Epigraph: To know with certainty the road you travel: From John of the Cross (1542–1591), *The Dark Night of the Soul* (c. 1579), chapter 16, section 12.

Dudley Fitts: The poet and classical scholar Dudley Fitts (1903–1968) translated many of the Greek tragedies. His major collection of original poetry is *Poems, 1929–1936*, published by James Laughlin's influential New Directions Press in 1937.

The Little Prince: *Le Petit Prince*, the most beloved work by French writer Antoine de Saint-Exupéry (1900–1944), was published in 1943.

The poet Middleton: Richard Middleton (1882–1911), from "Mad Harry's Vision" in *Poems and Songs* (1913). The full quote, which used to be a popular catch phrase, is: "I'll get you into heaven yet, you damned old fool!"

Every action has an equal and opposite reaction: The third law of motion formulated by Sir Isaac Newton (1642–1727) in his famous *Principia* (1687). Please, do not send me an angry email ... yes, I know, Newton was a notorious introvert, one of the last people on earth who would be guilty of "heavy partying with his chums." Still, I assert my right to imagine absurd things—the more absurd, the better.

E. Anabeth Miller: Since I never mention Ms. Lambert's first name or middle initial, I leave it to the reader to puzzle them out from this anagram. Have fun! Otherwise, her first name will be revealed in chapter 11.

That was in another country: Christopher Marlowe (1564–1593), *The Jew of Malta* (c. 1590), act 4, scene 1.

Jean Valjean: A reference to the novel *Les Misérables* (1862) by Victor Hugo (1802–1885).

The only thing faith and hope do not give us: Thomas Merton (1916–1968), a Trappist monk, from chapter 2 of his 1954 book, *No Man Is an Island*. In checking the quotation, I note that Tom changed Merton's gender-specific pronouns *He* and *Him* to *God*.

That beyond which a greater cannot be conceived: Anselm of Canterbury (1033–1109), *Proslogion*, where the concept is expounded in chapters 2–5.

Will no one rid me of this turbulent priest?: Several historical accounts report that on Christmas 1170, Henry II (1133–1189) said something to this effect as an aside to four of his knights who assumed it to be an order. Thomas Becket (1119–1170), archbishop of Canterbury, was then murdered by those knights four days later. The event is the subject of the plays *Becket* (1884) by Alfred, Lord Tennyson (1809–1892) and *Murder in the Cathedral* (1935) by T. S. Eliot (1888–1965).

a dark foreflowing song: From the first stanza of the poem "Southwest Passage" by poet and classical scholar Dudley Fitts (1903–1968), first published in *Poetry: A Magazine of Verse* (June 1930).

CHAPTER 9: A WALK IN THE WOODS

Epigraph: Your enjoyment of the world is never right: From Thomas Traherne (1636–1674), *Centuries of Meditation*, I, 28.

heart-easing Mirth: John Milton (1606–1674), "L'Allegro" (1631). You've read this poem if you've ever taken an English literature survey course. It's worth rereading. I confess that like Dr. Johnson (in his *Life of Milton*), I find myself respecting Milton distantly rather than loving him, though "L'Allegro" is among his most palatable.

While the higher things are indeed better … : Katie could no doubt have quoted this in Latin, from Augustine's *Confessions*, 7.13.19: *"meliora quidem superiora quam inferiora, sed meliora omnia quam sola superiora."*

Santa Teresa: The butterfly image is from *The Interior Castle* (1577) by Teresa of Ávila.

every creature is a word of God: This quotation from Meister Eckhart (1260–1327) is found in *Breakthrough: Meister Eckhart's Creation Spirituality in a New Translation* (1991) by Matthew Fox (b. 1940).

tongues in trees, books in the running brooks: Shakespeare's *As You Like It*, act 2, scene 1.

Francis of Assisi called the sun and moon his brother and sister: Francis of Assisi (1182–1226) wrote his song "Canticle of the Sun" (*Laudes Creaturarum*) in 1224.

When you stand before the Judgment Seat: I honestly have no idea where in the Kabbalah Sue Park found this quotation. But I like it. One of my favorite writers, Leonard Sweet, quotes it in his book *SoulSalsa: 17 Surprising Steps for Godly Living in the Twenty-First Century* (2000).

"As Kingfishers Catch Fire": This beloved poem by Gerard Manley Hopkins (1844–1889) can be found in any standard

edition of his works. It was first published in Robert Bridges's edition *The Poems of Gerard Manley Hopkins* (1918).

like a wolf on the fold: Lord Byron (1788–1824), the opening line of "The Destruction of Sennacherib" (1815).

Origen settled the matter: I believe Dunwoody got this notion somewhere in the book by Origen (c. 184–c. 253) called *On First Principles*. I would have asked Katie to track it down for me, but I didn't want to risk the humiliation of having her remark, "You haven't read Origen?"

Milton ... Shelley: The poems referenced are "L'Allegro" (1631) by John Milton (1608–1674) and "To a Skylark" (1820) by Percy Bysshe Shelley (1792–1822).

The world is a mirror of infinite beauty: Thomas Traherne (1636–1674), from his *Centuries of Meditation*, I, 31, which was not published until 1908.

the small rain and the great rain: Job 37:6 KJV: "For he saith to the snow, Be thou *on* the earth; likewise to the small rain, and to the great rain of his strength."

how way leads on to way: From the well-known poem "The Road Not Taken" (1915) by Robert Frost (1874–1963).

the female of the species: From "The Female of the Species" (1911) by Rudyard Kipling (1865–1936).

the snows of yesteryear: A reference to the poem "Ballade des dames du temps jadis" (1461) by François Villon (1431–1463), specifically in its most famous English translation, titled "Where Are the Snows of Yesteryear" (1872) by Dante Gabriel Rossetti (1828–1882).

One touch of nature makes the whole world kin: Shakespeare, *Troilus and Cressida*, act 3, scene 3.

pathetic fallacy: John Ruskin (1819–1900) discusses the "pathetic fallacy" in volume 3 of his *Modern Painters* (4, xii). The two examples given are both mentioned by Ruskin: *"dances as often as dance it can,"* Samuel Taylor Coleridge (1772–1834),

"Christabel," part 1 (1816); *"cruel, crawling foam,"* Charles Kingsley (1819–1875), "The Sands of Dee" (1850).

as a scroll when it is rolled together: Revelation 6:14 KJV.

the planet on which so many millions of us fight: If you've not read the essay "Dreamthorp" (1863) (from which this quotation comes) by Alexander Smith (1830–1867) please promise me you will do so soon. You can find it in one of those little blue Oxford Classics editions, *Dreamthorp, with Selections from "Last Leaves,"* or, as Ms. Westcott assures me about most everything, it's available online.

thus endeth my tale: Geoffrey Chaucer (c. 1343–1400), *The Canterbury Tales*, "The Shipman's Tale."

May all your guardian angels punish me if I lie: From the *Satyricon* of Petronius (c. 27–66 CE). I first heard this quoted in Latin (*"ego si mentior, genios vestros iratos habeam"*) at a Classics Department party by one of the professors who, after a few drinks, had started telling tall tales. The rest of us are still waiting for our guardian angels to punish him.

CHAPTER 10: THE DISCIPLINARY COMMITTEE

Epigraph: We suffer because we have no humility: This is found in Archimandrite Sophrony (1896–1993), *St. Silouan the Athonite* (1991).

blooming alone, all her lovely companions faded and gone: From the poem "The Last Rose of Summer" by Thomas Moore (1779–1852).

chaff before the wind: A common expression that comes from Psalm 35:5 KJV.

pierced for our transgressions: Isaiah 53:5, roughly from Young's Literal Translation (1862).

The old hour glass spins its thread of sand: from the "March" section of *The Shepherd's Calendar* by John Clare (1793–1864).

[his] soul to a strange somewhere fled: From the poem by Abraham Cowley (1618–1667), "The Despair," in *The Mistress* (1647).

"Charge of the Light Brigade": An 1854 poem by Alfred, Lord Tennyson (1809–1892): "Half a league, half a league, / Half a league onward, / Into the valley of Death / Rode the six hundred."

out of their own means: Luke 8:2–3.

women shouldn't even talk in church and should keep their heads covered: Ms. Lambert is referencing 1 Corinthians 14:34 and 11:6–10. I believe she leans towards the New Revised Standard Version.

Anyone who is angry with a brother or sister: Matthew 5:22 NIV, though I love Wycliffe's take: "Ech man that is wrooth to his brothir schal be gilti to doom."

our brother is our life: Quoted in Archimandrite Sophrony's *St. Silouan the Athonite*.

From love of our brother comes the love of God: I believe President Costa also got this one from Sophrony's *St. Silouan the Athonite*.

CHAPTER 11: MS. LAMBERT'S STORY

Epigraph: The place of prayer is a precious habitation: From John Woolman (1720–1772)—part of the conclusion to chapter 10 of John Greenleaf Whittier's edition of *The Journal of John Woolman* (1871). Woolman dictated this passage to a friend when he was quite ill and thought he was dying. Woolman is one of Ms. Lambert's favorite spiritual writers. By the way, I asked her if I might give her chapter the title "Dunwoody Inamorato," but she thought it too disrespectful. I stand corrected.

"The Wedding of Sir Gawain and Dame Ragnelle": An anony-

mous fifteenth-century poem. Chaucer (c. 1340–1400) tells the same story earlier in his "Wife of Bath's Tale" in *The Canterbury Tales*.

Let not injustice run faster than death: This sentiment is indeed from Plato's *Apology*, though somewhat truncated in Ms. Lambert's paraphrase; the full quotation, in Benjamin Jowett's translation, reads: "The difficulty, my friends, is not in avoiding death, but in avoiding unrighteousness; for that runs faster than death."

one-horned hellcats, malevolent pachyderms: Here the quotation is from Ms. Lambert's own *Pythons of Paris*, as is her description of the gargoyle Stryga.

Quasimodo: A reference, of course, to the novel *The Hunchback of Notre Dame* (1831) by Victor Hugo (1802–1885).

I love the Lord because he has heard my voice: Psalm 116:1 NRSV.

CHAPTER 12: THE ALL-FAITHS FESTIVAL

Epigraph: Both read the Bible day & night: From William Blake (1757–1827), "The Everlasting Gospel," written around 1788.

Woe unto you ... : Brother Jonas quotes liberally and noncontextually from a dizzying array of books of the Bible, more or less in the King James Version: Matthew 23:27, 13:42, 23:24; Romans 2:23; Isaiah 9:17; 1 Corinthians 1:18; 1 Timothy 5:20; Mark 13:13.

as a cloud with the morrowtide, and as dew passing forth early: Hosea 6:4 Wycliffe Bible (spelling modernized). Lovely, isn't it?

discern false prophets: I was referring to Jesus's words in Matthew 7:16.

hated of all men: Mark 13:13 KJV.

swell the gourd and plump the hazel shells: John Keats (1795–1821), "To Autumn" (1819). Most people remember this poem for its most famous line, "Season of mist and mellow fruitful-ness," but I find the swelling gourd and plumping hazel shells more evocative and less over-quoted.

Answering a fool according to his folly: This seems to be Dunwoody's own crisp paraphrase of Proverbs 26:5, which is quite apropos, since he was (as you know) translating Proverbs for the forthcoming NICE Bible at the time.

From each according to his ability: Contrary to expectation, the phrase does not come from Marx's *Das Kapital*; it is found in his 1875 *Critique of the Gotha Program*.

Thou shalt have no other gods before me: Exodus 20:3.

When thou art come into the land ... : Deuteronomy 18:9 KJV, 12:3 KJV, and Jeremiah 10:5 NET, respectively.

Nahab and Abihu: Leviticus 10:1.

faithless and perverse: Matthew 17:17 KJV.

"Every Praise to Our God": A gospel song by Hezekiah Walker (b. 1962).

Whited sepulchers: again, Matthew 23:27 KJV.

faith is a razor-sharp sword ... I vaguely remember Kierkegaard saying something similar, though I can't find the reference, but this also makes sense of what Jesus says (Matthew 10:34 NIV): "I did not come to bring peace, but a sword."

How good and pleasant when God's people live together in unity: Psalm 133:1 NIV. Again, one can appreciate Wycliffe's take on this verse: "How good and how merry it is, that brethren dwell together" (spelling modernized).

CHAPTER 13: INTO THE LABYRINTH

Epigraph: Whoever possesses the present moment: In his 2014 book *The Three Gifts of Térèse of Lisieux: A Saint for Our Times*, author Patrick Ahern attributes this widely quoted passage to the other famous saint of that name, Teresa of Ávila (1515–1582), though he provides no documentation. Graciela, who admires this quotation, admits that she has no idea where in Teresa's writings it is to be found and has her doubts as to its authenticity. But it is appropriate, so I'll keep it.

The gloaming spreads her waning shade: Lord Byron (1788–1824), "Elegy on Newstead Abbey" (1808).

Elizabeth Kübler-Ross's Five Stages of Grief: From the 1969 book *On Death and Dying* by Elizabeth Kübler-Ross (1826–2004).

Me and my loving, Love makes them both one: From "Love Is Life" by Richard Rolle of Hampole (c. 1300–1349). In Middle English the line is "For me & my lufyng lufe makes bath be ane," found in *The Oxford Book of English Mystical Verse* (1921).

Christ the tiger: From "Gerontion" (1919) by T. S. Eliot (1888–1965).

I am the way: John 14:6—invariable in nearly every English translation.

NOTES ON THE TEXT (BY DR. MARTIN BONHAM)

Scantlings of learning: Poet and scholar Austin Dobson (1840–1921) once wrote that Izaak Walton (1593–1683) tended to lean heavily on quotations (often misquoted) in his most famous book, *The Compleat Angler* (1653). Dobson's precise phrase is "the scantlings of learning with which he sought to dignify his book ...," from the essay "On Certain Quotations from Walton's Angler" in Dobson's *Side-Walk Studies* (1902). You see, I don't "make stuff up."

A NOTE FROM THE AUTHOR
CUPPERTON, THEOPHILY, AND FLIGHTS OF FANCY

Although Cupperton University is fictional, it has existed with great vividness in my imagination for many years. In December 2017, I planned to write a series of articles to explain how the study of the humanities and sciences could provide ways of approaching God that are every bit as valid as the study of theology. Then this thought occurred to me: Why haven't colleges created departments in which faculty members might teach their students about the spiritual aspects of their various disciplines? How, for instance, can we learn to love God more through biology, history, literature, sociology, art, and so on? At that point, another thought occurred to me: Why don't I create my own imaginary college with its own Department of Theophily—its department of "the love of God"?

From that point on I began to visualize, as clearly as if I could walk there myself, Cupperton University, with its two quadrangles of Gothic-revival sandstone buildings with their crisscrossing walkways of uneven brick; its shaded arboretum, awash with lilies and smelling of pungent wisteria and sweet lilac, with its wooden benches, jingling fountain, and flagstone labyrinth; its glass-façaded art museum, which visiting parents complain is much too modern for the rest of campus; its black squirrels hopping across South Quad where students lounge under majestic maples, scrutinizing their smartphones as if they were mirrors, which, in a sense, they are. When things had proceeded this far, I had no choice but turn it all into a novel.

Cupperton, as I imagined it, is located somewhere among the cornfields of the vast, bountiful, cloud-speckled Midwest, with four unambiguous seasons and spotty cellular connection —and distant enough from the nearest urban center to have created its own somewhat insular subculture. Alumni from such schools know what I mean.

About five thousand students attend Cupperton. As a private liberal arts college, it has, like so many similar institutions, vaguely religious roots, being founded two centuries ago by Episcopalians or Methodists or Congregationalists—no one seems quite sure. I suspect Ms. Lambert in the library would be happy to provide you with that information.

The school earns the right to call itself a university because of its music conservatory, its pre-nursing program, and, as you've gathered, its graduate-level Seminary and School of Theology, which, while not on a par with Notre Dame or Duke Divinity, produces students who could hold their own at a church-history trivia night against such schools as Marquette or Wheaton.

The school's colors are navy and gold, and its crest, displayed on the wrought-iron archway over the west entrance —and on the logowear for sale in the Student Stores—shows a night sky with gold stars against a navy field. At the lower end is a child's shoe, and the motto on the ribbon beneath it reads *GRADIBUS PARVULĪS AD ASTRA*—"By Baby Steps to the Stars."

No one is quite sure where the name Cupperton comes from, though again, you might ask Ms. Lambert. Some say it's a corruption of Copper Town—though the nearest copper mine is some two hundred miles away. Others insist that Cupperton is a namesake of the Italian city of Copertino, which was the home of one of the more dubious Renaissance saints: Joseph of Copertino, who is said to have had the unusual gift of levitation. That is, he could fly. As a result, he is now regarded as the patron saint of pilots, airline passengers, and drone operators—and not surprisingly, he is also the patron saint of those suffering from extraordinary delusions. Which gives an entirely new meaning to the term *flights of fancy*.

Whatever the origin of the name, that buoyant saint is appropriate for the university's newest and most controversial academic department: the one-of-a-kind, interdisciplinary Department of Theophily, which is about nothing if not flights of fancy, as you will have discovered in these pages.

So what exactly is *theophily*? From the Greek, it means "the love of God"—our love for God and, by extension, God's love for us. As Professor Bonham explains to his students, theophily is different from theology. While theology focuses on learning as much *about* God as humanly possible, as an object of study, of scrutiny, theophily focuses on how to *love* God more deeply with "all our heart, soul, mind, and strength." Two very different things. Studying something doesn't necessarily lead to loving it, which anyone who failed high school chemistry can tell you. As Thomas Traherne (Bonham's favorite writer) once wrote, "To study [an] object for ostentation, vain knowledge, or curiosity is fruitless impertinence, [even if] God himself and angels be the object. But to study that which will oblige men to love him and feed us with nobility and goodness toward men, that is blessed" (*Centuries of Meditations*, III, 40).

The word *theophily* has biblical associations. The writer of the Book of Luke and the Acts of the Apostles addressed both documents to a person named Theophilus—"lover of God"— about whom scholars know nothing, which hasn't prevented them from advancing conflicting theories and more or less casting Theophilus in their own image. But in the absence of evidence, as Dr. Bonham would point out, the name already hints at everything we need to know. Theophilus loved God or, at least, wanted to love God more—otherwise Luke wouldn't have been writing to him—and as Dr. Graciela Rojas said in her talk at the celebration banquet, "Wanting to love God more *is* loving God more." Each chapter in this book has tried to suggest some way of doing just that, for each contains a small and usually not-so-subtle homily on the subject of how we can love God more.

This novel, as you've noticed, is not like most. Readers expecting a well-wrought three-act romance or a spine-tingling suspense thriller will have been disappointed. *The Beautiful Madness of Martin Bonham* was written in the deliberately episodic tradition of "the novel of ideas," or "philosophical novel," in which each chapter is more-or-less self-contained and each presents a specific idea—in this case, about how to love God—with a new character usually provided to introduce each idea. Such novels used to be popular—Thomas More's *Utopia*, Voltaire's *Candide*, Dr. Johnson's *Rasselas*, or more recently, C. S. Lewis's *Great Divorce*. This means that the characters in this "theo-philosophical novel" support the ideas rather than the other way around. In a sense, the ideas *are* the characters.

Which is not to say that the human actors are unimportant. Each one reminds me of someone I've known, or, more accurately, many someones. They are all composites—except for Ms. Lambert, who is a very real librarian and gave me permission to use her name. Their various approaches to loving God are what interest me.

More to the point, most of the characters are also me, for each one lives and breathes inside me, and at some time or other I have shared their attitudes, enthusiasms, excesses, and misconceptions. This book, rather than being a "lives of the eminent philosophers" is more like a "lives of the immanent philosophers." We look within ourselves to see the world ... and to see its creator.

So thank you for spending time at the wholly imaginary but otherwise very real campus of Cupperton University. My hope is that you too, in your own mind's eye, can picture these oddball characters as they scurry across campus while the bells in the tower of Murphy Chapel chime the Westminster quarters; as they hang out at the CupperTea Café across the street from Phipps Auditorium or slip into the Student Stores for protein bars or ear buds or to order next semester's texts; as they cluster in shaded, ivy-framed doorways, having animated conversations; jogging past the graffiti-covered boulder in the center of North Quad; or as they peer up at you from their laptops in library cubicles. They are young and old, dignified and silly, religious or not, but most of all, they are not really *they*; rather, they are us—all of us—as we prepare for our own exams in that curious and sometimes perplexing life course on the subject of loving others, loving ourselves, and loving God. In other words, Theophily.

See you in class.

Now, some acknowledgments: As in everything I write, Shelley Townsend-Hudson is on every page. She has taught me more about God's love than anyone. Thank you to my daughters,

Abbie, Molly, and Lili, for their constant encouragement and listening. From among the things they will inherit from me someday, may Theophily be the one that means the most.

Special thanks to Linda Lambert, formerly instructional services and collection development librarian at Taylor University, for meticulously reviewing and commenting on these pages and for making editorial contributions, not the least of which is suggesting most of the biographical details of her eponymous character. She provided information about the inner workings of a university, and she did indeed conceive of the Hiss and Hearse Series referenced in these pages.

For reviewing all or portions of this book and making helpful suggestions, I would like to thank Julia McKee Bergquist, Jessica Dion-Steffes, Dr. Matthew Estel, Mary Hassinger, Miranda Gardner, Tisha Martin, Bethany Russell, Timothy John Stoner, Emily Van Houten, Virginia Wieringa, and Courtney Zonnefeld. Of invaluable assistance was Reverend Jon Propper, formerly of Park Congregational Church, Grand Rapids, Michigan, who was the inspiration for chapter 12, "The All-Faiths Festival"; and I extend special appreciation to Dr. James Ernest, publisher at Eerdmans, who made a key suggestion on an early draft, which turned into chapter 5, "A Visit from the Archbishop."

Thanks also to Dr. Chris Beetham, who checked my Latin; Dr. Nancy Erickson for her constant, joyful encouragement; and poet Brian Phipps for always asking how the writing was coming. Brian was one of the earliest and most enthusiastic advocates for this project. In gratitude for their contributions, three buildings on the Cupperton campus have been named in their honor.

The bits of sententious wisdom collected under the name of Dudley Fitts (Bonham's old friend, *not* the poet and classical scholar) come from three old friends of my own, Dr. Robert F. Gross Jr., Bob Moore†, and Duane Siebert.

Many thanks to artist Mark Sheeres for his beautiful map, the image of the labyrinth, the Cupperton University crest, and the cartoon on the next page.

To visionary author, editor, and publisher Rev. Dr. John Mabry—a heartfelt thanks for seeing the value in this book and for his lovely endorsement.

Thank you to Kelly Hughes of Dechant Hughes Associates for her amazing and persistent promotional work on behalf of this book. Thanks to Sarah Arthur, Traci Rhoades, Leonard Sweet, and Jonathan Wilson-Hartgrove for their kind endorsements; I encourage everyone to track down their books, each of which has a special meaning for me.

And special gratitude goes to my agents, Tim Beals and Pete Ford of Credo Communications. It's rare to find agents who love Medieval and Renaissance literature as much as I do.

—Robert Hudson, August 2023

Since our errors do not arise out of malice
but are the natural consequences of human weakness,
we hope we shall be pardoned for them
in this world and the next.
—Voltaire, A Philosophical Dictionary
(trans. Martin E. Bonham)

ABOUT THE AUTHOR

Robert Hudson was an editor for Zondervan/HarperCollins Christian Publishers for thirty-four years. He is the author of thirteen books, among which are *Kiss the Earth When You Pray* (poetry), *Seeing Jesus* and *The Poet and the Fly* (nonfiction), and *The Further Adventures of Jack the Giant Killer* (short stories). He and his wife, Shelley, play fiddle and banjo respectively in the old-time band Gooder'n Grits. They split their time between Grand Rapids, Michigan, and Old Salem, North Carolina.

"Stop calling me 'holier than thou';
I AM holier than thou!"